SMITH 2

TIMOTHY LONDON

Published by Soulpunk

Copyright © 2021 Timothy London

All rights reserved.

ISBN 978-1-9196547–44

www.timothylondon.com

To all the grown up punks.

1

Chapter 1: Everything is Normal

Miriam trawls, dead eyed, through the first editions of rival newspapers, searching for stories that can be stolen, adapted and inserted into her own paper's second edition. She is temporary assistant to the night editor. Not the most noble part of her career. But Bill, the news editor, who takes a personal interest in her progress, recommends a stint of death-watch duties as character building. His theory is that it will also keep her out of trouble.

The hangover has been pretty brutal. Eight months since she had been almost murdered, knocked unconscious, since she had almost broken a significant, history-changing story as well as (almost?) falling for some kind of errant spy in the shape of one, Stephen Smith. Bill had taken to calling her 'Magneto', due to the way she attracted this kind of trouble. Which also included the suicide of a corrupt council finance manager, Gerald Yorke, who had hung himself after she confronted him as a favour to Councillor John Kaspar, head of Redbridge Borough Council. Who owed her a dinner.

The change has marked her appearance, her mouth is a straighter line, eyes suspicious. Guarded. The plus side is that she is taken more seriously by journalist colleagues and acquaintances. The book of secrets had fluttered open in a breeze of weird activism and she had caught a glimpse, several glimpses, of how things really are that she almost wished she hadn't seen. And this has left its mark, for good and bad.

The night editor, crumpled old Tom Newton, who has been at the paper longer, even, than the proprietor, has sneaked up behind her. She doesn't know how long he has been standing at her back when he finally talks to her.

'Are you actually reading any of that, Miriam?'

She looks down and realises she has absent-mindedly turned on to the sports section of the newspaper she has been scouring or more accurately, glancing over.

She wakes herself up.

'Yes, Tom. Nothing, nothing there. Sorry. I haven't adjusted to the unusual hours, yet.'

'These hours aren't unusual. They are newspaper hours. My hours. Are you saying Tom Newton keeps unusual hours?'

He's not really annoyed, she knows. He has a different, less harassed way about him than the daytime editors. Probably impossible to maintain that amount of energy throughout the night, anyway.

'My body keeps on asking me why it's not somewhere warm and cosy. And my head… too much coffee.'

'I've told you before, Miriam. If you want to stay awake, keep off the caffeine – it only works for a few minutes. Drink water, fizzy water and bring fruit. Fruit!'

He magics an apple on to her desk.

'Now. Page five is waiting for you.'

He walks off, sipping from his water bottle. She replaces the paper in front of her with another from the pile on the floor by her chair. It sometimes feels as if it's her job to create

2

the news, not just report it. Pluck something that will satisfy her editors and the public out of thin air. Strangely, her experiences months earlier hadn't made the papers, or any of the media. By the time she had recovered, the news had marched on and she couldn't interest her bosses in the story. Partly, she knew, because she still didn't know exactly what had happened, but also because of a reluctance on their part to get enthusiastic about it. Even Bill, who hasn't mentioned it since.

Half way down page two she has just found a promising article on a double drowning in Herefordshire when her mobile buzzes. Her mum isn't normally up at this hour. She feels a pulse of expectancy. Not good.

An hour later and Miriam Taylor is on a shocked taxi ride to Kingston Hospital in southwest London, to be with her mother as she goes to identify her dad's body. Her dad is dead. Her mother was calm on the phone, but couldn't tell her very much. A phone call from the police: a man with credit cards and driving license in her dad's name has been found dead. That's all. That's enough. She knows it's true. As the taxi takes her closer to something dread she wants to turn it around, go home. Deal with this from a distance. Which, she knows, is impossible.

As it turns out, there's her mum, red eyed, but composed and obviously very concerned about how her daughter is going to take this. It's a competition in concern as they doggedly march through corridors, her mother talking in a remote voice, telling her what she's been told. Apparently a road accident. He had popped out in the car to get milk – you know how he hates anything upsetting his breakfast routine – and, somehow, he had been struck by another car, as he walked from the car to the shop at the all night petrol station. This car had driven off and he was eventually found by a petrol shop employee, already dead, having lain there for well over an hour. There is a hint of the efficiency her father admired in his wife, formerly his secretary, in her telling.

Arriving at the morgue. Standing with her mother as they lift a corner of sheet from his face, just one side of his face and, yes, there he is. That's her dad. Holding it in while she guides her mother, now overwhelmed by pneumatic sobs, to a quiet room, where there are only solo chairs, no sofa for a mother and her daughter to sit and cling on to each other and wrench it all out. So she pulls the chairs close and holds hands and stares at her mother's bowed head, the brown and grey hastily scrunched together with a red elastic band, as it nods with coughs of grief from deep inside. Miriam saves it up for later.

*   *   *

Under the old Mulberry tree, out of bounds. Hardly camouflaged, in his summer blazer, charcoal with the give away blue piping, the white crest over his heart. It hardly matters. Another, what, eight months and he'll be gone. The worst that could possibly happen would be that they force him to take his exams by himself or at the local Further Education college. He sits and waits, puffing at a roll up, enjoying the Indian summer sun.

Hearing them before seeing them. The 'left, left, left, right, left' in a cracked voice. If a voice could have zits… Here they are, sorted by size, tallest in front, marching in dust and desert colours, plain enough to see against the cropped grass of the playing fields of Hertfordshire. He stubs out the roach and eases himself up against the tree, saunters towards the company of thirty or so boys, who, rifles at sloped arms, are marching down the gentle incline towards a long, wooden hut, at the far border of the school grounds.

Head up, chin out, arms swinging, leading the platoon:

4

handy with a screwdriver and a spare fuse, the sergeant major, only ever known to the boys as Sergeant Major, or 'Sarn't Major!' A squat Glaswegian, marching with the stiffness only a girdle can bring. He has locked horns with this old soldier before, sensing a favour in his post – perhaps the ex-Master who had previously been an army chaplain and had approved the appointment had felt guilty; after all, a chaplain's post in the army doesn't often bring you into the line of fire. The Sergeant Major had apparently been a 'real' soldier. He joins them as they reach the hut and are formed into two straight lines at attention. The Sergeant Major looks doubtfully at the signed chit he has received from the unlikely soldier material that is Toby Flaxman.

'Do you want to join the cadets, Mr. Flaxman?'

'Sir, yes sir!' He shouts and is rewarded by a giggle and a wobble in the ranks.

'You'll need to take this seriously. If you mess about I'll speak to the Master and you'll be out before you can say, erm, 'Welwyn Garden City'… Seriously, Mr. Flaxman. Can you do that?'

'Sir, yes sir!'

'There's no need to shout like that, young man. We're not the American Marines. Now, if you're joining us I suggest you fall in, next to, erm… Mr. Findlay, here.'

Toby marches rigidly over to the tallest boy who stands at the end of the front line and energetically stamps to attention. One more look at the chit, a nobly shaken head and the Sarn't Major splits the boys into three groups.

'Farnish!'

A boy of about fifteen gives the Sergeant Major his full attention. Ten boys are sitting on a bench inside the hut, each holding their rifle, butts resting on the ground, barrels upright. Toby is standing, leaning against a post next to the

SM.

'You will share your rifle with Mr. Flaxman. You will each fire five rounds each. Is that clear? Now, step up to the range, lad.'

Farnish, clearly unhappy at sharing his target practise bullet allotment with the older boy gets into position, lying full length on his front on a raised, wooden platform behind four sandbags.

'Mr. Flaxman, if you would stand behind Farnish and watch what he does. Less chat, you boys. Farnish, five rounds at the target, in your own time.'

Bending behind Farnish, Toby sights along the rifle barrel. The gun cracks and jerks, Farnish feeds another bullet into the chamber and fires again. Toby can't help himself:

'Raise it, it's dropping too soon.' But why talk when you can shout?

'Mr. Flaxman! Do not distract the cadet! There is no talking on the firing range!'

Toby looks round. A couple of the boys are smirking. They look down when they catch his eye. What is a school like this without a pecking order? At the moment, in the hut, Toby is second only to the Glaswegian ex-soldier in rank.

It's Toby's turn. He makes the checks under the approval of the SM.

'Very good, Mr. Flaxman. I'm wondering why we didn't benefit from your interest in weaponry before now. Hidden talents, Mr. Flaxman?'

Looking down the barrel, through the sights. The place is warm from its previous occupier, the gun grip a little sweaty. He clears his mind then allows just the drips of memory back in. He hears Steve Blake's voice. He takes light breaths and enjoys the feel of the gun. The recoils are light compared to some of the weaponry he has been trying out lately, hardly any need for the ear defenders. The .22 bullets seem puny but

6

he knows, with accuracy, they can kill.

He misses the target completely, deliberately, one to five. The look of disappointment on the old soldier's face is to be savoured. The sniggering from the other boys silenced with a raised eyebrow. Seconds later he is free in the brisk sunshine and stretched shadows, walking away from the hut. He hears a shout, his name. He turns. Findlay is standing on lanky legs, aiming his rifle at him, grinning. A small puff from the barrel and the insect whizz of the bullet hitting the dry turf near his feet.

Findlay, clearly shocked at himself, already lowering the rifle, moving it away from his body, trying to disown it. The other boys stand around, almost as shocked. Toby stands very still for a moment then falls to the ground and lays still. A small thunder of cadet boots and he is surrounded. He can feel their breath and their fear. A voice asks, is he dead? A hand on his shoulder, lightly. He opens his eyes and looks up at Findlay, who's own eyes are watering.

'I didn't mean to Flacksy, it just went off, I was only trying to frighten you, where did I...'

Flaxman smiles at Findlay then reaches a hand up to the boy's throat, grabbing his collar, pulling as the boy backs away, standing up, resting his arms on Findlay's shoulders. The ring of faces are expectant, on tiptoes, Findlay's mouth is open. Flaxman pats Findlay's shoulders twice, a friendly pat, then turns and walks off. Findlay draws breath, ready to shout, with anger and relief but is pipped by the Sergeant Major, just emerged from the hut and looking, puzzled, towards the group of boys a few yards away.

'What's going on? Findlay? Company! Fall in!'

And the awkward young soldiers run back down the slope to join him, Findlay dragging behind. Perhaps wondering how to explain the missing bullet.

* * *

Crests and ties and even the size of a teacher's gown. In a school like Stedman: they all denote rank. The school is like a well ordered series of paddy fields in terraces, from the scummiest at the bottom, where the water has trickled down through the mud and fertiliser, to the freshest at the top, which is watered by the sweetest rain, straight from the mountains.

This gown says 'around the middle, nearer the top than the bottom'. Belonging as it does to Mr. Peters, a man who has been at the school long enough but not quite long enough for some.

'Flaxman, what happened at the shooting range?'

Toby stops on the stairs.

'Oh, it turns out I'm a rubbish shot, sir. Waste of time.'

Peter's voice is low, a harsh whisper. His eyes dart around, looking for listeners.

'You made me sign that form, made me lie for you. What for? So that you can play with guns? Well, that's the last time. You can do what you want Flaxman. I won't be blackmailed.'

Peters walks briskly down the stairs. Toby calls after him, sweetly.

'You will, sir. Yes, you will.'

A school like this is built only to bully those within it into submission.

In the pew, in the abbey twice a week, the boys are conscious of the huge weight of the cathedral roof, all light directing eyes towards the heavens, urging them to duck, to bow their heads to submit to the pressure of tribal ritual contained within the vaulted stone. Toby is aware he must try not to stand out now, that he is charged with a deep rebellion that goes beyond open defiance, but, in this place, he can't help but casually keep his head up, curious to see the teachers, the wives, the Master – especially the Master.

It says a lot about the permanence of the school's aesthetic that its first female head mistress retains the title 'Master'. She is staring at him, not in disapproval but interested, wondering. Toby is quite used to a certain kind of interest from older women, has been for a couple of years since his choirboy looks became firm-jawed and confident. This is different. Ms. Dacre is weighing him up, whilst the priest intones a prayer for unity in a mad world.

So, it's no surprise to Toby when Mary Dacre holds him with a glance outside the abbey and beckons him to come to her. In fact, he has made a point of waiting, dawdling, to give her the chance. Using a little Steve Blake trick, he moves in very close, well within the safe circle of social defence most people deploy, too close for comfort. With a questioning look.

Used, as she is, to gauche boys and young men, Mary Dacre is generally inured to displays of ignorance like this. But there's something about the confident way this young man holds himself, biceps brushing her shoulder, gaze not flinching from her own, that is vaguely unsettling. She seeks to deploy her power: he has, after all, entered her perfume zone, kept for intimate moments of influence, over boys and teachers alike, a secret weapon that is very effective in a mainly masculine environment. So she allows the closeness, for the moment.

'Toby, I heard something disquieting, about an incident yesterday, near the rifle range.'

She pauses, to watch for effect. There is none. Toby still looks questioningly at her. Maddening boy.

'The Sergeant Major seems to think there might have been an 'illegal discharge', as he put it. And, I heard from someone else, who was evidently observing, that this discharge might have been in your direction. Can you tell me any more, Toby? What happened?'

Somehow, she has found herself walking slowly alongside

Toby, towards the school. Alarmingly for her, he seems to be in control. She stops and takes a step back. Toby is smiling. Maddening.

'No, ma'am, I didn't notice a discharge. Can you tell me what was discharged?'

'Come on Toby, you know what I mean. Someone told me that Gareth Findlay fired his gun at you. The SM said there was a round missing. Something happened and you were involved.'

'Well, Mr. Peters thought I might make a good soldier, ma'am. He sometimes likes to put boys in certain roles, ma'am, as you know.' Pause.

'But it turns out, ma'am, that I'm a rotten shot so I thought I wouldn't waste anyone's time and left the cadets to get on with their… cadetting. No one aimed their gun at me ma'am. Apart from Mr. Peters, so to speak. At least, not that I noticed. Who told you this?'

'Never mind who told me, Toby Flaxman. I'm going to have to mention this to your parents and there might be an enquiry. This is very serious. You do know really just how serious this is, don't you? We will speak again later. Off you go.'

Instead of leaving on cue, Toby lingers a moment. He moves back, within the perfume zone and almost whispers:

'I think it's very dangerous, having guns at a school. Don't you, ma'am? But, please, don't tell anyone I said that, because people can get very upset. But guns, ma'am. And children, ma'am. It doesn't bear thinking about.'

He walks off, leaving her own cadences ringing in her ears. A very effective mimic. Was it an homage or a piss take? Maddening boy.

Toby is quite pleased with himself for a few moments before the self-chastisement begins. Alright, he must make a point of being as normal as possible for the next few days. As normal as is possible in this anachronistic place. But first, he must nip the enquiry in the bud. Wouldn't look good on his records. Bloody Findlay.

Bloody Findlay in the Master's garden, a popular smoking spot, due to the eight-foot hedges and several exits. Toby finds him standing with a couple of the younger cadets. Findlay looks startled. Then his jaw sets and his stance changes but his eyes remain darting as Toby joins him, nodding to the two boys.

'Make them go away.'

Findlay hesitates, then turns to the boys.

'Fuck off.' And they leave, quickly, flicking dog ends into the bushes.

'What do you want, Flaxman?'

'Were you trying to kill me, Findlay? Do you want me dead? Should I get protection?'

'No, you know very well, it was an accident, alright? I was just messing around and my finger, slipped. I didn't mean to.'

'You didn't mean to.'

'Look, it doesn't matter, anyway. Say what you want, no one will believe you. All the cadets will back me up. They'll say you did it. You fired at me. Ask them.'

Toby puts his hands into his trouser pockets, relaxed. He smiles at the taller boy.

'That's alright, Findlay. I wouldn't tell anyone about it. If you can keep your little chums quiet then you don't have to worry. I know that Groundskeeper Willy would prefer it was me and not one of his cannon fodder. Thing is, someone has already talked, to Dacre. Any idea who?'

Findlay frowns.

'That will be Farnish, the little scrote.'

'Will you have a word? Or will I?'

'What could you do? Freak him out? He would just laugh.

Everyone laughs at you, Flaxman. No I'll do it.   He'll shut up.'

It's tempting, tempting, to jab in the eyes, knuckle the kidneys, kick the shins, stomp the balls. But not now.   Steve Blake told him, to roll it up into a tight ball, this hate, and put it in his pocket for later. So he does.   With another smile for Findlay. The new, smiley Toby Flaxman. His mother would be proud.

*   *   *

Her capable mother would not be capable of coping with this, she thinks, as the civil servant, known as Sarah Cumberland hands Miriam a sheaf of A4 typewritten pages.

'Is this what I think it is?

'It's the Official Secrets Act, Miriam.'

'And why are you giving it to me?'

'We are asking you to sign it, before proceeding.'

'Before proceeding with what?'

'You have been named as the executor for your father's will. We need you to sign it and the solicitor, a Mr. Hale?'

'You've been doing your homework, Miss Cumberland. What on earth do we need to sign the Official Secrets Act for? It's my dad's will. Nothing to do with you.'

'It's just in case, Miriam.'

Stop using my name, it's my name, you can't have it.

'Your father may have records, of his time with BDP, that are sensitive and come under the Act's jurisdiction. These might be included in his will. You can't have access to these without signing and neither can anyone else.'

'Is that so? Are you sure? I think I'll need to check with someone who knows about the law, first, Miss Cumberland.'

Fit fifties. This woman has had an empathy bypass. She looks like she could run a mile or two, in her flat shoes, fitted slacks and very appropriate for her age cardigan. Scooped, to show the hollow scoops by her neck bone. A hunter-warrior woman. Civil servant, indeed.

'Look, Miriam, you're a journalist. You know how these things work. You don't want to upset us, do you? If you sign it now, get it out of the way. I know this is an upsetting time for you.'

'I buried my dad today. And you couldn't even wait one day to come round and threaten me. I think you'd better leave now.'

'Miriam, we can't wait. This is important. Sign it. Sign it today. I can come round later…'

'Don't even think about it. Now leave. Please.'

Infuriating woman. She's not even getting up.

'There is something more you should consider, Miss Taylor.'

More formal now. Serious. Bad. OK, fire away.

''We are aware you had a relationship eight months ago with a wanted criminal. This isn't the kind of thing you want to be generally known, is it? This man is wanted for murder, amongst other things. We are the kind of people who can help in situations like this. Much better that we are your friends…'

'You are really unbelievable.' She can feel it rising. Unfortunate for this woman that it's her who manages to finally pop the veneer of calm Miriam has formed around the hurt place inside in order to get through, to support her mother. The thing she has been saving up for a time alone. Pop. It bursts. The papers go flying as she stands, hands in fists by her side and hears herself screech:

'Out! Out! Fuck off! Get out! What don't you understand you stupid, stupid cow! Fucking leave! Now! Now! Now! Fuck. Off!!' And then she is pushing, handling her out of her parent's front room. Then her fists are no longer by her side and she is flailing at the woman's head, in the hall, by the front door until, amazingly, Miriam is suddenly still, held

13

tight, her right arm pushed up behind her, bent to her shoulders, her face against the wall as the full weight of the state leans against the small of her back.

Breathing hard, Miss Cumberland is by her ear.

'Calm down. Calm down. You'll upset your mother.'

Indeed, Miriam's mother is standing in the hall, watching with hand to mouth and red rimmed eyes wide. The civil servant lets Miriam go, brushes herself down and opens the front door. Miriam's tear soaked face turns to watch her leave and, beneath the sorrow there is a spark of satisfaction at the nasty red mark just above the woman's left eye. With any luck that will turn into a proper shiner. The door slams shut and she is left facing her shocked mum. Who holds out her arms, which is just what she needs, right now, as she contemplates the void in the present that is her dad.

Always plan your funeral, she is thinking. Earlier that day in the church. Otherwise, strong minded, religious minded relatives will take over and your family will have to sit through dreary hymns to a god you don't believe in and a vicar who never met you will repeat personal information and relate small moments from your life, which, when taken out of context, will sound trite and a little bit desperate.

The primary motivation for Miriam is that the day passes as smoothly as possible for her mother, who is mainly concerned with doing what must be done, as ordained by other people who know best.

Miriam is certain that her father would not have wanted this dour event in the local Anglican church, but she couldn't stop the momentum provided by relatives and funeral directors and even the organist, who hopefully presented her with a hand written list of appropriate pieces she could manage without too much trouble. So she practised nodding and is now wishing the day on and away.

The church is busy. Sitting next to her mother at the front, by various uncles and aunts and cousins she is aware of footsteps behind her, the shuffling and polite movement of an English funeral. She looks over her shoulder. Many people she has never met. Tanned faces of men in their sixties and seventies, with well cut hair, several with an upright military bearing, as she would have put the cliché if she was writing it up. Even a couple of bristly moustaches. The only thing missing is the odd row of medals and ribbons. A few couples of her parent's age. A small group of uncomfortable men who looked like they were allotment neighbours, witnesses of her father's late interest in the natural and organic. A family, also from the allotments, two woolly jumpered good-lifers, trying to keep three young kids in check. They deserved a smile, so she gave them one.

A light brown dome, moving along, sighted between shoulders of the congregation near the back, somehow familiar. The service starting, all eyes to the front, but not before noticing a smart middle-aged woman hurrying in to perch on the end of a pew nearest the door, checking her mobile. Miss Cumberland, as she found out.

At the end of the hand-shaking duties. Now thoroughly fed up with the relatives, the vicar, all these strangers who knew a man she could hardly relate to her father. A grim smile set, her mother finally helped away to the car from the grave side by an uncle, she is hoping to just, take a moment for herself. Eventually aware of someone at her elbow. It's the brown dome, accompanied by the rest of the bulk that supports it.

'So sorry for your loss, Miriam. He was a good man.'

Observing the pious purse of the lips, the dark eyes which ignore the emotional muscles of the rest of the face. This man, last seen bending over her, telling her he had called the ambulance as her head bled and throbbed on her bed, somehow responsible for the policeman or secret agent or whatever he was who had broken in to her flat, beaten her and killed his partner, a dark haired woman. Shot her. Shot the woman, right in front of her. Pistol whipped Miriam, knocked her unconscious. This man probably saved her life, in some way. But, somehow, was responsible for her life being threatened in the first place.

He knew her father, she remembers, or at least, that's what he told her. She feels afraid, suddenly.

'Please don't be frightened, Miriam. That unfortunate event involving my brother was absolutely nothing to do with you. A mistake.'

'Your brother?'

'We look very alike, but there is a year between us. It was he who helped you, in your apartment. He saved your life, Miriam. But it is myself who knew your father. My brother unfortunately never met him, didn't have the pleasure.'

Remembering.

'Oh, yes, Barry, said something about 'which one'... I mean...'

'You mean Stephen, of course. He asked you which one had approached you in the pub, the first time we met. He meant, which brother. Well, that was me. My brother you met later, in less fortunate circumstances.'

Barry Bolton. Stephen Smith. One and the same. The liar, the murderer and, for a short while, her lover. It sounds like something from a Mills and Boone.

This is something she would rather not have to deal with right now. As he must realise. She tries body language. Looking beyond the wide man in his immaculate Crombie overcoat, holding a bone handled brolly to keep off the drizzle. She notices instead, that he has moved the umbrella over her head, too. It doesn't feel like a gallant manoeuvre, more as if she has been incorporated, sucked into his gravity.

16

She tries again.

'Well, nice to meet you again. I should catch up with my mother.'

He doesn't move.

'Yes, of course, your mother. How is she bearing up. Such a sudden death. Quite unexpected. And they are so recently retired, hardly any time, any time at all.'

His head shakes in sorrow. His eyes penetrate.

'Unlike you, Miriam, your father's profession meant that he had to learn to be very quiet sometimes. Perhaps that's why nobody noticed him, as he lay there, at the petrol station. He was so quiet. I wonder if you have inherited any of those qualities. One would think they wouldn't be very useful to a journalist, but, sometimes, even someone like you could benefit from being very quiet. Like your father.'

She's not sure. Is she being threatened in some vague way? The great brown egg is shaking sorrow once more and the lips are tutting. Tutting!

'Oh, but please don't let me keep you from your duties. Off you go. You really are being very brave. Well done. Well done.'

He walks away, faster than would allow her to comfortably catch up with him, ask him just exactly what he meant, ask him his name. This is a graveyard, where processions are slow, the rain falls slowly and evenly, the gravel is level with the trimmed grass and the moss creeps across stone. She sees two men approaching, slowly, carrying shovels. It's time she left.

The doorbell. When finally the movement has ceased, with her mother upstairs knocked out by the normally forbidden sleeping pills her father kept for 'emergencies', when she is curled up in her dad's chair, reclaiming it from the entirely presumptuous vicar who had invited himself round for the wake and promptly sat himself down in what everyone else had recognised as hallowed space before proceeding to knock back the sherry and whisky and finger food whilst holding forth on the weather. The door. Someone and something else to deal with.

Steeling her nerves ready to tell who-ever it is to get lost, she opens the door to the very welcome face of Bill Freeman, her boss. He attempts a smile and the attempt is worth more to her than the hundreds of sympathetic grimaces she has encountered all day. As he shyly enters he looks pointedly at the door chain she neglected to use, then back at her, then at his watch.

'I hope you don't mind. I couldn't get away for the funeral. I know it's late but I wanted to see you before … are you still up?'

She's fully dressed, still in black and obviously still up. He has journalist's manners, worked into the grooves of his bearing over many years and small talk was dis-included many years ago. She brings him into the front room, sizes him up. The old fashioned look, everything creased, the clothes just the right side of comfortable, smart enough for the United Nations, casual enough for a pub in Soho, to go with Bill's old fashioned face, which is whisky and Guinness, Seamus and Windsor. Tired, but alive.

When he is settled on the sofa with a large whisky, his coat folded on his knee he finally looks at her, long and frank, as she hugs herself in her father's chair.

'When are you coming back?'

It's what she wants to hear.

'As soon as possible, Bill. I'm the executor of the will. We're going to try to get it out of the way quickly. Then I'll need to be here for my mum for a bit. But I can stay here and commute in. How long have I got?'

'Official bereavement leave? The management recommend

we allow a day for the funeral and a day to get over the hangover, but take as long as you like. When do you hear the will? He did make one…?'

'Tomorrow. We go to the solicitor's office at twelve. It all seems a bit quick.'

Sitting up, remembering.

'Bill, I was visited by someone who said she's from the government. She tried to get me to sign the Official Secrets Act.'

If Bill is surprised he doesn't show it.

'You didn't. Presumably.'

'No, of course not.'

'Good. Because then I would have had to sack you. What did she say?'

'She said, well she sort of threatened me, said they could hurt my career. It's to do with dad, with files. I don't know exactly what she meant.'

'Did your dad have a computer?'

'Yes, but it's an old PC, ancient. Surely he kept anything secret at work?'

'Miriam, the kind of things your dad was involved in, armaments, weapons manufacture and procurement, it's highly likely he knew all kinds of things they wouldn't want to be general knowledge. I'm not surprised they tried to get you to sign. But you don't have to. Just be aware of the, sensitivities here. And don't get yourself into any more trouble.'

'I can't imagine my father doing anything that, I don't know, is against the government. He was very patriotic, in his own way.'

Bill offers his empty glass to her for a refill.

'You should know better than that Miriam, after your experiences with Smith. It's all very complicated. Stay out of it. If you find anything, destroy it, delete it.. Just, get on with your life. I was thinking…'

Lightening up as much as he can, which isn't much:

'…when you come back, whether you might do some lifestyle features, interview some cooks and models, actors, for the magazine. Get some new experience. I'll take you off the death… er night shift and you can cover some of the happier stuff. Work with a photographer.'

'Bill, you know that's not what I want to do. I'm a journalist. I don't even read that stuff. I wouldn't have the first idea.'

'It's not your decision, Miriam. It's mine. As long as you're working at my paper you'll go where you're told.'

Perhaps realising where he is, the soft furnishings, the black bordered cards, the flowers. Not a newsroom, where he is, indeed, a minor king.

'I'm sorry. We'll talk about it when you come back. Miriam…'

'Yes?'

He's getting up.

'Use the chain, on the door. In fact, don't open the door unless you know who it is. Even then, be careful.'

His coat is on and he's almost out the front room door. She knows he won't answer, yet. But it's time to start asking.

'Bill, what is it? What is it that you won't talk about, that my dad wouldn't talk about? I'm a part of it all now. You need to tell me. I need to know.'

He's standing at the open front door now, back to her, looking about in the lamp-lit wet, pulling his collar up like a gumshoe detective.

'Not now, Miriam. Not now. We'll speak when this is over'

He turns for a goodbye glance and then walks off. She stands watching him. He calls:

'And lock the door.'

* * *

20

*   *   *

If ever there is a graphic example of the system of the governing class at its most raw, here it is, right at the roots. Toby is happily ignoring a tall, confident looking young chap who is talking to him as he looks around at the assembled esteemed visitors to the Stedman. Eventually his attention drifts back to the Head of School, in time to hear:

'Look, Tobes, I know you're not happy about this and, to be honest, neither am I, so just get on with it, then slope off as soon as you've made your presence felt with the staff. As long I can say you attended and helped out a bit then we're both happy. But, please, try not to upset anyone, especially the OS's. OK?'

Toby is wearing a prefect badge. He has earned it with two weeks of good behaviour, attendance and regular conversation. The Master has decided to try to reward him with some encouraging responsibility, even though she feels uneasy about him being here at such a high profile event. He is determined to keep her and Steve Blake happy. This is a test he will pass. All he has to do is be polite. He nods at the elegant young man watching his face, waiting patiently for an acknowledgement. Fine.

Be polite. To a collection of snobs and bores, ex-service men and still-serving judges; professors and clergy; business men and politicians. All of them with a heightened sense of entitlement due to being back in the place that made them.

Moving back, away from the main entrance to the lobby he watches the teachers, pupils and ex-pupils milling around. In his dark suit he could be a very junior partner in a law firm or at an accountants. He prefers wearing this to the blazer that makes him a target on the streets of the town for the boys and girls from the comprehensive schools. All Stedman boys have to run through their adolescent years from the hoi polloi. It creates a secret hate that will serve them well in future years as they lock up or order around or send to hell the lower classes who tormented them out of the shops and parks. It's the very solid bond between the old boys and Toby's generation, solidified in fear like all the strongest allegiances.

Although Toby came to this realisation by himself he is grateful to his mentor for agreeing with him. Steve Blake knows. He says he experienced what Toby is experiencing. And he was as desperate to escape as Toby is. He lied but how would Toby know that? Steve Blake is a brilliant liar.

There is a firm tap on his shoulder. Toby turns to see a stooped tortoise of a man, one arm holding a well-worn, Mahogany walking stick, peering over the top of half-moon spectacles. His tanned pate is almost completely bald but there is a thin moustache below his beak.

'Excuse me. I do hope I'm not disturbing you. Have they moved the trophies?'

The voice belies the image. To Toby old is old, in fact, anything above fifty-five is old. But if he were to close his eyes he would hear the voice of a virile cricket commentator, or perhaps a cricketer recently retired, someone used to being listened to, a captain and an issuer of the definitive statement. Toby's instinct is to tell him to fuck off.

'No, they're still where they were. Did you… I can take you, if you want.'

Polite.

'They have definitely been moved. They used to be in the corridor by the Master's office. They're not there now. I looked.'

'Yes, they are. Opposite the door.'

'No, they're not. I looked.'

Looking around, everyone is busy with everyone else. This beaky man obviously belongs to him. He starts moving off.

'Follow me, I'll…'

'Not so fast.'

A horny forefinger reaches his wrist, hooks into his jacket cuff.

'I'm not as young as you, young man. Now, which way?'

Feeling as if he has been chained to a rock Toby walks towards a corridor leading off to one side of the lobby.

'Where are we going? The long way? I want to see the trophies, not the gymnasium.'

They have paused. This is going to take forever. Toby seeks patience from within.

'When were you here last, er, sir?'

' I visited last time I was back in England. Ten years ago. Why?'

'I think they did some building, before I came here, renovations. The Master's office is down this way now.'

Although he doesn't look very pleased with the information it at least spurs movement. Not a word is said until, further down the corridor they stop by a large, floor to ceiling, glass cabinet, filled with cups, shields and trophies. Toby wonders if he can leave him to it, but he finds he is still a captive. After a long couple of minutes, gazing intently the horny forefinger taps at the glass near the middle shelf.

'I knew it. It's not there. It's not there because he didn't get it.'

At this moment there is a small commotion from the end of the corridor in the direction from which they have just arrived. A stocky figure of medium height is limping towards them, calling out:

'It's there, right where I told you it was!'

Limping into their orbit. Fresh faced, a sporting man, child face almost unwrinkled, plastered over a boxy head on the wrecked body that once flew across turf carrying ball and javelin. Slightly breathless.

'I told you. I told you. They moved the bloody trophies, just went to where they used to be. Bloody computers in the

Master's office.'

'The computer room.' Toby offers. He is ignored. The pilgrim who he just guided makes a little cackling sound at the back of his throat.

Standing back with a malicious smile below the beak as the captain of all sports examines the cabinet.

'Where is it? Bloody thing. Where is it?'

He turns to Toby.

'Where is it boy?'

'Where's what?' It's not going to last, this politeness.

'Hockey. County champions, nineteen fifty-one. It used to be here.'

Toby knows if he speaks then he won't be able to help himself. He shrugs, instead.

'Stupid! Where is it?' and the captain bangs on the glass, his face turned florid. Several trophies topple. The tortoise laughs out loud, wickedly.

'I told you! It was never there. Because you didn't win it! I won it, in nineteen forty-nine. You lost it!'

Triumph versus distraught. It's a familiar scene to Toby in these corridors, normally played out with younger participants. Instead of walking off he is now interested enough to see what happens.

The sports captain is raging, spit on his lips, eyes bulging, limp-stomping around the case as his tormentor laughs louder, shaking like a dusty old tree in a breeze. This is fun. A lunge, the Mahogany stick is suddenly swinging, the tortoise man is falling backwards, landing on his back just as the glass cracks, smashes, the handle of the stick laying waste to the school's glories.

A moment.

One hand still on the stick, eye twitching, high flush on his cheeks, looking down, the captain of Steddon School field hockey team, nineteen fifty, at the captain, nineteen forty nine, who appears unconscious, arms across his midrift, a swatted fly by the Master's door. A voice, familiar, unexpected and wonderful – how did he get there without Toby noticing?

'Alright gents?'

A tall, slim man, apparently out for a stroll in the corridors, casually observing the small chaos. Kneeling by the unmoving old man, feeling for a pulse. Standing, looking down at the surviving captain, who's mouth is slowly opening with, perhaps an excuse, but pre-empted by the new arrival:

'Dead. Well done.'

A captain's stammer:

'What, what do you mean, 'well done'? I didn't do anything!'

'Yes you did. I saw you push him, you were going to hit him but you're stick got caught in the glass.'

'It's not my stick! Don't be so bloody preposterous! I wouldn't hit Bloxy!'

'I saw you. And so did this young man here. Didn't you?'

Toby knows enough by now. If an opportunity presents itself, act, quickly.

'Yes, you were going to hit him. With the stick.'

The tall man beckons with his head for Toby to join him. Stepping over the body, Toby can't help smiling at the sight of Steve Blake, who gives him instructions.

'Go and tell someone that there's been an accident. There's no need for anyone to know what really happened here - is there?' Addressing the last part to the completely flummoxed Old Stedonian, still holding the stick, staring from Toby, to Blake to the dead man, his mouth making an O.

A quick, fascinated glance at the swatted Bloxy and Toby runs back down the corridor. Blake regards the killer calmly.

'Someone will be in touch in the near future, Captain

Saunders.'

'What do you mean? How do you know my name? I don't know you?' Cheeks puffing, looking for his outrage.

Blake just points, his finger touching the rectangle of paper stuck to the old soldier's breast pocket that bears the legend of his name. Saunders looks down and Blake flicks his nose gently, before walking off, apparently oblivious to the pitiful bellow following down the parquet and plaster.

'You won't get away with it! Who do you think you are! I didn't touch him! Stupid!'

Standing on tip toes at the back he casts his eyes over the sea of grey and flesh to spot Blake, there, inches taller than most around him, apparently paying close attention to the Master's speech, welcoming the Old Stedonians for this extraordinary Founder's Day, a celebration of eight hundred years of unbroken educational achievements. Captain Saunders is long gone in a taxi, slightly better for a few sherries in the Master's room, but still pop eyed and paranoid, catching sight of Toby but thinking better of making a noise, just allowing his mouth to make goldfish bubbles as his eyes tried to leave his head.

The old captain's adversary of the decades has been removed in a private ambulance, after having blessed the school with its seventh heart attack in seventy years.

Noticing that Blake is wearing a school tie. Was he a genuine old boy? How did he get himself invited? They are clapping now and the Head Of School is on stage doing his impression of a Victorian philanthropist caught in a middle manager's body, dressed by Saville Row, asking everyone to please make their way outside to the Old Gateway.

Toby waits by the exit and gets into step with Blake who doesn't acknowledge him until they are slightly away from the crawling crowd.

'In a minute you will need to snitch on one of your schoolmates, in your own year. His name is Findlay. Any problems with that?'

No!

'What has he done? How do I know?'

'Say you heard him boasting about it on his mobile.'

'He hasn't got a mobile.'

'Yes, he has. Don't worry. Be confident. No one will know it was you who told.'

Blake wanders into the throng standing around the small wooden stage set up by the ancient wall of the Old Gatehouse. As he moves off Toby thinks he hears him whisper: 'you'll enjoy this!' but he's not sure.

The choir is regimented into two rows on one side, singing Benjamin Britten's *Flower Songs*. A microphone has been set up on the stage, where the Master, Mary Dacre, wearing a beatific smile and a two-piece in autumnal colours stands next to a tall, thin bishop, his purple/violet shirt shining in the light. The sun has come out. The bishop, in small, rimless bifocals, smiles pleasantly into the middle distance. A gentle sense of expectation fills the air. There's been a death, we can all relax now, the worst has happened and here we are, here the school is. The choir finishes. The most feminine of masters steps up to the mic.

'Ladies and gentlemen, Old Stedonians, pupils, teachers and guests. Here is Bishop, the Right Reverend Iain Althorpe, who will unveil the plaque.'

And she gracefully steps back. Some might have noticed her look over her shoulder and wrinkle her nose. Has the Bishop farted, wonders Toby.

The Bishop takes centre stage.

'Before the unveiling, let us bow our heads for a short prayer.'

'Lord, we thank you for taking care of this wonderful

school. We hope that your light and your love will fill the hearts of the boys and staff who are here, now, and who will come to this school in the future…'

Toby is looking fully into the eyes of Mary Dacre, who glances over her shoulder again, then back at Toby.

'…to be filled with knowledge and to experience their first faltering steps into the world with the benefit of a superb education and that, with your protection, the school will continue to thrive for another eight hundred years as it has, to this day. Amen.'

Waiting, while the amens are murmured and eyes squint open in the autumn sun, which casts the crowd in beams and causing hands to shield brows. The Bishop tugs at a velvet rope hanging next to a small set of curtains, they slide apart easily to reveal the plaque, which is almost completely obscured by thick streaks of brown matter.

There is a moment and then the Old Stedonians erupt; rice pudding spilling slowly and steadily from the pan, a sound, a range of hungry farm animals, a noise, a cold engine on a cold day, that once put the fear into an Empire: the polite anger of the British that needs to vent in the most efficient and proper way possible.

Now Toby understands. He catches a glimpse of Steve Blake, who is smiling to himself, not too subtly taking pictures on his mobile of the stage, the plaque, the faces around him. The Head Of School has rushed on to the stage with a tea cloth, but one look at the mess on the plaque and he is left, cloth in mid-air, looking around for permission to, leave it for the cleaners or the caretaker.

Mary Dacre shoos him off the stage. She helps the Bishop step down and then pulls the curtains across the shit-laden bronze. Ignoring the microphone she calls out.

'Ladies and gentlemen. Due to…what has happened here, I suggest we adjourn to the canteen where there are refreshments. Please.' And she gestures, with her arm out, towards marshalling prefects, some of whom are having a hard time not laughing. Toby hangs back. He looks for Blake, who has disappeared. Should he do it now? The decision is made for him.

'You know something about this, Flaxman. Don't you.'

It's the Master, suddenly in front of him. Toby has never seen her quite as... ruffled. She is accusing him with eyes and angle, her chin lifted. Well, this is easy, too.

'Yes, I do Master. Can we go somewhere more private. I have a confession to make.'

2

Chapter 2: Extra Normal

Boredom the only enemy. Peter and Ann feel like old friends already. Not with each other – of course they are old friends. They're married, have been for a long time now, very successfully. No, with him. His old friends, Peter and Ann, the Garveys. They don't know why, except that, they agree with him. Totally.

He crosses his legs like Peter has just crossed his, in the English, testicle crushing style. They sit near the hearth, filled with logs, ready for winter, toes pointing at the mantel while he reads the bound report and Peter watches. He finishes the last page, sits with hands upon the paper like a magician doing a trick. Changing the physiognomy. Peter makes a half full bottle of whisky appear from the side of his chair and passes it towards him. More magic.

'Can I pour you another tot, Steve?'

Reaching for his empty glass, holding it out. He's going off whisky.

'It makes for a sad story, Peter.'

'Indeed, indeed it does. Year on year, for the past five. I don't know how they manage to keep it going. Millions. Down the drain.'

'It doesn't matter, though.'

'I know it doesn't. Fascinating though, isn't it. What a word in the right ear can achieve. If you buy shares tomorrow, you'll get them for peanuts. But I can guarantee, in ten years time, you'll be able to retire on the results of say, ten thousand, on those alone. You should.'

'Should I?'

'You could fund some of the enterprises with just one of these.' Leaning over, tapping the top of the report.

'Do you?'

'What, take advantage? I can't be too blatant. But, sometimes, when I can create enough distance... how do you think we can afford this place as well as Wales?'

Joining them, Ann sits on the arm of her husband's chair, loosely letting her hand fall to his nape, to play with the soft curls there. A handsome couple.

'Peter is very careful. We both are. But it really is too easy, once you know the right people. And we do.'

In front of the hearth, contentedly waiting on his master and mistress, Steve Blake imagines a wolfhound, head on paws, eyes switching between the two who love him most.

'You two should get a dog.'

They both laugh. Good old Steve. Ann answers.

'I'd love a dog. A big old wolfhound. A family dog.'

'Seriously. The right kind of dog is better than an alarm. You'll need something. Which reminds me. I brought them. One each. They're easy to use. Let me get them and I'll show you.'

As he gets up he takes in the shine of excitement in their eyes. So far, a good choice.

In the hall of this great, complicated, Georgian and Victorian shell. Everything replaced apart from the outside walls, the ambience and the inhabitants. Peter and Ann could easily be the living embodiment of any number of well to do historical residents, apart from the fact that Ann is a highly paid barrister in her own right, next to her husband who is a solicitor. And there are no servants in the quarters upstairs where Smith will be sleeping later that night, although a cleaner will arrive tomorrow at ten in the morning when they have both left for their journey to the office at Lincoln's Inn Fields.

He takes two boxes from the shoulder bag he brought with him which was left hanging next to his coat on a peg. It's a windy night. The big front door rattles and he can hear twigs and leaves tapping the roof of his car outside. Apart from nature, it's very quiet here, a good forty yards from the main road that leads into the light streams of north London. An exclusive island in a private sea.

Ann has sat down next to the imaginary dog, on a rug in front of the hearth, sipping a whisky. In her jeans and slipper socks and several layers of sweatshirt and T shirt, she makes for an advert of successful aspiration. She couldn't be more comfortable in her skin. The same age as her husband, she has kept herself fit in mind and body and, he thinks, is the brains behind their partnership. She's bored, as well, which gives him an open window to climb through. Peter happily tags along, borrowing her ideas and ideals. Without Ann, Peter would not be on his list. Together they are perfect. An intelligent couple in early middle age, with an address book, between them, that would be worth killing for. Which he has considered. Which is still an option, if these two class traitors revert to their tribal loyalty.

He hands them two guns, grip first. Matching Browning High Powereds, evil looking hardware favoured by police forces in Europe for decades, for that timeless killing look.

Peter weighs it, passes it between his hands, figures out how to open up the chamber. Aims along the barrel.

'Bang. Very easy, isn't it? Just like the movies. Another

32

solution solved. Bang.'

Ann has placed the pistol on the floor next to her. She holds out a hand.

'Bullets, please.'

He passes her a cartridge. She slots it into place.

'How do you take the safety off?'

She figures it out for herself, stands and walks behind the two chairs on which the men are sitting. Peter turns to watch, frowning. Steve takes a sip from his glass.

She empties the cartridge into the logs in the fireplace. Twelve shots that leave the room ringing. Luckily there were no ricochets. He'll mention their possibility before she gets another cartridge. Nothing is said. Peter looks at him and he passes a cartridge across. Peter slots it in. Stands and moves back. He is grinning like a kid. This time Steve Blake picks up his glass and moves well away from the fireplace.

Outside, the garden rustles, crackles. Occasional leaves, ripped from the branches, float see-sawing to gravel and lawn. The sound of the great bowl of central London is a low thunder constantly rumbling in the background. Sirens punctuate and an airplane full of dreams flies across the millions of lights. There might be other creatures around but it is the humans who are having all the fun tonight, as with every night. Owls and foxes and half-sleeping pigeons stir at the crack, crack, crack, followed by bursts of laughter coming from the big house under the ivy. Blake-who-is-Smith casts his net with bangs and bullets at two thirty in the morning.

*   *   *

Making his choices for various reasons. Irony and humour, as much as use. They all become resources, whatever their talents. For instance. Here's Abe Humphry.

Not the nicest of flats, but in the constantly up and coming area of Tottenham he is buried deeply enough. Smith-known-as-Blake has paid the rent for a year and Abe has the place to himself. A bed, a fridge, five different pay-as-you-go mobiles. A West Indian take away two doors down for endless supplies of curry goat and pattie. Empty cans of Redstripe piling into the biggest binbag he could find. Instructions to avoid the CCTV ring of Hackney just down the road. Stay on the buses and overland trains. Stay in at night. If Abe plays his cards right he will have a small fortune to buy himself a ticket and a fake passport to somewhere without an extradition treaty. Is he grateful? Not at all. Abe is a man who accepts his fate: what God brings to the table is what he will accept.

Smith sits on the other chair in the tiny kitchen, a beer, untouched, on the formica top watching Abe roll and puff endless joints, suck Redstripe and shrink inside his track suit. He has asked for the whole story, how the diminutive Abe came to be inside for GBH, committed on a large African gangster (probably Nigerian) known as Gee Gee Aguta, hailing from Bethnal Green way. Abe is coming to the end of the tale.

'Gee Gee wasn't dead. I knew that, I saw him twitching. But he can't walk proper anymore, affected his brain. Can only see out of one eye. Like a stroke, I suppose. I'm not a violent man, Blakey, you know me, I'm not. But when my back's up. I'm not nice.'

'Remind me not to play golf with you, Abe.' Abe responds with a wry smile.

'Anyway, if any of Gee Gee's mob see me now, I'm dead. So, even though I hate Tottenham, better to be here than in the east. Cheers.'

And he drains the can.

Smith hasn't touched his.

'What have you got for me, Abe.'

'What have I got for you, Blakey old son? A word, a

whisper. Boxing match, good odds. Put it all on him, the Irish.' Passing over a crumpled betting slip on which is scrawled a name. 'And put this on it for me, if you don't mind.' Passing back a bundle of twenties, the same money Blake had given him earlier for 'expenses'.

'Sixty quid. I'll triple that.'

Smith doesn't mind, it's what he was expecting. A little motivation. Now, what can he, himself, afford to triple, without bringing too much attention? The little man will know. It's what he's here for.

Abe Humphry, staring into the smoke from his spliff.

Abe knows there has to be a pay out of some kind. This quiet, tough acting guy, Blakey, isn't doing it for love, or even tips at good odds. He's got something in mind, probably iffy. But Abe knows enough to keep his mouth shut, in one confined space or another. So he leaves the questions for a time when there might be answers. Besides, he likes him. Better to carry on liking the man, drinking Red Stripe, smoking a spliff.

* * *

No one likes a screw. But they are a necessity. Even the villains understand that. Those who work in the prison service have a lot of the qualities that Stephen Smith is looking for: loyalty to each other; they mind their own business and tend not to engage in casual chat with strangers; they are normally resentful that their work is seen as the nasty side of law and order; they are taught institutional tactics of violence. They normally drink too much, have rotten personal relationships and are susceptible to blackmail. Perfect. And this one has access to a positive army of small time crooks, thugs and outcasts. Even better.

At first, Dan White is sure that Blake-who-is-Smith is a secret millionaire. The way he parachutes himself into the life of the officer in charge of rehabilitation of Young Offenders, Liverpool. The way this pleasant guy in, what? - his forties? - has access to ready cash. Dan knows he's not being bribed, though: the money has gone towards practical things, much appreciated by both him and the YOs, stuff that will possibly make a difference: a bang up to date lathe; a hydraulic garage lift, to get them under the car without a trolley; several computers, chained to the desks and already fitted with a library of bookmarks for engineering sites, diagrams, tutorials in mechanics, engineering and HTML. The only provisos are that Smith-who-is-Blake's name be kept out of the press and reports (he is an 'unknown benefactor') and that Smith be allowed to observe the workshops attended by the YOs, coming up for remand, which Dan manages by swinging an observer's pass, normally given to government rep's from various departments. It's a small thing to do for the returns.

Actually, he enjoys Smith's visits and so do the lads. The man has an easy manner, but he's not soft. Plus he's a mine of info. Once, when a tutor didn't turn up, Smith took a class of hopeful mechanics, explaining, on his own BMW, how to replace a faulty alarm unit and how a car that has been disabled can be reset without the need to return it to a trade garage. Genuinely useful stuff.

All from a chance meeting in a pub! Blake-who-is-Smith was standing there, at the bar and they just got chatting. He never normally talks to strangers outside of the scene. During the odd game of darts or pool, he makes a point of keeping the small chat very small. He certainly never tells anyone what he does for a living. But, somehow, Blake guessed. Initially making him for a bizzie, then talking in admiring terms about the difficult job beginning after the arrests, after the court and the verdict has been read. Absolutely.

So Blake-who-is-Smith successfully chats up this amiable

father of two, recently divorced prison lifer. Dan White finds himself, over several more coincidental meetings at the pub, talking openly about his frustrations with his job. With a beer belly that belies the intelligence and commitment, dark eyebrows below a thick mat of grey, White isn't kidding himself, but he can't help it: he fancies Steve Blake, in fact, he's a little bit in love.

Does Dan, the snappy dresser, lathered in lotion on a Saturday night in the Curzon, notice Smith from the corner of his eye? Does his subconscious put the features together to make a safe passage for their friendship, for later, when they meet in the pub? Smith knows a bit about psychology but he's in a hurry, so just the one cruise round is all he allows himself and he got lucky. With Dan, the old self-denying queer.

Somewhere in the file of this man's memory is an illegal liaison with a prisoner, probably a young one, hopefully a teenager. Smith will eventually help his new friend open it in his presence. With any luck he won't have to use it; White seems to be onside already, as an outsider, an intelligent man with a conscience and a will to do, something. He doesn't need to be a team player, there are enough of those. He just needs to be useful and brave, or motivated enough to put his fear to one side.

Enough tickling around. It's time that soft, south Scouse accent wrapped its vowels around some truths. They have just finished clearing up after a workshop, Smith's fourth time. The tools are accounted for. The machines are off. They sit in Dan's office, sipping mugs of tea.

'We lose a couple next week, Steve.'

'Who's going?'

'Richie and Will. Shame they didn't have longer, I think they were picking it up really well, specially Will.'

'Nice lads, too.'

'You wouldn't say that if you know what put them in.'

'Bad?'

'Bad. Violent, both of them. Will was worst. I can't say exactly, but don't let that bumfluff face fool you, Steve. Catch him on the wrong night…'

'But they're smart. Will's intelligent, sharp. Surely there's a better use for someone like him.'

'How do you mean 'use'? He's never worked a day in his life. Perhaps if he had a few more sessions in here he could get himself a grease monkey job at a garage. Apart from that, I'll be seeing him again in a few months.'

'He'll be getting used while he's outside. Someone will be taking what he steals and fencing it, taking a cut. Someone will be using him to distribute drugs or to settle disputes. Even in here, he'll be getting used, as someone's muscle, as a fixer. But he's better than that. I could use a young man like that and help him to help himself. Know what I mean?'

'I'm not sure, Steve. I don't even know what your business is, not that we don't appreciate what you've done, the money, the gear…?'

Smith gets up. He looks through the glass of the office window into the workshop. It's empty. He slowly walks around, behind Dan's chair and puts his hands on Dan's shoulders, kneading them gently, boxer-trainer style.

'It's alright mate, I'm not into the boys, I don't want to put him on the game. Too young, right? But they have skills, and so do you, Dan. If I can connect a man with the skill to a man with a need for a man with the skill, then everyone benefits. You, for instance, have worked hard and found yourself in this unique position, a command of your own, away from the dregs and the monotony. You're making a difference. That's what I'm all about, Dan, making a difference. Balancing the scales of justice.'

He massages a bit harder. Dan is obviously uncomfortable.

'You can help me find talented individuals, bring them on, like the propagators do to the baby plants, make them grow faster, stronger. Choose the good ones, do a little weeding. Then, when they're ready, I can provide them with some fulfilling work.'

Calmly moving away, back to his seat, relaxing with full eye contact with the older man across the desk.

'And as you are acting as my consultant I can help with some cash payments that you can put towards your retirement. It's all perfectly legal, but a bit below the radar. Nothing in writing. Just give me the odd pointer, who's shaping up. As you did with Will and thanks for that. How does all that sound?'

Dan gathers himself. He had hypnotised himself with possibility.

'Bloody confusing. What work? What kind?'

'Well, Will is obviously getting the hang of engineering. He's a dab hand with the lathe. His maths skills are excellent. So I would find work for him in that field. Probably not a permanent position, but one that would ultimately benefit him far more than another course at an FE college.'

Getting up, ready to leave now.

'You could come and have a look, once I've got him into something. Check it over, make sure you're happy there's nothing unethical about it. Think it over. I'll call later.'

Solid Steve, Respectable Mr. Blake. Off he goes in his solid car. Leaving Dan the prison officer man wanting, wanting to say yes, even if it's a little bit dodgy - anything is better than another lonely pint tonight, waking up tomorrow with the sofa pattern dented in his cheek, the taste of a take-away on his tongue – if there's a chance those strong hands melt the tension in his shoulders, one more time.

As Smith drives away, he senses the give, as Dan White's will bows to basic human need and he likes the man for it. A collection, a tribe, a gang. He wants to like his people, for all their faults. He wants faulty operatives, not efficient managers. Real people. Too long spent with the nihilists of of his previous employment. Wriggling through the crevasses between all the gangs: the police gang, the law gang, the toffs and the merchants and the bishops. His gang will fit right in with everyone else. Their strength will be their weaknesses, all together. That, and their ability to use a gun.

He calls Dan White on his hands free, as he drives.

'Dan, Steve again. Dan was there anyone else?'

'How do you mean Steve?'

'Any other young men, perhaps they stayed in your mind, because of one thing or another in the past. If they're out and you're still in contact, perhaps we could help they, too. Any ideas?'

'Oh. Yes, come to think of it. There might be one or two. In fact, there's one guy in particular. I'll have a look, see if I've got an address or a number.'

'Great!'

Of course you will. Here's the excuse you've been waiting for Dan. Lovers reunited. The truth.

*   *   *

Slap! Right cheek. Slap! The left. A small blossom of red. The slap, on the beat, sixteen bars til the end of the routine so, bent right over, legs apart, giving it all away for the third time this evening. Lilly, everything shining, from dazzling teeth to polished shins, via slinky vulva, all the hair concentrated on her head.

The track finishes. The MC/DJ raises the cheers and applause:

'The lovely Lilly! Let's hear it chaps! Lilly! Coming up in five minutes the delightful, the athletic… Tedi!' And he plays another bass heavy tune, keeping the pace even, like the flow of beer and spirits in the club.

Smith drops a fiver in a beer glass and receives a cheeky smile of thanks from a sweet girl in mesh and nylon who is pacing round like a colt learning to walk, in vertiginous platform heels. Browns used to be the classiest strip joint in Shoreditch. Now it's one of only two left and its days are numbered.

The last time Smith was trawling the sleaze around here was years ago, looking for some emotional numbing, pissed and flying on ecstasy. Back then there were numerous pubs with unlicensed strip shows, often taking place on beer sodden carpets, inches away from scummy blokes who, on returning to their homes, would beat off to the memories before taking to their frigid beds and falling into a lager and pickled onion sleep.

Even though Smith tried to place himself ironically in this crowd as an observer, not an enjoyer, he knows that, really, simply by being there, he is making it all happen. The slave prostitution. The hints at pedophilia with some of the youngest looking girls.

He had stood, leaning on the bar in a tiny pub lounge watching a girl who looked fifteen, rows of punctures in her arms, spread herself over a pool table, the balls still on the stained green, as a woman who looked like a hybrid of ancient East End harridan and glamorous pub landlord dressed in Diana Dors' soiled underwear, stood over her, talking, telling her how to move, how to pose. Next to Smith at the bar a young man in a track suit put his back to his charge as she earned them their next fix.

All for the pleasure of five men in anoraks and donkey jackets and the ironic Mr. Smith. Or whatever he called himself back then.

But if this was a gutter that he found himself in it was nowhere as low as he had fallen. Compared to the looks on the faces of his 'clients', bound to the simple wooden chair, ready to sell the stories of their souls, dripping in pain, compared to them, the essence of defeat in this young stripper's eye could be mistaken for hope. Which was why he was there, back in the day: steeped in booze and pills, trying to give himself a rest from the sights and sounds of agony which had become his nine to five.

Compared to those mucky shit holes Browns was a palace, back then. Now it feels like a heritage experience. Pretty soon, the professional women of Hackney will have committed this surviving bawd from London's previous moments of gay violence and abandonment to a mention in a Peter Ackroyd book. Meanwhile, the city boys are having their Saturday night, various old school villains are reliving Soho times and Smith waits for Tedi to pass around the pint glass.

Here she is.

'You're back then. Should I be flattered?'

He spotted the accent immediately last time and flummoxed her with some fluent Croatian, which seemed to equally delight and annoy her. Tedi is on a mission to make money and doesn't welcome distractions.

'I'm hoping to see something new, this time.' As he slots a twenty pound note into the glass. Flash tippers aren't unusual here, but there is a code. Too much and it looks like a punter might want more than just to look and a word is had with one of the beefy guys at the door and with the proprietress and the MC and a taxi is booked. The over eager punter might find his way out blocked for a few minutes while the young lady who interests him heads off into the night.

'I doubt it. You must have seen everything last time. If you didn't, get closer this time.'

Walking off, with a squeak of buffed latex. She manages the stilts with the balance of the gymnast she trained to be. In some ways, the best part of the show is Tedi walking the glass round. Some of the girls resent going on before her as she distracts the punters from the stage. Smith certainly enjoys himself, following her a few paces behind as she takes her position by the stage steps, waiting for the MC and her track to start up.

Strange how a gymnast in her prime makes way for a supple woman in her prime. Is she spending all her good health, all her muscle strength in her youth only to have to spend her older age in agonies of arthritis? Smith is at the lip of the stage and she holds his eyes with hers as she parts her legs, lifting one up, knee behind her ear, as she licks the tip of one finger and slides it down, over tensed stomach muscles to her crotch where she fakes a wank and her eyes act out an orgasm, before spinning herself upright and then bending over backwards, her head near Smith's as she gives the men at the other side of the stage a good look too. Oh to be born a woman in the west. Failing that, a visa will do. Smith is surprised to hear a dedication.

'That was for you.'

At one side of the long, horse shoe bar, away from the flying TV sets showing sports activity from various channels, the girls are allowed to congregate in twos or threes and relax for a few minutes on the tall stools and, very occasionally, accept a drink from a regular. The way they relax their bodies sends a message and, despite the fact that they are still only dressed in the strips and clasps of their stage gear the punters ignore them. The green light is off.

Smith is the opposite side of the bar. A small woman, glamorous in hours of tailoring and hair sculpture, proper and expensive, discreet jewels, the epitome of East End class, doesn't serve but watches quietly and mentions and gestures and things happen. Smith catches her eye.

'I'd like to buy Tedi a drink. Is that OK?'

He waits while she sees him. As good an examination as the best of Scotland Yard. He is summed up and passes muster but with a question mark. Money, but where from? Either way, he is blessed with a dazzling smile and an instruction.

'Orange juice, darling. No ice.' A pretty young barmaid has the glass in front of him in seconds, then it is whipped away together with his money. He watches the glass arrive next to Tedi, who is sitting, one elbow on the bar at the other side, the glass goes to lipstick lip, sipped, put down then ignored. She tosses him a casual smile over her shoulder before returning to chat with another stripper, two perfumed athletes awaiting their cues.

Did he arrange to be there? If he did, he has conveniently forgotten, in order to be genuine.

'Hey! You dropped your mobile!'

She hadn't noticed. His car is shining in the rain shower, engine purring, door open and he is on the pavement holding up her phone. She is hidden beneath an umbrella. They join each other and she decides to let her guard down a little. Just enough to look him in the face.

'Oh, it's you!'

He seems to be genuinely surprised. But how would he recognise her, fully clothed, hatted, beneath the umbrella? He is embarrassed. Cute.

'Sorry, this looks really… sleazy. I saw the phone drop then I… well, cheers.'

He starts to walk away.

'Hey! Thank you!' She catches him up.

'Don't worry. It's not sleazy at all. I need my phone. Thanks.' Should she?

She does.

'How come you speak Serb-Croat so well?'

'I'm a translator. I spent quite a bit of time out there. I spotted your accent, don't get much opportunity to speak it nowadays.'

He's getting wet. His car is illegally parked. She's got to get home.

'Give me a lift.' Mad, she must be. If Nicky finds out she's dead. Still.

'Where to? Where do you live?'

'No, it's stupid. I live miles away in Greenwich.' New Cross, actually.

'Are you sure? You don't know me.'

'I trust you. You can speak to me in the car, we can have a conversation.' She walks towards the car.

It helps, to be good looking, apparently well off. Respectability is an expensive suit, that's all. If you can afford it, you can have it. Smith has got plenty of money. Not technically his, but who's worried about little details like that?

How can he use a beautiful, athletic Croatian stripper? Let him count the ways.

*   *   *

Then, when he's feeling like this there isn't a thing he can't do. Intense empathy, a super power.

On a train to a place, one of a few, where a small case contains thousands of pounds, Euros and dollars. It's expensive, this adventure. It has financial implications. Soon, he will need to go shopping again. In fact, it's one of the regular activities he's planning for his people: once a year, rob a bank. Or an institution. Or... someone.

Casting around the carriage, heading south, towards the sun and sea. Any one of these people will do. A couple of students, lost in battery power, headphones and mobiles and laptop, as committed to communication as any unit of soldiers on the front line.

A mother. Her baby. Stroking and caressing it to quiet. A refugee on a secret road; a wrong-religion duo in a cupboard under the stairs; a Hutu or a Tutsi family remnant, saving their horror memories for another day, hiding in a bush. Don't cry.

In matching grey and beige, an elderly couple, their hands entwined on the seat, warming their love, fighting the world and its expectations to keep together, to keep alive. He has the experience of fifty years in a workplace that chaffed his hands and calloused his nerves. She has the muscle strength built by three births and nursing her mother to a comfortable death.

Survivalists all. Anyone will do.

His eye alights on an overweight man in creased chinos, sweater and cheap windcheater, eating a home-made sandwich from some greaseproof paper. He looks out of the window as he eats, never at his food and jots short scrawls in a small notebook parked on the table next to the greaseproof paper. A trainspotter!

But Smith will never know if, in his arrogant mood swing towards complete and utter self belief, he could have made this a fighter, a possible killer, out of a man who's primary interest is all things trains, whether this man could be enjoined to join his gang. He is beaten to the punch.

A tall man in a long, tan overcoat and what look like tweed plus fours which end in socks that, in turn, disappear into ten hole work boots, a surprisingly cool look, is suddenly standing next to the startled train spotter. This man holds his own notebook, a school jotter, open in one hand in front of him and he begins to speak, clearly, above the rattling bogies.

'Ladies and gentlemen, forgive me for interrupting your journey. I am not asking for money, I am not begging. I am not mad, at least, no madder than any of you. And I am not drunk or on drugs.

I merely want to read you a poem, to which you can listen or ignore and it will be over before you know it.'

He clears his throat. Most people in the moderately full carriage have given him a glance then got back on with what they are doing. But a few have cocked an ear and are waiting expectantly.

He starts.

'Six! Six times, turned around.

Taken to the place, where my clock is unwound.

Where the shock joins the sound

Of teeth that are grounding

The rubber bit, as the shock hits:

One, two, three, four, five, six.

And when I return

With my soul burned and seared

My silence elec-tricked to my ears

Licked, fixed, locked in tears.

I count the days with finger clicks.

Before it starts again. Six.'

And here, he clicks his fingers, loudly, six times, before smiling to himself, looking around, acknowledging a brief, tender clap from the mother and, finally, looking at Smith, a full, frank stare that is followed by a confident walk, almost swagger, until he is looking down at Smith. Who looks up from his seat.

'Bravo.'

'May I sit down?'

Smith gets a good look at the young man as he sits next to him. His skin a yellow brown, tight curled, scrappy beard and moustaches, thick framed glasses, a cloth cap perched above delicate ear-ringed ears, two white, shiny badges at the lobes like flat pearls. He holds out a hand.

'Sherriff Clarke. Nice to meet you.'

Smith is delighted to meet him.

'Steve Blake. I enjoyed your poem.'

'I know you did. The only one. Everyone else was ready to patronise or hate or, even worse, ignore. I think you understood. I think you knew what I was talking about. I think you might have even experienced, the same. The shock. Am I right?'

Smith notices their hands are still locked together, like a Japanese handshake, sealing the deal. Of course. But we can't have this overeager pup thinking he is in control. He squeezes the poet's hand harder.

'You said you're not mad.'

'They cured me.'

'They cured the incurable? I don't think so. You are managed. And showing obvious signs of not taking your managing pills.'

The handshake is flipped, suddenly, into a soul shake, Sherriff's other arm embracing Blake's shoulder, banging shoulders, as he laughs loudly.

'I knew it! I knew it! You do know. I can always recognise another, a brother nutter. So.'

Settling down, old friends already.

'Are you cured too?'

Spreading his hands on the pull-down table in front of him, Smith speaks to the back of the head rest.

'Sherriff. That's your real name. You're twenty-nine. No, thirty-three – you have young skin. You were brought up by adoptive parents in a seaside town in the south, in Essex or Kent. You don't remember your mother or father. If you smoke marijuana you hear voices but you enjoy it too much to stop. You think you can self medicate with joints and it's better than the drugs they give you, which make you slow and depressed and unwell. In London, you have a small room near Hoxton in a hostel. You hang out at various bohemian gatherings where you have a reputation for sometimes being unreasonable. Some people also think you are talented, unfortunately, none of them own a publishing house so you remain poor. You've run out of money so you're heading home to rest, get some cash and pop in to the clinic for a short spell. You are a vegetarian. You have a girlfriend who never sees you when it gets too bad because you take yourself away. Which is what you're doing now.'

The thick frames are cocked to one side. Smith remembers the grip, which was powerful. He slowly turns to stare solemnly into the cloudy lenses. He begins to smile. A moment. Then Sheriff joins him in a grin, which shows two gold teeth next to his canines. We'll have to fix those, with some basic white – too showy. The poet is nodding his head.

'Yes sir, yes sir. Very good. You see, you know. A little bit dangerous. I can tell. You might be police but you're too… weird. You look straight but I can tell. You're, what? Not a doctor. Not a professor. You're a bad man. But you don't scare me. What are you doing?'

'What are you doing?'

'Poetry.'

Smith whispers:

'I'll tell you a little bit now and a bit more later, when you're out. Will you remember?'

'I always remember, unless they shock me.'

Sherriff Clarke waits, seriously, for his life to change. Smith tells him how it will be:

'I want to recalibrate the world. Like a gun. I want to zero the sights. I want accuracy, I want people to get to where they need to be, like a bullet hitting its target. And I'm looking for others to help. The first thing will be a robbery. A big robbery. And, Sherriff? …I'm not mad, either.'

Their hands are entwined again. Smith can feel a ring on

Sherriff's middle finger digging into his own. The train is pulling into a station and the poet is getting up.

'You're a poet, too! How will I contact you? Give me a number.'

'Don't worry.' Smith smiles. 'I'll find you. Should be easy enough in...' he looks at the station board.

'...Chatham.'

Sherriff, calling as he walks backwards down the carriage:

'By the way, you were wrong: go and look in a bookshop – it's called Pebbled! Green and brown cover! By Sherriff Clarke! Not all my friends are poor! And I don't have a girlfriend – I'm gay!'

*   *   *

Is this the future? A nine millimetre bullet, apparently quite ordinary. Brass. Hollow point. Looks like a bullet. But at the very tip, for those with sharp eyes, is a tiny piece of clear plastic. Whitmore clicks the mouse and the plastic lights up, a pin prick of green. He clicks the mouse again and the bullet trembles lightly.

'That's it searching, tiny weights shifting about. If it had momentum it would be like a beagle, searching for its electronic path.'

'Like a guided missile.'

'Like a tiny guided missile.'

Another click on the mouse and the bullet returns to normal.

'Of course, it couldn't work. The cap exploding would ruin the fine precision. Imagine a similar explosion behind a guided missile, in an enclosed barrel, a very hot one, too. Impossible. But plausible.'

Smith tosses the bullet a few times.

'What's it like as a bullet?'

'What, instead of a MacGuffin? Fine. You wouldn't notice

the difference. It will kill a man as easily as any other bullet. As long as you don't miss.'

'Oh, I won't be firing it, Whitmore. I have an expert marks-person in mind.'

The sound of a hand saw in the room next door. Whitmore kicks the adjoining door shut.

'Bloody Wolfy. He thinks he lives here.'

A door bell, from outside the room, somewhere else.

'Bloody hell. It's all go. That'll be Lee. You'll stay, of course?'

Leaving to answer the door before he gets an answer, Whitmore leaves Smith feeling pleased with the situation. He only needs one of these little winged monsters. Or, what he means, to himself is, this one just needs to be found inside the right person. Then all will come to pass. The bullet is not just a bullet. It is a magic button. He can afford to celebrate, he thinks, as a strong Cork accent enters the room with a ruddy faced young man in red overalls attached.

Whitmore, with his white coat cape-ing behind him ushers in his friend Lee and they are already arguing. The sawing has stopped and moments later a strong jawed man pokes first his head, then the rest of himself into the small laboratory.

Whitmore diving beneath the rough hewn bench on which sits a delicate looking lathe, various electronic equipment filled with meters, visualisation units, wires, cartridges, casings and jars. Scales. Tiny tools. Petite welding unit. Solder. Coming up with a handful of beer bottles, passing them out as the small room bubbles with loud male voices, introductions, bottle tops pinging from the edge of the worktop. A cacophony of Cork. And Smith laughs out loud.

The understanding is in the tone and the repeating, as the strong hash joint works its way around, soon joined by another, the two fire sticks chasing each other in a circle of appreciation, it's all 'wits thatchya say?', 'what are ye on about?', 'like I say' and 'fuckin sayit again, I don't understand.' As the working men puff the communion of fellowship and bamboozle each other with flying syllable, Smith is happy to realise he understands as much as any man. Lee, sombre, in his red jumpsuit like a baby faced action man:

'So I finish the field, record time, record, t'inking, I'll just take a powder, man, head to the Priest's Head, because it's nearby…'

Interrupted, full throated by Wolfy, the builder, who looks as Spanish and Irish as a cartoon, with a full flush on his cheeks and the blackest curly hair, flecked with the light blue of the wall paint, same colour.

'Ya dirty skiver!'

'…no. No, I did me work. A man's entitled, after his work. Isn't that every man's right?' Turning to Smith who nods enthusiastically.

'But, anyway, did I even make it to the car? Did I fuck. It's himself, turns up, starts getting to shout at me, pointing at the tractor and I'm saying, what? What?'

'What?! What?!' From Wolfy and Whitmore.

'And he says, you fucking fucked up my fucking tractor, you fucking fuck, you…'

'Whit's that?'

'The tractor! He says…'

'Who says?'

'He does, the gaffer.'

'What's thatchya say? Look after what?'

'The gaffer! Fucking deaf man. D.E.E.F. But it's the new one, with the suspension that rises and lowers, like a Citroen, right?'

'What the fuck are you on about, Lee. A flying tractor?'

Observing from the ceiling, Smith is himself for a while,

Stephen Smith, looking down at this unscientific scene, matches and lighters flaring in a room with gunpowder – gunpowder! – high explosive, with booze and strong drugs. Four men, filling the world with their presence. There should be a woman watching, to see that all this needn't lead to violence, the competition, the threats, the chins jutting, insult battling insult. Gunpowder. Men can talk their lives as well as women, as long as no one organises them beyond the basics, organises them to go to war. Other men.

So, a brief rest for Stephen, before he gets back in his chariot. What do these men think about a scientist, a ballistics expert and electronic engineer – a small genius – making miracles in the extension of his terraced council house on the outskirts of Cork whilst his missus is out buying chips and his kids watch cartoons of American kids on the TV next door? It's all the same. Lee drives a tractor, or a combine harvester or a huge lorry; Wolfy hammers and saws and chisels beautiful lumps of wood into practical surfaces with barely an adornment; Whitmore creates a radio controlled bullet that will never work and they all accept Blake-who-is-Smith into the circle on a recommendation. Well he's here, isn't he?

In the garden, standing next to Wolfy who is in a philosophical mood, as they pass a new joint between them, listening to Lee playing with the kids on some computer game thing as Whitmore has a good natured argument with his wife, who Blake still hasn't met. It's past eleven and Wolfy has been talking solidly for an hour. He will never talk so much again.

'You see, Steve. All a man needs are the bones. A family, for better or worse. Food. Shelter. A drink. And a motorbike. Do you ride?'

'I have done?'

'What did you have?'

'Honda Three Fifty Four. Was my favourite. You?'

'Harley. MT three fifty E. Ex British Army. Went like a motherfucker.'

'What happened to it?'

'Trashed it like a motherfucker. I was stupidly riding it in the snow and ice, to get the milk – can you believe it? – to get the fucking milk. Ended up bent round a wall. Broke my leg, too. But, though, I miss that bike.'

Has Smith had an idea? Well, why not, his extended family could encompass the universe. Here's a man with a hundred uses.

'Are you a Catholic, Wolfy?'

'Born one. I'd say I'm pretty much an atheist now, ready to rot in hell. Why? We don't bring up religion too casually in Ireland.'

'I know. It's not casual. Have you got a lot of work on at the moment, Wolfy?'

'You're using my name a lot – now I know I should be suspicious. Come on, English boy, what do you want? I finish here, at Whitmore's and that's me. Nothing on the table. The future's not too bright. Are you offering me work?'

'Yes. A bit different from what you normally do.'

' A bit different? And you want to know if I'm a Catholic? You're not robbing a bank, are you Stevey?'

He can't help but smile widely, like a wide-o from the south east. Wide. Here under the Irish sky. Put it in words.

'Not a bank. Like a bank. You get to ride a motorcycle… there's money…'

'I'll do it. Fuck, don't say any more. If you ask me again tomorrow I'll say no, when I'm sober. Don't say any more now. I'll do it. Give me the details later, but I'm saying yes now. I want to rob a bank. I want to ride a motorbike. I've got nothing to lose. I'll even build you a wardrobe, too.'

54

'Good!'

'Great!'

'Yes…'

'Fucking mad, man. Yes. Let's do it!'

A pact sealed with the shared saliva on a roach, as serious as a lover's kiss, in the garden of the suburbs of the city of Cork, under the Irish Atlantic sky. Whitmore enters the garden from the door to his lab, joins the robbers.

'Don't listen to him, Wolfy. He'll say one little thing, next thing you know, you're making magic bullets and getting yourself involved in something that might be just a little bit illegal.'

'Oh, it's definitely illegal. I know it is. But I don't give a fuck. Man's got the right attitude. Anyway, what's the worst that can happen? I do a little time. Won't be the first time, won't be the last.'

The worst. Smith is remembering, the pops and rattles of automatic fire, the tip of flames and billowing smoke above roadside bushes in a lane, south of London. How two of his last bank robbers were immolated and peppered by petrol and brass and lead. Well, Wolfy is a much nicer guy. He'll try not to let anything like that happen this time. There are other ways to tidy up, apart from with flame and death, not as final, perhaps, but possible. He'll do his best.

Fortune to fortune, once the wheels are in motion, like money to money, the movement attracts men and women of quality, magnetised by the blur.

In the morning Smith finally meets Mrs. Whitmore. Who is this Patrick she's talking about? There's a lot of Patricks in Eire. Leaning on an elbow, hair tousled. Checking his watch. Eight o'clock AM and already he can hear Whitmore in his lab, buzzing away at his day job, which is making and adapting dentures. He's whistling. Through the hangover he figures out that Patrick is Patrick Whitmore and that Mrs is a little suspicious. She has brought him tea and her suspicions by way of breakfast.

'He won't tell me anything about it, but he's got the bullet casings and the gunpowder. We're not insured. Did he tell you what happened last time? How did he get away with it, telling the Gardai he was an old IRA man – as if!? What if he'd got the wrong man, a proper policeman? It's not as if he's even going to use them, he just likes the… science of it. Making it work. You better not be using him, Steve Blake. You better not be fucking him over, because if you are, you'll have me to deal with, you know?'

Looking at the formidable woman he could imagine the threat would be enough for most men. She is tiny, immaculate in pressed snow white track suit and trainers, blonde hair streaked with cream and brown, sovereign ring reigning over the lesser rings.

She checks the door to the lab, which is shut. Whispers.

'You're mighty smooth tongued. But I can tell bad, I can sniff it out. I grew up with bad. You don't believe in heaven or hell, mister.'

One of her hands, surprisingly, in his hair, sorting the nest of black frond. Suddenly, viciously grabbing it. Then her mouth, pressed to his, a tongue sliding between his teeth. He is aware of his morning breath. He can taste tobacco, menthol, mint toothpaste. He allows the kiss but doesn't move. She finishes and slaps his face, almost gently.

'If you come back, mister, I'll fuck you… then I'll fuck you up.'

She gets up.

'Be gone by the time I get back Steve. I mean it. I don't trust you.'

Mrs. Whitmore. Tongued by a woman without a Christian name. Her better half opens the door and looks round.

'Was that the missus? Do you want a tea?'

'Throw it.' Smith does as he is told. The bullet wings high up into the air. Whitmore points a box with a stubby aerial in its general direction and slides his finger over a flat ribbon contact. The bullet dances as it drops, zig zagging back and forth before falling on to the lawn.

'That'll do.'

'That'll do.'

Somewhere on the ferry, the bullet and controller sit in a VHS tape machine which sits in a padded box in a sack of parcels in the back of a lorry.

Smith leans on the railings watching the port of Cork recede beyond the dancing grey waves, which are already swilling the disinfected slops of beer, sick and oil back and forth across the decks. A pint of Guinness appears at his elbow. He takes it and smiles his thanks at the already guzzling Wolfy who, too, leans on the bar and looks back. Finishing half the pint with a smack of the lips.

'What a sight for sore eyes. Wouldn't mind if I didn't see the fucking place again.'

'What about your family?'

'Fuck 'em.'

Wolfy's idea of any trip begins with a pint, to celebrate escape. Smith looks at his newest soldier's thick fingers, nicked and decorated with dark splinters. Who would win in a fight? He would; Smith would. Wolfy wouldn't stand a chance. It's all about the hate, delving deep inside to summon up the primeval hate. Wolfy loves life, loves his life. He cares too much, for all his strength. Smith craves death – he sees it as an answer to all life's ills, the biggest ill: being born. He knows this – it was teased and beaten out of him when he was being prepared for his previous employment. Some things are best left hidden, perhaps. An intelligent man with a propensity for violence, they're always causing trouble. The firm's psychologist really should have known better. They all should.

He taps his glass to Wolfy's then drains it in one. Wolfy spits, long and dark into the Irish sea before finishing his. Then he launches the glass into the waves. Smith hesitates a moment, then follows suit. Wolfy thinks he hears the glasses collide, but he doesn't say anything. Even if he is impressed. He decides he will keep the chat to a minimum from now on.

*   *   *

In the house at the end of Milford Street there is a queue of one at the bathroom door.

The landing is lit by a low energy bulb in a fringed shade, silvered by dust, hanging from a ceiling which has no colour. The light it spreads, bulbous on the pate of a wide, bald man who paces three, four steps, back and forth by the bathroom door. Americans call it 'the bathroom'. In this case, the room is both British and American versions and one brother is using it for the former while the other brother needs it for the latter.

Quilted dressing gown over comfortable sweat pants and shirt, leather flip flop slippers that slap the thin carpet, The Times folded under one arm. Back and forth.

'Every bloody morning! Why don't you get up earlier?'

Through the door, the muffled, jolly sound of a man enjoying his ablutions, his shaving, voice contorting with his gurning as he creates smooth surfaces to scrape with a Bic.

'The same could be asked of you, brother.'

'You know I always rise last, brother. It has always been thus. You miserable cunt!'

And here, he slaps the door with the paper. His brows are knitted together in an evil V above his nose.

'Hurry up!'

The sound of shaking jowls through the door.

'Oh, stop it! You'll make me cut my throat.'

'Give me the chance, brother!'

'Why don't you use the bucket?'

There is a bucket, an old hospital bucket, kept in a cupboard under the stairs for emergencies. The bucket has seen use from both ends of both brothers, catching the results of epic bulimic excess. It is a fabled object in their house, used to taunt and goad as well as to illustrate particularly memorable days and nights of celebration.

'Fuck your bucket! Come on! Open up! You must surely be finished!'

'I am done when I am done. Go and use your time more usefully. I have the whole of my head to shave yet and I've barely started.'

Venom in the spit, the globule of gob, which is aimed with force at the door. Loud enough for the other brother to hear, eliciting quiet chuckles.

'Cambridge cunt!'

'Oxford cunt!'

The Oxford cunt slaps down the stairs, negotiates a dreary hall of overcoats and umbrellas and the same flock wallpaper which warms every wall in the house, and through a door, into an office space in which are crammed two dark desks in a deco style, facing each other, respectively behind which are two dining room chairs. He sits uncomfortable down behind one of the monstrosities and opens a drawer in the desk.

The old brown file is a dossier. Pictures and type, dates, addresses, more photos, always one step behind. A stubby, manicured finger traces across a photo of Whitmore, the Irish dentist/armourer as he leaves his front door, kids running in front; a photo of Dan White, official, in his prison officer's cap; several photos of Steve Blake, AKA Stephen Smith, in his current state, taken from CCTV cameras and older, clearer photos of him as a younger man, passport shots with various hair styles and colours, bearded and otherwise.

The finger stabs Dan White.

'We know who you are. But who are... you.' And the finger stabs Whitmore.

'We shall have to find out.'

From the same drawer he takes a small laptop and opens it on the desk, over the dossier. A few clicks and some fumbling on the keyboard and a voice from the laptop speaker.

'Yes boss.'

'Go to Eire and find out who this is.'

'I thought we know who this is, boss.'

A tut.

'Don't annoy me, Parker. Find out what Smith wants with a dentist. Speak to him. Pull some teeth if you have to – he can always repair himself afterwards.'

The laptop lid closes.

'A dentist. Perhaps he's looking for another Bassett.' Bassett, Smith's loyal torturer, did all the physical stuff whilst Smith interrogated in one of the many languages in which he was fluent. Poor Bassett, who's body was launched from a cliff top just days before he was due to retire.

Hearing some sounds of motion upstairs, perhaps the bathroom door opening, Bassett the memory dissipating into the needs of a stomach full of shit to unload its contents fast..

'Ah. At last.'

He lets out a long and noisy fart, lifting one fat leg on the chair.

'If it's not too late.' Calling. 'Are you out yet?! '

3

Chapter 3: A Tickle

These two well dressed, anonymous men. Possibly one of the least pleasant aspects of their job, they would both agree, is dealing with government sanctioned professionals, especially these two.

The scrape of wooden chairs on parquet, a school sound familiar to all four secret individuals. A cheap room for shoddy work: just the regular four walls in cream, a bare bulb from the high ceiling, the London traffic through part-opened double glazing. On the flimsy, formica covered table top sit four laptops in front of the four men. The two brothers, sitting opposite each other, somehow surrounding the other two, who also sit opposite. One could be a white haired politician from the 50s, a long, graceful commander who looks like he served on a destroyer in the second world war but was actually a hippy in the 60s, for a while, at least, in hair length and style, although he never did quite manage an LSD trip. Strange how an economics grad can end up head of MI5, a few older heads have muttered in gentlemen's clubs in and around the West End. But it makes perfect sense to anyone who knows him – an almost digital understanding of facts and figures allows a clinical diagnosis, which can be interpreted and explained by everyone from agents with guns to politicians with budgets. Perfect.

His literally opposite number has a grudging admiration for the neat plans of MI5 now. In the chaos of the rest of the world, he must sit on a tossing boat that flings him and his shrinking group of multi-linguists from port to stormy port, always in the wake of American inspired debris, always in thrall to Israeli technology, always in fear of Russian thuggery. The shitty end of the secret stick. He wears dark bags beneath his sorrowful eyes and inspires distrust in patriotic fellow workers: how could someone who looks so… latin, be in charge of MI6?

A brother speaks.

'If my brother had kept a proper eye on Mr. Smith we would not need to be here, of course. But, as it is, here we are and it is best that we all pool our resources to find out what he's up to and then kill him. Agreed?'

This kind of language is only ever spoken as a translated code in the notionally accountable world of military intelligence and such frank speech causes some shifting about on seats from its two representatives. The ex-hippy speaks, with a slight northern twang, possibly from Blackpool:

'We are a long way from authorising any such action, which is possibly a little extreme. The information you have provided is thin, to say the least. Added to what we have it's not enough to make a firm conclusion of any sort. He talks twenty-one languages. So what? He has some money, perhaps a few hundred thousand. So what? So does anyone who owns a house in London, potentially. He's smart? So what? Lots of people are smart. He's freelanced for various agencies including the one opposite…' A nod. '…and he might know a few things. So what? Unless he finds a way to bring them to various people with the right impetus what he knows is useless, sensationalist conspiracy rubbish. I'm tempted to say, let's wait until he relaxes, sticks his head above ground and then we'll put him away for the robberies. He'll be in his seventies by the time he gets out and no one will give a damn.

'Right now, we don't have the resources and you really haven't given me a reason to do anything at all.'

Two brothers sigh and look at each other. The dark latino speaks, surprisingly, with a strong Belfast accent:

'Smith has worked for us all over the place. He's unusual because he has heard and understood Croatian fascists, Russian trade officials, Venezuelan army officers, all kinds of Arabs – if he puts it all together, he has a serious amount of info, plus he's probably insane, so there's that whole...' The dark eyes flick across the two brothers who are sat, hands folded in laps, beatific expressions on their egg-faces. '... unpleasant thing.

'Really, the easiest action would be, find him, find out what he's been doing, make him disappear. End of.'

Another brother speaks:

'But what a terrible waste of a wonderful resource. Perhaps all he needs is some TLC...' The other brother snorts.

''What he needs is some BFB – big fat bullet – in his head. Brother, I know you are fond of him, for some strange reason, perhaps he is the son you never had, but he has caused all kinds of upsets. He knocked off three of my boys, caused mayhem in the home counties. He's a bank robber! He couldn't be any louder if he took a megaphone to the top of Big Ben. We are being noticed, brother. And we can't have that.'

All four men pause to ponder that most terrible of possibilities. Here's MI5:

'It's simple, really. We can't afford it. With the new financial restrictions in place and the prospect of having to explain to certain people exactly what he did for us. I will have to say, do what you will, but I'm not going to put anyone on this, distraction, or spend a penny sorting it out. Essentially it's your problem, gentlemen.' And with this he sweeps a long fingered hand around the table.

But here's MI6:

'That, if I may say so, is quite typical. We are meant to be cooperating. We are meant to have the same goals. Alright, I know that's impossible. But this is an extraordinary situation. Smith isn't an agent on the periphery, an online whistle blower; he's an ex-manager and probably the best there's been. Honestly, John…' he uses MI5's Christian name affectionately, gesturing to the brothers. '…look at them. They never sit down together. We never sit down together. All of us in one room, this is unprecedented. Smith has the potential to do great damage and we can't afford to let anyone else get involved. He's got to be removed.'

Both brothers lean forward together. Which one speaks, Cornelius or Horatio? Both, in turn.

'Help us find him. Then we will have a little chat…'

'Find out what he's been up to…'

'Find out who else is involved…'

'There was that woman, that journalist, for instance…'

'And he's been speaking to a prison officer…'

'And a dentist…'

'We can talk to all of them!'

'Sort it all out…'

'Then things can get back to normal…'

'How they've always been. You, us, everyone else, cooperating…'

'Getting on…'

'Maintaining the status quo.'

'After all,' says the most genial brother, 'it's what we're here for, isn't it?'

'Just help us find him, we'll do the rest.'

The reluctant ex-hippie gets up, steps to the window. A net curtain trembles to the traffic rumble. He talks from where he stands.

'I'll give you one man with a limited budget. But in return, I need a favour. Someone in a big arms firm, one of ours, has heard a rumour. He met someone from Canada who has been offered a prototype of a new kind of munition. We need some hard facts from the Canadian. The details are at the normal place.'

The relevant brother, the Cambridge cunt, looks happily interested.

'How much?' Even though the mathematical ex-hippie from MI5 understands and even appreciates the question there is something about having to deal personally with the smug features of the brother that sticks in his craw.

'The normal payment. Through the normal channels. And don't take the piss. We want the whole recording. Everything.'

'Including the screams? Including the slicing and the squelching?'

MI5 is already leaving.

'Everything.'

And he's left. MI6 is on his way, too.

'Gentlemen, it's never a pleasure. When you get Smith, let me know. I'll have someone there, in case of eventualities. Don't forget. Oh, and that Canadian? We'll be watching, too.'

The door shuts quietly behind the second secret man and the brothers are left in the room alone.

'They don't trust us, do they?'

'I don't trust you. You don't trust me. No one trusts anyone. That, I think, is the status quo. Long may it last.'

'Amen, brother.'

*   *   *

He might have to let Dan White go. Spotted as soon as he enters the street where the prison officer lives: a black van, too new, too shiny, windows smoked and parked too well, diagonally across the street from White's front door. Two aerials. Pulling into a vacant spot he sits and waits. Then again, this could be fun. He makes a call on his mobile.

'Dan? Steve. I'll be a little late. Did your guy arrive? Good. See you soon.'

Dan replaces his mobile on to the kitchen top, next to two steaming cups of tea. He takes the tea through to his small living room, hands one to a young man sitting on the edge of a sofa.

'There you go, Dean mate. One sugar, right?' Sitting down, looking at the lad affectionately. It's been two years. He looks alright, filled out a bit. When they met, Dean was a scrawny youth who hadn't finished growing. But there was a light of intelligence in his eyes, a watchfulness, that Dan spotted immediately. Now he looks a little uncomfortable, but he's clean, dressed in new sports gear, looks healthy and strong. Dan knows there's no chance, not now. But just being in the general proximity of someone he had loved so thoroughly makes him quiver inside. But he's holding it together. This is his gift, back to the young man who had given him love. Steve Blake is going to change his life, he is sure, for the better. Dean sips his tea. It's up to Dan to make the small talk.

'So, how's it been? Are you settled?'

Dean's voice is lower than he remembers, but still quiet.

'Kind of. I left my sister's. Got a room now. Good landlady, leaves me alone.'

He sips.

'No work, though.'

'Well, hopefully we'll soon have that sorted. Mr. Blake's

running a bit late. Shouldn't be too long though. Tea OK?'

'What job's he offering? If it's another work experience I'm not interested.'

'No, he's talking about wages. Wages and training. He's a good man. You'll like him.'

'Is he like you?'

'What, a prison officer? No…' Dan White knows that's not what the lad meant and he's a little bit hurt. Surely it meant something to him, something more than, typecasting?

'You know what I mean. Is he queer? Is that what this is about?'

'You mean, queer, like you. You're queer, too, aren't you Dean? You told me you were. You seemed like you were.'

'Look, I was young, yeah? I didn't know what I was. Still don't.'

Dean smirks and suddenly looks coy, dipping his head to look at Dan through calf eyes. Lovely eyes. He hadn't forgotten.

'You're teasing me, Dean.'

'Course I am, you soft cunt. Of course I'm gay. Bent as a nine bob note, as someone once said. Gayer than you are. I haven't got any kids or a wife. You have.'

Dan relaxes. This is more how he remembers things. There could even still be the spark of something… There's a knock at the door.

'That'll be Mr. Blake. Just be yourself, lad. He'll see you're alright.'

At the door, through the frosted glass, White is surprised to see the shapes of two men. Perhaps Steve has brought a colleague. He opens it to two strangers, men, probably in their thirties, in suits, who White immediately spots as force, of some kind. The shorter one nearest him holds up a wallet with a card. He has a Scottish accent.

'Mr. White? DC. Graeham. This is DC Bryant. I wonder if

we might have a word.'

It's not unusual for White to deal with the police – he is often the first port of call for officers tracking down an ex-offender suspected of a new crime. But it is unusual for them to come round to his house on a Saturday. And these two, well, they don't seem the normal Liverpool cop. The hair is wrong, for a start. Almost a bowlly cut, like the Scallies from two decades ago, but a bit smarter, shorter on top. These look like Mormons. He keeps his arm up, barring the way.

'What's this about lads? I'm a bit busy. Can it wait til Monday?'

'I'm afraid not. Can we come in?'

'It's not very convenient. I'm expecting company.'

'We know. That's why we want to come in.'

'What do you mean?'

'You're expecting someone, probably calling themselves Stephen or Steve? He's a wanted man, an armed robber, name of Smith, Stephen Smith. We're here to pick him up.'

'You must be joking! Steve Blake's not a robber! He's a business man.'

'They're all business men. Can we come in?'

Something not right, very not right. He leans out and looks up and down the street, which is quiet.

'If he's an armed robber, where are the rest of you? Where's your back up? Why aren't there more of you?'

'They're hidden away. We don't want to frighten him off. Look, we need to get inside now or he'll see us and it could get very messy. Please.'

The pressure, the weight of doing the right thing by the law plus the insistent stare of the Scottish cop – he gives way and moves to allow them in. Graeham walks right past him and opens the door to the living room. He looks around the door and returns to White.

'Who's this? Who have you got in there? What's he, a rent

boy? You about to have a session with Smith? Is that it?'

Outraged, White opens his mouth, only to exhale in pain. The silent, bigger cop has knuckled him in the solar plexus, hard. Doubling up he hears Dean's voice as Graeham disappears into the living room.

'What's going on? Dan?'

Then the clear sound of flesh being hit by something hard. White feels a hand grab his collar then he is being shoved and pulled until he finds himself sitting next to Dean on the sofa. The young man is unconscious, a nasty red mark by the side of one eye, a tear of blood in the eye's corner. Dan's got his breath back.

'You dirty bastard! Why'd you do that for? He's done nothing wrong!'

But the tall cop is standing in front of him, slapping a short, black cosh into a gloved palm in a cartoon style. The Scottish cop is at the window, looking out, wiping his own matching, weighted wood in leather, the kind of vision that would get certain men excited down at the Curzon.

'Don't, Whitey, just don't. He enjoys it. It's all I can do to stop him murdering anyone. Don't give him the excuse. Just sit there nice and quiet until our man turns up. Then you open the door and we do the rest.'

The motion of the cosh is at his eye line. White allows his anger to be replaced by fear. He glances at Dean who remains unmoving. He can see his chest rise and fall – thank god!

Then DC Bryant speaks:

'If you move, you fucking poof, I will smash your head in. You're too old and too slow and you know it.'

An accent from somewhere near the Thames, a thug plucked from a mass of sixteen or seventeen million people. As far as White is concerned it's London. London and Scotland, invading his Saturday afternoon, just when things were looking up.

He can hear his mobile buzzing in the kitchen. Graeham goes and gets it, brings it back, looking at the display.

'It's him.'

The buzzing stops. Then the ding of a text arriving. Graeham holds it in front of White's eyes. It reads: 'sorry won't be there for another 10 mins.'

'We might as well have a cup of tea.'

Graeham goes back to the kitchen and soon White hears the electric kettle heating up. Dean is still. Bryant stays standing in front of him, slightly more relaxed now, arms by his side.

Even though it's only been two years since he moved in to this house, White has become accustomed to its sounds. It's a quiet neighbourhood. Sometimes, when the telly's off and it's late there are only the sounds of the house and his thoughts to keep him company. So he is surprised to hear the clear sound, to him, of the back door opening, the plastic Tescos bags of recycling being disturbed, his kitchen lino being scraped. These sounds being masked by the boiling kettle. White is tensed, but still not ready for the terrifying scream that comes from the kitchen. He has a flash of Bryant's open mouthed face, Dean's rigid leg kicking Bryant in his crotch followed by the young man launching himself upwards, his head making contact with Bryant's face, before, his own instincts kicking in, he is up on his feet and landing a blow to the tall cop's head himself. It's seconds later and he has Bryant's arms locked behind him as Dean hammer's the stomach, then the face, then the stomach with his fists and Dan acknowledges the surge of animal joy that fills him. A blast from the past, prison riots of yesteryear.

So the voice, calm and amused is as shocking as the violence was moments ago. Dean stops and turns. They both see Smith, holding a rolling pin, gesturing to the staggering Bryant, talking to Dean.

'You'll break your hands like that. Always use something. There's generally something handy. Only use your fists...' here he swings the rolling pin and Bryant becomes a dead weight in White's arms. '...if you really have to.'

'I promise I will explain as soon as we have taken care of these two.'

They're both alive, these cops or whoever they are. They've made a considerable mess in the kitchen and on Dan's living room carpet. Almost as soon as Bryant hit the floor Smith has been in motion, pulling black bin liners from under the sink, cloths, washing up liquid. For a moment Dan had looked from the door to the kitchen and understood the scream he had heard what feels like hours earlier: Graeham (if that's his real name) is unconscious on the floor, a small gardening fork suspended by one prong in his eye socket which leaks blood, slowly. Amazingly, he's not dead. Yet. Bryant, the side of his skull caved in, is also still alive. Thankfully no arteries appear to have been involved and Dan catches himself thinking like this, not because of the cleaning but because he already feels like a murderer. Having dealt with many killers over the years it's as if he is finally slotting into a comfortable space that has been waiting for him. He looks at Dean.

Dean seems frozen, in awe. Even in these extreme circumstances Dan can't help feeling both proud and jealous of the fact that Dean has obviously immediately fallen under the spell of Smith. There is something special about a man who can be so violent and so calm and, even, pleasant, almost caring. Obviously better to be on this side of a mad man... Then Dan begins to take in what Smith is actually doing.

'Steve... you can't put them in the bags... they won't fit, the bags are too small... besides, they'll suffocate.'

'Don't worry Dan, they won't suffocate. Dean, take his legs, there's a good lad.'

'Dean! Don't touch him! Steve, what the fuck are you doing? You've hurt them really bad. We've got to call an ambulance.'

'Dan.' Realising he has to pause for a moment at least, Smith lets Bryant slip back on to the carpet. He pulls a gun from his jacket.

'Steve...' the tone is both sorrowful and angry and afraid.

'Dan. Sit down, you too Dean. Let me explain what's going on here.'

He fires, casually into Bryant, at his heart. Bryant twitches then lies still.

'Fuck!' Dean's eyes are bugging.

'These two men are here to take me somewhere else where they would have tortured me and then killed me. Before leaving here, they would have killed you. It's complicated, but basically, they are part of a violent gang, a very well connected, very violent gang. Somehow they got a bead on me and connected me to you. For which I am very sorry. Ideally, you wouldn't have discovered the situation in quite such a cruel way. But here we are. You now have the choice, both of you, of waiting until I leave and trying to explain exactly what happened. Or of trusting me until I've got rid of Tom and Jerry here and then I will tell you all of it. Either way, they're dead and you are both alive. And for that, I am truly thankful.'

Smith looks at White, at Dean. He nods then goes into the kitchen. They hear another shot. A kind of hysterical laugh escapes Dean's lips.

'Fuck!'

Dan automatically lets his mouth work without completely engaging his thoughts.

'That's alright lad, take it easy, easy. It'll be alright. Just sit still, like a good lad.'

Smith enters carrying the body of the Scottish cop,

wrapped head to toe in black bin liner, over his shoulder. He walks through and out to the corridor. They hear him dump the body by the front door.

Soon he is back, shoving Bryant's head into another bin liner, splitting several bags and taping them together around the body. Dean is suddenly there, kneeling by him, helping. Nothing is said. When Bryant is fully enclosed in shiny black, Dean takes his feet and Smith leads the body into the hall. Then they are back, Smith sweating slightly, momentarily touching Dan's shoulder in a reassuring way.

'Now, Dan, do your neighbours pay you much attention? I'll tell you what – turn the telly on, there's a good chap, something noisy like a war film, nice and loud.'

When Dan doesn't move, Dean finds the remote, points it at the small TV in a corner and surfs channels until he finds a western.

Smith is in the kitchen. The tap is running. He comes back in, drying his hands on a tea towel.

'Dan, Dan, nothing has changed. You've still got your job. No one is going to arrest you. You've done nothing wrong. I know you're a bit shocked...' A bit! '...but now we need to just keep it together until we're somewhere, where I can explain just what's going on. So we're going out, through the back garden, then we'll get in my car and then we'll find a nice pub. OK? OK?'

No, not really.

'But there are two bodies! Steve! You killed them. I can't... and Dean! What about Dean!'

'Dean will be fine, won't you Dean?'

Silent, but nodding. Dean is holding a bag of frozen peas to his head. Dan hadn't even noticed him go to the freezer. What to do? What to do?

Apparently, what Smith wants him to do because he finds himself locking the back door as Smith stands near, smiling, looking around, over the fences of the other rectangles of garden in the dimming twilight. They leave together, three men of varying age, on their way to some male relaxation, closing the garden gate, walking down the alley, one wall the back of some garages, the other past the gardens of the little terraced houses. It's a good neighbourhood, a place where he's happy for his teenaged boy and girl to leave and come back late. Not the sort of place to witness a passionate kiss between an overweight, middle aged man and a fit looking young guy in his early twenties.

The taste of Dean's tongue in his mouth is delicious. He is amazed to feel his cock harden. Dean is grinning at him. This is madness. They walk quickly to catch up Smith who is smiling fondly at the two of them from the end of the alley.

He finishes his drink and looks at the effect his words have had on Dan White and Dean. Dean speaks first.

'Is that all then? Yeh, no problem. I'm not doing anything right now. What next – assassinate the queen, yeh?'

White is really staring. Obviously the booze has helped his confidence return, masking the dull ache in his stomach.

'You're serious aren't you?'

It's just a pub. But somehow, Smith has turned it exotic. The customers, all men, are all possible killers, gangsters, spies or terrorists.

The blood, the split bone, the dead features stretching the black plastic: what had been witnessed and was undeniable becomes the proof. The explanation fits. Another wallet. Another ID card. Who else and why else? If Steve Blake says he is an undercover agent for HM government agency, what else could he be?

Where were the cops? Where was the back up? The two men who had invaded White's house were working alone, like criminals. And he wants to believe Blake. It's just about plausible: a truly undercover operation, with co-opted agents, civilians in fact. If it's possible to win the lottery, and it is, then you can meet a man like this, become involved. Watch as a man is shot in front of your eyes.

'Go home, Dan. Think about it. Charge your phone. I'll call you tomorrow. Don't worry. They won't send anyone else. They don't even know what's happened yet. Dean?'

'Yeh?'

'Come with me. I'm, going to teach you how to use a gun.'

'You think I don't know already, Steve?'

'I don't know. Show me. Let's go.'

And he's off, leaving Dan White nursing his empty glass, not even attempting to stop his ex-jailbait lover from following along. Not a problem. What can he say? By the time he gets home, Wolfy will have cleared up the mess, loaded the bodies into a van parked in the still warm spot previously taken by the team from MI5, taken it somewhere quiet and torched it. Tomorrow, when he calls him, the prison officer can decide whether it was all a bad dream or the start of an adventure. If he's still alive.

Outside the pub, in the car park, Dean has his suspicions of the superhero status of his strange new mentor confirmed when Smith suddenly levers himself on to the bonnet of one of a row of ten parked cars and, leaping from bonnet to bonnet makes his way down the row to the end car, nearest the exit. As Dean watches, Smith, standing on the bonnet coaxes a shocked looking man out of the car at the point of his pistol. Smith smiles at the man as he frisks him, several items are removed from his pockets, before he is allowed back into the car, allowed to remain alive as a symphony of car alarms set Dean's blood racing around his charged body. Like falling into a movie. Like dreaming awake. Ridiculous.

If Smith is conflicted about not putting a bullet into the

man's head he doesn't look it.

They are travelling at speed along the M62 motorway and Dean is buzzing. In his lap are the various possessions of the surprised man in the car park: a nice mobile; a wallet, with an ID card, insisting the owner is a Louis Gray, Squadron Intelligence Officer, RAF; a Walther P99 pistol. It's the latter, which is getting him most excited.

'That's yours now.' Smith tells him, whilst tapping a number on his hands free. Dean is only half paying attention as Smith has a conversation on a faulty connection.

'It's me... can you hear? ...yes, that's right. Listen... you need to get out, no I said get out. Leave. Right now. ...because there are people on their way now. If they... ...can you hear me? ...no, listen. If they get you, they will hurt... I said hurt. Torture you, damn it! They'll hurt you... maybe kill you. Yes... yes... No don't get the ferry from Cork. Don't say it... no, don't, not on the phone. Just get across and I'll find you. Send them to her mum's... listen. Just do it, right now. ...yes, I know. I'm sorry.'

Half an hour later and Dean whoops as the car they just used to cross the Pennines lights up the branches of the trees in the cul de sac by a small park on the outskirts of Wakefield, petrol flames of blue and yellow reminding him of the joyriding climaxes of his youth.

Minutes later and they are settled in a two-seater minivan parked nearby, heading for London on the M1. It's all action adventure go! with Steve Blake.

Dan White looks at the spot where a dead man had lain, just hours earlier. The smell of washing up liquid still in the room. He had returned via the back door, walking quickly through the kitchen. He hadn't gone to the hall, the front door, to check if the bodies were there. He knew they were gone. Death had left the building, for the moment.

Sitting there, for an hour, just staring. Looking at his hands, which had punched the man. Looking past them, at the floor. He works through the five minutes or so of violence and murder. Then the walk along the alley, the kiss, the explanation in the pub, all a tailing dream on the end of the five minute collision of events.

At the end of the hour he has set himself a test. A cup of tea. He fills the kettle. Turns it on. Beneath the work top is the cupboard where he kept black bin bags, for the bin. He'll need some more now. He takes a cup from a hook on the wall. A teabag from the box by the kettle. He opens the fridge.

The kettle boils. He pours, mixes, stirs. Drops the teabag in the sink. He notices spots of crimson, tiny dots at the base of the tap. Wetting the washing up sponge he scrubs the hard scabs, they eventually smear away.

He sips his tea. Good. He won't need to call the police then. For the first time in his adult life he has absolutely no idea what will happen.

He thinks of his kids. He's not doing it for them. Or his country. He's doing it for love. Of life, of Steve, of Dean – for himself.

There is a knock at the door. The kitchen clock tells him, too late. Of course, if there were two, there can be three, or more. He has his mobile in his hand. He speaks.

'Steve. I'm in. There's a couple of lads would be spot on, with a bit of help. Well, they've got nothing else to do, that's for sure. I'll speak to them tomorrow. Call me in the evening. There's someone at the door now, so I'd better go.'

Does he leave the phone connected on purpose? Is the sound of the frosted glass cracking, the phone being dropped, the front door being opened, pushing some heavy weight to admit someone with treble toes, tapping on the lino, the frisking sound (how can it be so obvious? Yet it is.) The musical sigh of a last breath. All the concrete noise of accusation? Of recrimination? Oh Steve, you must have known. How could you?

It's a fucking mystery. Dan White, who never quite came out, even though his wife knew and his kids, really if they were honest, did too. What happened to Dan? Spies and bad people prefer neighbourhoods where the TVs are loud and the curtains stay drawn, where the demographic is mind your own business.

4

Chapter 4: Practice

It's a small, modern flat in a large, old building. Mr. Peters has made his place a friendly, warm haven, for the boys who are sometimes too sensitive to flourish in the rough and tumble of communal shower beatings and dorm humiliations. Many is the time he has sat patiently, sympathetically listening to how rites as old as the school itself are kept alive and performed, often at the expense of the weakest, most fragile boys.

Indeed, it could be said, and as by way of justification, he sometimes tells himself, that what sometimes follows these chats is another old tradition, dating back to ancient Greece, where an older man can describe, via words and deeds, another, more sensual, more caring world to an unhappy youth, freeing their young minds from the doubt that, somehow, they are abnormal. It doesn't happen as often as school fable tells it, but it does happen. Toby has seen it.

Two years previous. Toby, still soft faced and sweet on his second visit to Peter's love pad. The word had gone out, years before then, even, that, amongst certain boys, the odd ones, the misfits, the book readers and the thespians there was a teacher who they could trust, who wouldn't bellow or pass on confidences to their parents. That sometimes, certain boys were chosen to spend precious hours away from the school, at his home, eating, reading, quoting, relaxing. That, if you became part of this group, you earned a kind of protection from some of the more odious, hard edged elements of the school, like the incessant bullying from boys and tutors, like the insistence that all boys take part in the traditional wall game (where several hundred boys, divided into their houses, battle, with muscles and feet and fists, to wrestle a ball made from a pig's bladder from one end of the school grounds to the other).

In the spirit of Wilde, the Romantics, the poets, boys have gathered at Mr. Peters' place for years and, every now and then, Mr. Peters falls in love with one of them and tries his best to fuck him up the ass.

Fizzy, pink champagne. To dizzify and delight a boy. Toby and Bruce, enjoying the rare privilege of sanctioned boozing on school property, as Mr. Peters looks indulgently on. The stereo is turned up loud: the pulses of The Ride of the Valkyries seem to coincide dramatically with the battle scenes from the film Zulu, moving across the wide screen mounted on a wall. The most gorgeous Michael Caine, mutely wording in his best posh, streams of half naked Black men falling under the guns of the British fighting square. Toby and Bruce, mock fighting on the sofa, their glasses filled at regular intervals. They're pissed.

The music changes, a piano piece, the mood quietens. Bruce is in the toilet, throwing up. Mr. Peters is sitting next to Toby, gently stroking his hair, murmuring in his ear, offering all kinds of wonderful things – a trip abroad, how would he like that? They could go to London together, stay at a nice hotel, see a show – how would he like that? Stay, tonight. Don't worry, he'll sort it out with the Head of the House. Stay.

They can have a wonderful time together, because, you really are, Toby, a wonderful young man.

Then the hurt look, not from the reddening ear where Toby's fist had connected, but from the rejection and the defilement of the peace in his sanctuary. Mr. Peters, backing off, not saying a word, moving immediately back to his chair, holding his ear, frowning at Toby, but smiling warmly at Bruce who returns, queasy faced, shirt flecked with spew.

The tutting, clucking mother hen teacher, helping Bruce to his bedroom for a lay down, to sleep it off, all the while looking at Toby, showing him – this is what you're missing, you ungrateful boy – taking a glass of water from the kitchen, returning, finally to speak to Toby.

'You can go now, Toby. Bruce needs a bit of a sleep. I'll see you in class tomorrow.'

Not closing the door, flicking the snib and slamming it, holding it tight shut by the letter box, in the corridor outside the flat, listening as Peters closes the bedroom door inside. Waiting. A minute. Two minutes. Then padding back inside. Waiting again, outside the bedroom door. Was that a moan from Bruce? Waiting, listening to the insistent, muttering Peters, the bed sounds, Bruce saying 'no, no' and Peters answering, 'yes, yes.' Opening the door, a crack.

He can't see. He opens the door a little more, he sees Bruce's socks, his feet, poking from the crumple of trousers pushed down to his ankles, he watches as the feet turn, soles up. He opens the door all the way.

Mr. Peters, oblivious, naked apart from a pair of white ankle socks, spitting on his hand and rubbing the saliva into his rigid cock with one hand, whilst his other explores Bruce's anus with a finger. Fascinating. The only thing to hand is the empty glass, rolled from the bed to end up by the door on the floor. Toby picks it up and flings it against the wall above the bed's headboard. It crashes. Peters ducks, flinches and, for a moment, there is a frozen tableaux , a scene from a vase, glazed thousands of years ago, Bruce's back arched as he pushes upwards, Peters, one hand on one of Bruce's ass cheeks, the other on his own cock, staring in horror at Toby. An involuntary grunt from the teacher. Drops of semen flick from his urethra and fall on to Bruce's buttocks.

Toby finds the sight of the teacher, contorted face reflecting the torture of the switch between terror and pure lust, amusing. He smiles. Bruce, suddenly sober is looking with disgust at the mess on his behind, is suddenly thumping the teacher's back with his fists.

'You bastard! Dirty fucking queer bastard!'

Pulling up his trousers, getting from the bed to the door, pushing Toby to one side, tears streaming from shame, shame, shame.

For a moment, teacher and boy observe each other. What did Peters think would happen now? Toby lifts his hands to his face, mimes a camera. Click! Then runs after Bruce, who he can hear flailing through the flat.

Catching up with Bruce, on the stairs, stopping him.

'Bruce. Stop. Listen. Take down your trousers. No, listen, do it.'

Bruce, already defiled once, absolutely not about to let it happen again.

'Bruce, listen. Get the spunk. We get the spunk. Then we've got him. DNA. '

Toby has a glass, an empty champagne glass, ready to catch the drops. Bruce is beginning to understand, but…

'It's too late!' Almost sobbing. 'It's soaked in! The bastard!'

'Alright, don't worry. It's on your pants. Even better. Keep them.Don't wash them. We'll go back, put them in a plastic bag. Hide them. We can blackmail him! Blackmail the bastard!'

OK. Bruce understands. He understands, but never recovers. Over subsequent weeks, he becomes withdrawn. It's noticed. There are appointments, with teachers, with the Master, with the school psychiatrist. Bruce remains mute, hardly answering. He is officially 'troubled'. His parents are called and they remove him from the school. Last heard of being home tutored in France.

The pants stay, buried in a bag, in a box, under the Old Mulberry Tree, where they are, now, as Toby makes his way to the sensual haven and home of Mr. Peters, who is about to do another little favour for his tormentor.

With what he knows now, Toby feels, combined with the increasing strength of his muscles, his bones and his will, he could crush Peters physically, mentally. And he senses Peters recognises this and, almost, enjoys the sensation. But Toby doesn't allow him to wallow in the feeling.

'I need to get something from the Sergeant Major's office, sir.'

'No, out of the question. I told you, I won't be blackmailed any more, Flaxman.'

It's a little game. Toby is tired of playing. Each time he asks, Peters refuses until he is reminded of the evidence, of what could happen, what probably would happen, about how a nonce is treated in prison. This is the last favour, so he is impatient, unwilling to play.

'Let's not fuck about, sir. I need to get into the caretaker's office. You need to give me the key.'

Peters is petulant.

'I don't have the key.' He sniffs. 'So, I can't help you.'

'Get the key. Give it to me before tea. I'll be in history with Mr. Pleasance. Call me out and do it then.'

Peters is surprised by the tone. Here's a young man who has already left the mental precincts of the school. He nods.

Toby pauses. Is this what it's like, then? Is this what Steve Blake meant when he said that power works? Just don't get emotionally involved. Try not to enjoy it. Use it in the same way you use a key to open a door. He's using Peters to open a door, literally. He likes it. Peters means nothing to him. He leaves.

There are always unexpected bonuses, it seems, once the plan is in motion. Getting Findlay expelled was one. How Smith had arranged for the plaque to be covered in Findlay's shit was a total mystery he didn't feel entitled to ask about. But the tests proved it was so. The mucky boy was taken from the school by his mother, who practically held her nose as well as the open car door, as Findlay miserably ducked into the Rolls.

Toby had kept quiet. Part of his agreement with the Master was that she should keep him out of it. He didn't want thanks. He didn't want to be quizzed. He had noticed a softening in attitude towards him from both the Master and some of the more hard-core teachers who had long harboured suspicions that he was a borderline delinquent. It had been amazingly easy to dob Findlay in it. In the shit.

In the Master's office he simply told her:

'I saw him do it. I didn't say anything because he threatened to shoot at me again. I was sneaking out to smoke a cigarette. It was late. I'd been revising and I wanted to chill... to relax before going to bed. And he was there, with a plastic bag. He saw me. That's when he said, 'if you say anything I'll shoot you and I won't miss this time', so I just went back in. But I had to say something. It's just so, disgusting. Please don't tell him I said anything, will you?'

Assured by the sceptical Master of his safety. It was less than a week later that he watched the Findlay family Rolls Royce drive out through the Old Gates, past the now shining bronze plaque (cleaned by a young Polish man, working for a specialist cleaning firm – shit job, Toby thought at the time: shit wages) as he wondered on the wonder of the wonderful Steve Blake.

Another unexpected bonus: the Sergeant Major's service revolver, an old Webley, oiled and loaded (ready for what, precisely?). Not to steal – Toby has no need of more weaponry. Smith has already told him he can get pretty much whatever standard small arms he requires or desires. No, here's an opportunity to make a small adjustment to the barrel, one that might come in handy. It meant a trip to a hardware store, to get another key cut and to buy some Rhino putty. Then another early morning visit to the caretaker's office. Wadding the putty into the barrel, just inside and out of sight, blocking it completely, then replacing the gun in the back of the cupboard, wrapped in oilcloth, behind the box of cleaning chemicals.

So now he has two copied keys, one for the caretaker's office. The other for the door at the top of the stairs in the Old Gatehouse, giving access to the roof. He's waiting now, for the last two sets of instructions from Smith. He knows where and when. In another two weeks he'll know who, and what with.

*   *   *

In two weeks Abe has learned a hell of a lot. He's learned at least partially what Smith has got in mind. He's also learned that horses can be companies, boxers can be small countries, that 'good going' can mean a war and 'weight loss' can mean bad investment. Abe Humphrey has surprised himself by becoming a money man. A proper money man.

It was a simple proposition: Smith visited him. They had their normal chat about this and that and Smith brought him his share of his winnings. Getting a nice little nest egg, too. Taking it easy, spreading his bets, but not killing it, not yet.

Then Blakey does a switch: it's not about sport, Abe, not really. It's about money. And if it's about money, what are they doing pissing around with a few thou here and there when they could be doing the same amount of work for a whole lot more?

Where's the money, Abe? That's what he had said. And Abe knows where the money is, he can smell it, floating up the A10, all the way from the City of London. He's scored enough from those city boy mugs over the years. Money to burn. But they never seem any brighter than him, just took a different route when they were younger. He thought he preferred sport. But now, he realises, it's never been the sport: it's the money, just like Steve Blake says.

So for two weeks now he's been reading, at the internet cafe, books, the Financial Times. It all makes perfect sense. Remove the noughts and the 'plc's and it could be a bookies. It's a scam, that's all. There's those who know and those who don't. There's mugs and punters. There's the lucky and the smart and the unlucky and the idiots. Abe Humphry is definitely smart and he's beginning to find out, even if he's not quite in the know.

Applying basic principles. What they're after is three, two, hopefully just the one opportunity, the big one, to make a killing and get out before being tempted, like some addict, to blow it all on something else. Smith has told him to look. Look at everything, but, especially look at what, after money itself, is a mainstay of the British economy: armaments.

What an eye-opener! It's as if Hackney Council subsidised the races, paying for owners to buy horses, giving them the money to do it, then paying for the jockey's training, then letting the new owners and the jockeys take all the winnings and all the glory! In return for owning the haulage company who relay the hay that the horses use as fuel? What's the sense in that? Why would the British government give money to some tin pot little country in the Middle East in order that they use the money to buy weapons and ordnance that they don't need? In return for controlling shares in a factory in the middle of nowhere that makes a reverse thread screw... he's finding out. He's finding out it makes a lot of sense, if you're in the armaments business. Subsidised betting! He'll have some of that.

Smith calls him up.

'How's it going?'

'Blakey! Smart. Very chipper. I'm enjoying myself. Did you know the threat of a revolution in Chad is enough to raise prices of shares in FFE&BC? So, buy now!'

'OK, Abe, I will. Listen, Abe. I won't be around for a couple more weeks. But you'll be getting a delivery soon. And I'm going to ask a favour. It will mean going south of the river. You OK about that?'

Abe appreciates that Smith understands him. He doesn't have to. A favour. No problem.

'What is it? This favour.'

'I want you to be a knight in shining armour. Going to rescue a damsel in distress. You'll get the details soon.'

'What, by carrier pigeon? Snail mail?'

'You'll find out.'

He rings off.

Not long later, there is a knock at the door. A delivery. For one, a Mr. High Rise. Not a blink from the courier. High, low, all the same to him. But for Abe, High Rise means a lot: best part of twenty grand, to be exact. Winner of the 1998 Vodaphone Derby. That's his name alright, Mr. High Rise. Had he mentioned it to Steve? Must have.

From the well-packed box, he opens a Samsung netbook, apparently fresh from the factory. Apparently not. It's charged. There is a dongle already inserted in its USB port. He turns it on. Not a big fan of modern technology he is pleasantly surprised to see, flickering across the screen, his new name: 'Mr High Rise' then 'click here' and there it is, a series of instructions. So thoughtful, the basics, how to operate the laptop, how to change passwords, how to access the internet, with some more added, probably by Smith for their peculiar relationship: never use your real name; never use my real name; never use anyone's real name; don't visit porn sites; don't send emails. And instructions on how to leave and access comments on various sites. A whole mini-communications system that would have gob-smacked Batman and astounded Sean Connery's 007.

Finally, the favour. An address. A photo. Very tasty. Another photo: he might need his golf club. A day: today. A time: he'd better leave now. He rolls a small joint for the journey.

London is shadows, breathing misty rain. Even after travelling the best part of two hours Abe is still not out of the natural bowl that clings to the swampy atmosphere siphoned up, through clay and concrete and tar. The London cough. The London peculiar. Good to hide in, as the busy world passes by, heads down, caps pulled low. He stands for a good five minutes, looking at the house, a modern council/housing association build, the kind meant for that first rung but which end up as buy-to-lets as soon as the first default notices land on the doorstep.

What Abe sees are curtains, drawn. Cracks of light around them. Nothing more. He walks across the road and knocks the door.

If she is surprised to see a sweaty, stocky man carrying something long, wrapped in newspaper and parcel tape Tedi doesn't let it show, too much.

'Yes?'

'Steve sent me.'

'Steve? Oh, Steve.'

Steve, who she had taken, on a whim almost, to her bed, via her living room floor, a few weeks ago, from whom she hadn't heard anything since. The same Steve who hadn't left a number, or a surname. Possibly, the same Steve (was it him?) who had sent a post card of Mljet Island with a message in Serb Croat, which read like poetry, like a promise: 'there will be a wind and you will fly – the wind will bring you to me – I will show you the other side of the water – and you will be free'. The same Steve she had put from her mind, because good things didn't really happen to her and she is on a mission, to make money, to make a life.

'So, Steve sent you? What... do you have something for me?'

'Can I come in?'

The little man looks at his watch, it's a big watch for a little man. She notices his wide wrists, showing in the gap between his soaked, over-size varsity jacket and his gloves, golfing gloves. He is a strange sight, his head shrouded tightly in a sopping hood. But, then, how does she look, dressed as she is for work? Towering above him in her pin heeled boots, dressing gown open to reveal the reveal of her costume. Suddenly conscious, she wraps her arms around and pulls the gown closed. Nicky will be back soon, ready to take her to Shoreditch.

'What do you want?'

The little man looks a little disappointed. He looks around. The street is empty.

'Look, if I can come in it would be better. Wouldn't it?'

'Would it?'

'Yeh. Cause your... is it, Nicky? Well, Nicky will be here soon and not very happy to see you talking to a strange man on the doorstep. I'm right, aren't I?'

'How do you know Nicky? Who are you?'

'I told you – Steve sent me. Steve Blake. I've got to… I'm here to help. Oh, Christ…'

A car is pulling up next to the house. Suddenly Tedi looks scared.

'Look. You'd better go now. Go! Don't come back.'

She is motioning with her hand, shooing him away. He ignores her. She notices the long tufts of light hair that are stuck to his forehead. He looks like a boy. But then, he looks like a much older man. The car door slams. A tall, wide figure is ambling round, coming into the light from the open front door. The little man talks again, quickly.

'Look, it really would be better to go inside…'

Then the driver is upon them, removing the hood from a puffa jacket, revealing the angular face of a woman in a trucker's cap. When she speaks it could be any gangster anywhere. The homework of a thousand hours in front of pimping TV, knocking balls around in various subterranean bars, a couple of years in Holloway Women's Prison. Plus steroids and a mean disposition. But all useless when being pummelled with a two iron wrapped in soggy brown paper.

It takes moments, as he knew it would. That was never going to be the problem. Dealing with a dead weight of someone who he knew was going to be much bigger than him, was and is. Sighing audibly, panting a little he tries to grab a handful of slippy puffa, giving up and grabbing the woman's two, short blonde pigtails that poke out from under her cap. Rain and blood and man made materials conspire against him.

'Give us a hand love.'

She has her hand over her mouth. Lord. Has he got to deal with this one too? What's this all for, Steve? She's shaking. Hysterical. No. She's laughing. Wicked cow is laughing. Then she's helping, the two of them hauling in the unconscious Nicky, dumping her on the floor, Abe kicking her legs away in order to shut the door. In. Good. He looks at Tedi. Her gown is undone again. He grabs an eyeful. She doesn't mind. Fine mesh body suit, thigh length boots, shiny, latex bra. Fit bird. Not his league, even for money. But he can see what Steve sees in her. Still smiling, she aims a kick at her pimp's stomach. There is no reaction. But he knows his swing – she's not dead. Maybe brain damaged, like Gee Gee.

In control now. She looks at the little man. He is literally steaming in the heat of her hallway, standing next to the radiator. She laughs again.

'Come in. Wait, while I get my things.'

Simple decisions. Very simple when there is no choice. She has nowhere and there's no one else to help her. The spark of trust she felt with Steve Blake-who-is-Smith is alive within her. It's enough. If she has a new pimp, better a man with a smart car, plenty of money, good looking, smelling expensive, who can organise this unlikely little hard man to rescue her from bonded sleaze work, from this bully pichka, this cunt, who hadn't let her go since she was sold into the work two years ago. Boyfriends, mafia, this lesbian maniac – all the same. It's all about protection. Perhaps Steve Blake will protect. Perhaps he won't.

She is ready. Everything important in a large shoulder bag. Instead of the dressing gown she wears a long coat. She stands waiting for the little man to lead the way to his car. He is distracted, looking at a local telephone directory. He sees her.

'Oh, right. Do you know the number of a good cab firm? My name's… he remembers Steve's instructions. That's alright, this isn't online, this is real life.

'…my name's Abe.' He puts a hand out. With his hood off she can see a child/man face, spidersweb wrinkles at the corner of his eyes the only clue to his age. She shakes his hand.

'Tedi.'

'I know.' A smile, one each from both of them before Abe is smothered by a tumbling puffa jacket from which something expels between a screech and a roar, the door to the hall crashing against the wall. Tedi sees the quick curve of shiny steel as Nicky poises for a moment, ready to stick it into Abe, who is pinned beneath her, half on a chair, Nicky's elbow at the side of his throat. Tedi moves, swings her bag at the knife hand, which flicks back and, for a moment Tedi is caught in the hating glare before she realises the handle of her bag has been sliced, before she realises the tip of her thumb is missing. But it was enough.

For Abe to punch and push and slide his way from under the woman, but not enough for him to get clear away. She moves again and he is face down, her knee on his back, the knife at his throat. Tedi holds her thumb but the blood pumps out. She staggers, falling back to lean on the wall. Nicky is staring at her.

'Who's this, bitch? Is this your new man, bitch? He doesn't look very handsome, bitch. He doesn't look very happy, bitch. Shall I make him smile? Do you want to see your new man smile?'

Nicky, her bunches freed of elastic, her cap off, blood caked around her right ear, her chin swollen from the golf club. Looks every bit the part. This is why she had stayed, because Nicky is capable of this. The knife is poking flesh. It's a wicked, curved blade, like a small pirate's sword. Tedi has seen it work before, striping the face of a man who had tried a bit harder than most to get into her knickers. He was drunk, didn't deserve that. Who does? Not this ball of a baby man, caught, unmoving like a mouse, hoping not to be noticed, perhaps. But what could she do?

Open the door, perhaps. Out of the corner of her eye she has noticed the letter box push open slightly, a gloved finger trying to prop it open. She decides. Nicky screams:

'No!'

And the door is open. Two loud shots later and Nicky is rolled on one side, next to Abe, the two of them almost spooning. Abe has his eyes shut. Tedi, though, is getting a good look at a smartly dressed woman, attractive, rich looking, eyes full of pupils, blowing on the end of what should have been a smoking barrel, the business end of a shiny hand gun with a pearl grip. When the woman speaks, the accent is cut glass, pure confidence oozing from every syllable.

'Hullo. You must be Mateja. My name is Ann. How do you do. And you must be Abe. Abe! You can open your eyes now. And this must be... my god! I've killed her!' Glee and hysteria, no doubting the enjoyment.

'I've always wanted to, well, wondered what it would be like...'

Ann kneels for a closer look.

'Well! Look at that! Right in the head...' Instead of standing back up she heavily sits down next to Abe, who is pushing himself up, touching his neck where there is a pin prick (a knife prick) of a blood drop. They both look at Nicky, at what was Nicky.

Ann has the gun in her hand, on the floor. Tedi points to the gun.

'Should you...?'

'Ah, yes.' Ann puts the safety on. She smiles, first at Tedi, then at Abe. Then back to Tedi.

'Steve sent me. You don't have anything to drink, do you? Something alcoholic?'

*   *   *

Sweet caresses. The skin to brain signals switching from repel to embrace. Relax. Tedi on a hotel room bed as Stephen

Smith the enigma introduces Steve Blake, the concept, the solution, the action. She's not stupid, she knows she's being groomed, stroked, literally, into submission, but it doesn't feel like that. Despite herself, she feels empowered. He doesn't want anything from her that she isn't prepared to give. What does he want? It emerges, slowly, so slow that the ridiculous notion seems like an inevitable situation. Join us, we're good people, you don't have to do anything, you can always leave. OK. Look at your life, what has it been? Bad, hard. What could it be, with friends, money, action, making the world a better place? It could be... what I want. Rob a Swiss bank, with guns and explosives? Why not?

5

Chapter 5: Grandstand

Captain Saunders is outraged. Outraged! Not an unusual state for the captain. This particular outrage is all the more enjoyable because he will finally divest himself of the nagging doubt that, in his retirement years, he had become a brutal murderer.

As he finishes his tale, sitting comfortably on the shiny leather pad of one of the Master's guest chairs, he even realises he has forgotten the, outrageous, fact, that the Master is a woman. Who sits, hands folded, elbows on desk, chin resting lightly on knuckles, listening and, like all politicians must do, all the time, deciding the best course of action for herself and what she represents.

'So, Captain, you think it was Gareth Findlay who showed you to the school prizes? A tall boy? Quite thin?'

'Yes, yes, must have been – who else? Why would he try to blackmail me, if it wasn't him?'

'These are very serious charges, Captain Saunders. Do you have any letters? Any proof?'

'No, of course not! I told you, it was a phone call, well, three phone calls. Poor old Bloxy – to use his death in that way. Evil, positively evil. There we were, chatting away about old times and then – poof! – that was it! Keeled over. Smashed the glass.'

'And who was this other man you mentioned? The old boy?'

'Never seen him before. Obnoxious fellow. Old boy, school tie. Practically accused me of murder. Probably put the whole idea into the boy's head.'

'Would you recognise him, if I showed you some photographs, for instance?'

'Doubt it. Had one of those faces. Could be anyone. The point is, miss, Master, er, the point is, it wasn't me! Bloxy just...died. Right there. One minute he was laughing away, the next...'

'Well, thank you Captain. As soon as today's proceedings are over I will contact the police and let them know. Can I keep this?'

She touches a sheet of typewritten paper on her desk.

'Of course. To the best of memory, you understand. Should have recorded it. But, you know, don't expect that sort of thing, on the telephone. Certainly not from a fellow!'

She shows the, now, less outraged old soldier out the door and for a moment, stands, scanning his typewritten memory of the phone conversation during which, apparently, that troubled soul Gareth Findlay, had tried to convince the old soldier to intervene on his behalf at the school or risk being exposed as the murderer of another Old Stedonian, Bloxy Bloxham. Just what Findlay thought would be achieved she isn't sure, but boys never cease to surprise her with their idiotic actions and ideas. She folds the paper in half and puts it into her handbag. It's a handbag kind of event: the centenary carols at the end of term, for once taking place outside, by the Old Gatehouse, and not in the cathedral. It's a fine night and she is determined neither the weather nor the disturbed young man who was both Cadet Under Officer and the school's crack shot is going to spoil it. Pulling on a long, warm coat with a voluminous fur collar she leaves to take personal charge of her festive army.

As the choir sings Silent Night, in the original German, of course, Master Mary Dacre fixes her smile to serene. A frosty English night. Perfect. Here is the whole school and several hundred old boys, esteemed guests and family, their faces lit by the old glow of midwinter, powered, probably, by a newly throbbing nuclear power station somewhere on the south coast. All around the Old Gatehouse, entwined in its ivy, and in the nearby trees are fairy lights, hundreds of tiny candle bulbs, lighting the wintry breath of the crowd. Hanging from posts in glass jars are a hundred candles. A large fir tree, tastefully bedecked in oversized decorations and supporting a silver star is on a block next to the wide, low stage on which will sit the dignitaries and leaders of the school. Pride of place, in the centre, a kind of throne awaits her, as soon as everyone has found their place.

Someone who knows his place is Captain Saunders, sternly shaking the hand of a big, upright man who looks to be in his fit and healthy late sixties. General 'Sticks' Hemmings, who hasn't the faintest idea who this officer class cliché is, grants a moment's attention before dismissing the captain with the hint of a salute. The captain marches off to his place, with most of the audience, in the rows of chairs seated in a rough horseshoe around the stage. The general nods to the patiently attending Head of School who has the privilege of showing General Hemmings to his seat on the right of the Master. His arrival on stage seems to signal a shift in proceedings, as the hubbub of chat, quietens to a murmur and the choir comes to the end of the carol.

Mary Dacre is aware, as she stands once more to address her audience, that the last time she stood in front of the Old

Gatehouse was an unmitigated disaster and one more of those and she will be teaching in a comprehensive in Preston. But, gazing out at the quietly composing faces of the well shod and warmed core, she feels confident. The scene is lovely. There are children who could have escaped from the richer ends of a Dickens novel. There are parents and grandparents who will be happy providing to the exact hearts' desire of these kids, some of whom are already attending nursery and year one at the school. And this is a unique occasion, to be remembered and savoured for a hundred years.

Into the gap between the stage and the chairs of the majority, a procession, some carrying more candles in jars. A donkey, led by a ten year-old pupil. A donkey! Carrying a blonde Mary, borrowed from the girl's school down the road who, in turn, carries an actual baby, sleeping contentedly in a bundle of swaddling, followed in ascending order of height, by a Joseph, three shepherds, three kings of the Orient and the rest of the cast of the nativity, including a very domestic sheep and goat. To one side, a woman, possibly the baby's mother, looks poised to rush in and catch the infant, who, it would be uncharitable to presume, is earning her a few pounds for this personal appearance.

As the Christmas characters position themselves Master Mary Dacre steps up to make what will be her last public speech at Stedman's School.

As he walks into the shadows behind the trees Toby is surprised to feel quite Christmassy. It's a nice time of year and he always enjoys the family ambience during the two week holiday. He's quietly confident of enjoying it again this year, unlike poor old Findlay.

When Toby was eleven he was taken, with his sister by their parents to Cyprus. His memories of endless snorkelling and adventuring on the beaches there would be in stark contrast to those running through the mind of General Hemmings, DSC, as he watches the children and young people work their way professionally through the traditional British nativity play.

It's Christmas Eve, nineteen seventy four. In front of Major Hemmings, as he was then, a group of about ten children of different ages are singing kalantas, jangling a pastoral backing outside the door of half a house. One side of the building has been completely demolished. The naked living quarters on one side have been partially covered by sheets of tarpaulin. There is a bloody stain on the wall, near the door.

In the cab of a lorry, sheltering from the thin rain, the major watches as the door opens and a youth appears. He shouts at the children who move off a little, down the narrow street opposite. He takes a step from the door and picks up a stone and throws it at the now running gang of kids, shouting at them again in Greek. The driver, observing, sitting next to the major in the cab turns on the lights of the lorry, blinding the young man, who, when he takes his hands from his eyes, the major can see is in angry tears.

'Turn those off!'

It's the kind of human evidence that gets in the way of good soldiering, he finds. When he tries to concentrate on movement and supply, what and who goes where, he remembers images like these, especially when he is tired and he is distracted, forced to think about the locals as more than just a strategic problem. Keeping a cool head and, it's got to be said, doing his very best to be brave, has got him a good reputation as an up and coming big hitter in the British Army. He needs to be completely focused on the mission (*which is?*) and not the peripheries, (the people of Cyprus and their lives) if he wants to keep climbing the slippery pole.

Back home, that's another story. It's the people who make

life worth living. On the small inherited estate, his family, the kids, his wife – the various workers and neighbours, a small valley of English rural delight that gets more perfect the further away from it he is. The idea that home, the local village, his own house, for goodness sake, could ever be a semi-ruin, pock marked with bullet holes, stained with British blood is ridiculous. The order of life changes very slowly at home.

Which is why it is such a shock to discover, almost simultaneously of both his wife's affair and her breast cancer on his return from his tour in Cyprus. But, in a way, even this situation lends itself well to his life view, as he knows he could never make love to a one breasted woman and he could never live with a wife to whom he didn't make love, at least once a year. It has little effect on his career – the seventies were the decade when divorce became common place. His children are old enough to go to Oxford in the next two years, he is a new bachelor and, on his return to Cyprus, he feels free to indulge himself with several local women who's needy wheedling he offsets with gifts and help with accommodation in the homes of some of the better-off Turks who are now north of the border, probably in what was a Greek house.

Catching syphilis was a good reason to stop rambling and he is soon wooing the handsome widow of an Egyptian businessman (an English woman, though, of course), and they are married in a small ceremony at a registry office when he brings her home.

The major becomes a commander and then a general and he finds himself increasingly at home as his children marry and his first wife dies.

Spending more time with politicians and finding he has a knack with business, himself, it's unsurprising that, shortly before retiring he is offered a post as Non-Executive Director at Markham Austin Engineering, who specialise in ordnance – bullets and shells – which he takes, after a decent interval (well, three months, to be precise) after leaving the army.

Here is a man, not inherently an evil man, who has managed to disassociate himself completely from the results of his orders and his wages. Ironic then, that his brain and a bullet are introduced to each other in such an intimate manner, moments before his death.

Toby watches his first kill topple magnificently from the stage, his mouth still open, ready to say, 'ladies and gentlemen'. He feels a little bit fraudulent – after all, if he'd had a large, heavy object to hand he's pretty sure he could have just dropped that on the general's head to achieve the same result. But, no, it wouldn't be the same result. As Smith had carefully explained, it's not the death, it's the bullet, the special bullet. The death is the telephone ringing; the bullet is the message, delivered, loud and clear: we've got something that you're going to love!

The shot had been louder than he was expecting in the still night air. Scrambling back across the roof to the trap door, he hears the growing tumult below. Shouts giving way to a scream, then more screams, then pandemonium. As predicted by Smith, several hundred people running for cover, the presence of so many ex and current members of the military shouting orders, countermanding orders, provide excellent cover. The one person he expects to see before taking his place in the chaos appears as if he has been given stage directions. Steve is brilliant! How did he know?

The Sergeant Major looks up the stairs, at the figure all in black, carrying the rifle with the outsized barrel. He is too stunned to raise his pistol at first. Toby smiles.

'You! You're not Findlay!'

Acknowledging, no, he's not. Toby stays where he is, the

rifle pointing downwards. The Sergeant Major lifts the revolver, finally.

'Drop your weapon, lad. You'll not be going anywhere now. Put it down or I'll have to shoot you. Don't make me do that.'

Savouring the look on the old soldier's face. This will be two in one night. As he lifts the rifle and looks down the sights at the SM, seeing the expression change from pity to fear to anger, the pistol now aimed squarely at Toby. Who holds his breath. A bang and the Webley clattering to the floor, the Sergeant Major holding his wrist, blood dripping from a hole by the base of his thumb. Then once more, Toby allows the butt of his rifle to find the light bruise over his shoulder blade, he squeezes his index finger against the hard trigger and the caretaker of Stedman's School falls to the ground, half his face missing.

Follow the instructions. He steps over the body. Leans the rifle against the door. It was Findlay's rifle, bought for him by the school. He really was that good, was Findlay. Findlay's rifle, Findlay's fingerprints. Where is Findlay? Who can say? Perhaps he is with his parents, who, of course, would lie for their son, for the family name. Is there enough proof to send him down? Probably not, but it will be messy and there will be a fuss. The whole incident will be unmissable. Comparisons with the end of the Lyndsey Anderson film, ... If. A very meaty story, full of mystery and intrigue and the whiff of something perverse, the smell of shit.

Stripping off the black jumpsuit, the balaclava, stuffing them into a black polythene bag. Deciding not to be the one who discovers the Sergeant Major's body, Toby slips out through the side door and locks it behind him. And is almost frightened out of his skin by the voice of Smith, speaking to him from the darkness.

'Good shot. Both of them. Give me your clothes.'

Toby hands the bag over.

'Now run, run and hide, as far away from here as possible. Go!'

Ducking, as if from a mad gunman, Toby flees into the panicking crowd trying to leave the school. He won't see Smith again for months now. But he doesn't mind. It's begun! Can't stop us now.

*   *   *

A different kind of companionship. Surrounded by memories, familiar sounds and smells. Returning from his holiday at the clinic, Sherriff appreciates the warm embrace of his adoptive mother but is happy to be alone for a while, whilst she is at the shops.

The constant drug haze that envelops the cream walls, the streams of unconnected bullshit chats with other inmates, all made a welcome fog and the voices receded into the deepest recesses of his consciousness. There, as a flimsy whisper, to provide the inspiration, but not the madness. Everyone agrees, he'll be fine for a while, so he makes his own way back to this solid house, well away from anything busy but central enough and feeds and smiles and sleeps and gets ready to meander back to a bohemian life in London. Normally.

He wonders if the electricity is sparking in his eyes, if it's been remarked on. He is charged. That strange, wonderful man on the train had sent him a message, somehow tracking him down, how, he knows not and cares less. And an envelope full of money. Five hundred pounds. In the time it takes to write three sentences he will join the ranks of Blake and Milton as a commissioned poet and stand next to Byron as a revolutionary activist.

The envelope is on the table next to his notebook, open to a blank page. The notes spill out in a fan. Written on the envelope, in pencil, are the instructions:

'Create a song of freedom from the heart of the people. Tell them, it has begun.'

Tell who? What has begun?

Sherriff thinks he knows. Looking up, through the net curtains at the window, above the roofs of the houses opposite. Arcing gulls. Early Spring in a pale blue sky. The skylines drawn by jet planes on their way to and from Gatwick airport. Escape. Freedom.

He writes:

'Where I walk
The concrete fresh
The snow untrod
The sand unimpressed
To where I go
Or what comes next
Come with
Find out
Who guides our steps.'

He pauses and enjoys the wood of his pencil. He blows on its tip. Then writes:

'Why wait? Just fucking do it.'

He scribbles the line out then pauses again. Then writes:

'We do what we do from love.'

Folding the notebook into the pocket of his jacket, Sherriff picks up the plastic bag at his feet and launches himself out of the house. The paintbrush tings the paint tin in the rhythm of his marching as he heads towards the docks and his appointment with a freight train.

6

Chapter 6: Everyone's An Expert

The ivy surrounding the walls surrounding the eight people comfortably. In a few days everything necessary - apart from a passport for Sherriff Clarke, the most unique looking of them, something which Smith had hoped to solve with a Mediterranean solution, but which had been foiled by another period of high alert at airports and docks – everything had been prepared, including the introductions and initial bonding.

Anything left to do would be sorted out by the robbery. Money and the creation of a tightly knit band of desperadoes will keep the momentum.

Sherriff left with them, very early in the morning, after a communal breakfast which Smith transformed into a ritual, passing steaming bowls of coffee along the people sitting on the benches, either side of the long table in the Garvey's kitchen diner, urging them all to pass and share and calling for a quiet moment's contemplation during which he listened to the group's breathing as it synchronised into a regular, calm rhythm.

The house can easily accommodate everyone. Six bedrooms, a study, and a warm, dry basement, with plenty of quality cotton sheets and bedding, thick walls and carpets to allow the padding around of various hour-keepers and liaisons, including, not surprising for Smith, an early morning visit from Ann, with a glass of anise, to freshen the breath and a body already warmed with anticipation and the blessing of her husband, which rode him for a muffled half hour before departing, apparently satisfied to return to the marital bed.

Whether Peter appreciated the taste and smell of another man or if it inspired more frantic fucking, Smith didn't know or care. The important thing was the commitment, sealed in sweat and desire, of the more powerful part of their partnership, Ann, and what that meant to his plans. He has a second in command now.

Tedi, settling into the unusual softness of her bed, coming to terms with the fact that the choice is hers to make, without violent persuasion or blackmail but, also realising, she has no choice. The decision made for her by Steve, that strange man who has engineered her release and prepared her road. The death of her lover-pimp sealing a kind of contract she has agreed to without realising. He seems to know what she wants before she does. He knew of her secret dreams of stabbing and broken bones, of Nicky choking on her own blood. And he had sent not just one, but two demonic angels to realise them. You can't beat that kind of power, so she humbly submits and is delighted to find out she is both appreciated and loved.

So much, so fast.

Sleeping easy, in a shared room, Abe fits himself around the bulky presence of the wilfully reticent Wolfy, fills in the silences with facts and figures of sport and commerce and takes in the grunts that indicate the big bloke's understanding – that they are both in a strange land but that these beds are worth almost anything, that their lives are turning vivid, because of the classless Smith, who slips between the wine cellars and exotic cuisine of two lawyers and the bacon and eggs of their experience.

By himself in wonder and awe, Dean enjoys a Viagra hard on every night and half the days that no amount of masturbation cures. The pure luxury of experience since leaving Liverpool, the memory of the white hot nerves that speed the violence and action to his brain – a young man, fitting the suit life has tailored for him, finally, on the front line. Where pain and joy are high contrast. His loyalty to Smith is also his gratitude. He's going to Switzerland, for fuck's sake! To rob a bank, for fuck's sake!

Sherriff also lies awake, in love with his life, head teeming with the tadpoles of culture and info and action initialised by a poem on a train. The talk, the noble, romantic faces of these people in firelight and candlelight and by the light of dawn several times, when he has found himself hoarsely crying out the love he has for words: Sartre's words; Rimbaud's words; Poe's words. All the dark words he can net, that belong to him. He has never felt so well and he glories in his state.

When they depart for Swtizerland, the others are showered with a cloud of blessings from Sherriff's best wishes. Speeding them on with just a look but one which contains all his love, as he himself heads down through the underground to plan the lines that will celebrate this European campaign in his room full of old London dust, off Old Street, in Hackney.

Smith's bedroom, in the maid's quarters in the uppermost part of the house is devoid of even a single, lone thread, a crumb, anything larger than a mote of untidiness. The bed is as fresh as a hotel's after the mid morning maid has prepared it for a new guest. He was there, as his converted friends can witness. But if they can witness, Blake-who-is-Smith is trained to make sure they can't prove.

Locking the door behind him, the key trembling ever so slightly with excitement and a little fear, Peter Garvey doesn't know that this will be the last time he touches the wood and stone of this most significant result of his inflated fees.

The house sits lonely through the day as, somewhere above, its owners fly first class, first due west then, swinging suddenly around, due south, towards the Alps. In the evening, the heating comes on for a couple of hours accompanied by the anti-burglar device which turns the house lights on until midnight. This happens daily, right through the summer months, and on, through autumn, until, finally in the middle of the next winter, a power cut trips the burglar alarm and upsets the rhythm so that the house remains completely still for a very long time.

*   *   *

The consecutive blessings of five sons, fired from his wife's womb at twelve month periods, starting when he was just twenty five, brought a kind of local fame to Guy Christeler. Through the years, watching the boys grow, with staggered daily pauses of ten to twelve hours, five days a week, whilst at work at De Luxe Rent luxury car rentals and at the beginning and end of every Saturday filled him with a sense of wonder, for which he thanked god every Sunday in church, accompanied by the bowed heads of his sons, in descending height, like the Von Traps.

With the death of his wife just after their youngest son's eighteenth birthday the legend grew of his neat dynasty, all of whom work for him at De Luxe, all of whom continue to live with him in the large house on Anton-Graff Strasse, perched on a rock outcrop, overlooking the city. It was as if he ordered his circumstances from a shop. Five strapping young men, all completely eligible, polite, hard working and loyal. And a new wife, twenty years younger than the previous model.

Good health, wealth and a reputation for solid business combined with his rank in the Swiss Militia of hauptman, captain, are a fortified redoubt of respectability which he is unused to having assailed, especially by a door to door salesman, with an unplaceable accent. Looking up, squinting, the trim, fresh faced, part-time soldier is polite and mildly curious.

Smith, meanwhile, is acutely aware that he doesn't sound like a local. But with a large percentage of the city of Winterthur, just a few miles from Zurich, coming from all over the world he doesn't see it as a problem. Dressed in the smart work clothes and baseball cap of a car valet, carrying a bag of 'tools', he has positioned himself with the bright morning sun shining over his shoulder, into Christeler's eyes.

It's a short conversation – but Smith knows the subject will interest Christeler, who is always keen to check out anything he perceives as competition in the luxury car game. He doesn't even get to the prices before Christeler hears the less than graceful Wolfy making his entrance through a back door. With his head turned, distracted, it's easy enough to push him into his house at the point of, what later turns out to be a piece of pipe. Moments later and Christeler is lying, face down on the floor. Wolfy, under strict instructions not to talk looks to Smith for the next move.

Smith leans in close to Christeler, who is far from cowed. Speaking in German.

'If we are still here when your wife returns then there will be a problem. Tell me where your gun safe is and we will leave you tied up and alive. It will only be a few hours of discomfort and then your wife will untie you and you can ring the police.'

It is a very reasonable and sensible proposal. Christeler buys time, to think it over.

'What do you want with my gun? I can't tell you if you are going to hurt someone.'

Which is a very reasonable thing to say – perhaps the poor

hauptman might be implicated in a murder.

'I will be very upset if all I find is your gun, captain. All five of your boys are in the militia. One of them is a sharpshooter, I believe. Now. You've had a moment. There's nothing more to say. Where is it and what's the code?'

The boys. He knows about his sons, he knows that his wife won't be back for hours. Christeler makes the sensible decision.

'Beneath the stairs, there's a false panel that slides. The code is 6568YV.'

Smith writes the code on a flyer for the annual summer fair and hands it to Wolfy who disappears back into the house. Smith, taking the belt from a coat hanging in the hallway ties Christeler's wrists and ankles together. Hogtied. Remembering the knots, from the days when it was normal for him to converse with men (always men) who were hogtied. Not so much a conversation, perhaps, but communication of sorts. His man Bassett taught him the twists and turns, the over's and unders required to keep a man in one spot, where he can be tickled with pain until he laughs out the truth, involuntarily. Bassett, known as 'Allsorts', after the liquorice sweets, of course and because he tortured all sorts of people.

Wolfy returns, carrying a heavy bundle of what looks like elongated squash rackets in padded cases, strung together with a length of webbing and a black leather hold-all. Christeler manages to bend his head round and give a sideways glance at Wolfy as he struggles with the guns.

He sees a big man, shaggy hair, perhaps Spanish, perhaps Swiss. He makes a note of his face.

Tutting, Smith shoos Wolfy to the front door. Taking a magazine from a rack of mags and newspapers by the door, Smith flicks through, searching, then, finding. Placing the magazine, opened on to a page with the picture of a man, a smiling company director with thinning blonde hair, at least fifteen years older than Wolfy and dressed in a suit, on the floor in front of Christeler's face.

Then, another visit to the rack, this time for a newspaper, separating several sheets, balling them tightly then, one hand holding the back of his head, forcefully shoving them into Christeler's mouth, stuffing it until even the dribble is soaked by the newspaper, wrapping the torn strap from a large umbrella around his head, tying the paper in place. Keeping his weight on the Swiss man's body, holding his head still Smith takes his small piece of metal pipe and starts jabbing at the side of Christeler's head, just behind his ear, using the edge of the pipe which soon mashes the skin into a bloody pulp as Christeler writhes in pain beneath him, gagging and trying to scream through the wad of paper.

Pausing, Smith drops the pipe and, reaching with his fingers, pulls open Christeler's screwed shut eyes, holding the lids, so that the poor man has no choice but to stare and drip tears on to the face of the smiling man inches from his nose.

Retrieving the pipe, Smith nods again at Wolfy and they leave by the front door, although Smith pauses to choose a set of keys from others hanging on several hooks next to the coats.

A few seconds later and Wolfy is driving Christeler's SAAB down the hill, towards the centre of the city. He doesn't look at Smith.

'That was pretty vicious.'

'You don't really want to be identified, do you?' Smith is smiling gently.

Wolfy drives. He thinks. Then he speaks.

'Fair enough.'

Smith replies.

'Fair enough.'

Peter looks surprisingly healthy for a well-paid solicitor, used to fine dining and elongated business lunches. But he comes from healthy stock, a long line of breeding that specialises in carefully chosen mares and fillies to keep the blood strong. He is dressed in the best Alpine all-weather jacket and trousers and makes good progress with just an empty knapsack to carry.

The bus stop across the road is revealed as the bus draws away. The unlikely couple of Dean and Tedi stand, looking around until they see Peter who, as soon as he sees them notice him, moves off down the street. Dean and Tedi walk in the same direction, staying to the other side of the road.

Arriving by train earlier in the day Peter had found a tasty breakfast of hot chocolate and waffle near the station and then hiked out across Winterthur towards the outskirts in the southeast until he reached the rendezvous by the bus stop. Feeling a little peckish now, but thrilled to be finally in action, he strides with hearty steps and pink cheeked vigour, soon leaving Dean and Tedi behind. For a few hundred yards the three of them walk through wooded suburbia until the houses give way to a grass field and then forest and the road ends at a T junction, connecting with a thin road that bounds the trees.

Peter turns right and walks until he reaches a yellow diamond sign, painted on the side of a tree at which point he turns into the woods and, after a few steps have obscured him from the road, stops and takes a small compass from his pocket. Orienting himself due south he crackles through the trees and leafs, whistling quietly through his teeth the theme from Bonanza.

Meanwhile, Tedi is also looking at a compass, Dean watching over her shoulder. Despite having covered many miles together Dean is still slightly in awe of this woman, who has managed to make her practical jeans and walking boots combination look impossibly glamorous, and is happy to walk along behind her in the wafting cloud of perfume, the same perfume, incidentally, as worn by Peter's wife. Dean could be any European student, although the monkey swagger which Smith had asked him to 'work on' would still give him away to any passing Scally, of which, luckily, there are none apart from himself, in these clean Swiss woods.

Having turned left along the T junction the job now is to join Peter by heading east-southeast through the woods. More used to the London Tube map and a 'you are here' arrow, Tedi gives Dean a quizzical look and a half raised eyebrow, as if to say, 'man – do your man thing'. Which he manages and they head off in the direction of his pointing finger.

Minutes later and they come upon Peter leaning against a tree, whittling a stick with his newly bought Swiss Army penknife, still whistling. He catches sight of Tedi, who has caught a couple of stray twigs in her hair, her face flushed from the walk and adjusts his whistle from tune to male approval, just audible enough for her to catch. Her fierce glance results in a mime of apology from the solicitor, who is well used to saying unpleasant things to people he must continue working with. Dean finds it amusing. Posh people are meant to be more polite but a bloke's a bloke and a fit bird is a fit bird, even in a forest.

As a testament to the respect they hold for Smith, there are still no words, only gestures, pointing, nods and head shakes as they move off together through the forest. After ten minutes the clear sound of fast moving traffic helps guide them. Soon they are walking along the edge of the forest, looking down through the trees at cars speeding along the A4, to and from Zurich. Ahead is a tunnel through a rocky hill, crossed above at its edge by the one lane road which has swung round the edge of the woods they have just traversed. The tunnel is named, with a distinct lack of Swiss romance, A4-336-HX, on a small embossed sign screwed into the rock.

Rolling back her sleeve, Tedi shows her watch to Dean and Peter. Five to two. Early. They find some bare rock in the trees and perch. Dean takes a bar of chocolate from a pocket and shares it round. Still nothing is said. Which pleases Smith immensely as he watches from a few feet away. Without bothering to be quiet, he walks quickly to join them, their startled faces each registering different degrees of happiness at his presence, the arrival of the guru.

'OK. There's no one around. Dean, go up that way, a few meters along the road you'll find Wolfy with two cars. Take the SAAB. Start the engine and wait. Tedi, you'll wait by the top. If you spot any official looking vehicles coming along the motorway let us know. Just describe them as best you can. Anything with florescent stripes or markings, lorries with cones, anything. Keep the phone on and move if you lose signal.'

Dean and Tedi move off straight away, Dean with a 'yes boss'. Smith opens the knapsack he is carrying in one hand, removes two orange and silver, florescent waistcoats with numbers on the back, hands one to Peter, followed by a white safety helmet. Smith leads Peter to a steel ladder at the side of the bridge. As he turns around, ready to climb down he tells Peter:

'Remember, this is our bridge. We own it. So act like it.'

'Gotcha!' Peter is enjoying himself.

The two men climb swiftly down the ladder and walk along the side of the road into the tunnel. Cars rush by only a few feet away but Smith could be surveying a meadow with an engineer's nonchalance. He wears one ear piece of a hands-free mobile and he can hear Tedi's breath on the microphone as she keeps look out somewhere above. He finds the sound oddly erotic in these unique circumstances. It's the kind of detail that makes life special.

By a metal door, flush against the walls of the tunnel, Smith takes a short crowbar from the knapsack. As Peter uses his body to shield him from the view of oncoming drivers, Smith prises the large padlock from the door. Seconds later and they are inside a small room, or a large cupboard, lined with metal panels bolted to the concrete. Smith inserts the crowbar into the edge of one of the panels marked with a stencilled HX, after a few attempts, he prises a corner away to reveal the small, metal door of a safe. Struggling a little in the confined space, the two men pull at the panel until it is hanging half off and the door is cleared.

Sliding the edge of his glove off the back of his left hand, Smith makes a note of the numbers written there, on the flesh, in biro. He beckons to Peter to kneel by the safe door, where there is a combination dial.

'Fancy being a safe breaker?" Peter needs no further encouragement. As Smith repeats the numbers, Peter twiddles the dial and the door clicks open.

As he is passed several bundles of orange, plastic tubes to place carefully in the knapsacks, Smith allows the solicitor some basic information.

'In the event of an invasion the Swiss intended to destroy the tunnel infrastructure. A few years back they decided there was no real threat so they removed most of the explosives from the tunnels and bridges. Then they, very quietly, put them back, or, replaced them, with newer, better explosives, most of which they got from UK firms, saying they needed it for the new Gotthard tunnel.'

The tubes were followed by a sealed, polythene pack. Smith carefully slices it open on the edge of the steel panel. Inside are coils of wire and two small, metal devices which look like digital alarm clocks.

'These are just the detonators.The bulk of the explosives are sealed in the concrete. The initiating tubes are slid down a channel in the concrete and set off with these timers. But they are all we need. After all...' He smiles at Peter.

'...we don't want to hurt anyone, do we?'

It's not the robbery itself. It's the getting away. Impressed with this vital element, Smith's group, still waiting for fate to grant them a name, are looking forward, an hour in the future, to boarding trains and planes, hiring cars and buying a motorbike and leaving Switzerland as fast as possible.

The robbery is almost a detail, so confident has Smith made them.

Perhaps, under an objective scrutiny, they all might have been more wary, if not downright scared; if, for instance, Dean had overheard an old lag boasting about it, he would have scoffed at the lies; if it had arrived as a sheet of evidence on the desks of Ann and Peter they would have wondered how the robbers ever thought they would get away with it. Abe certainly wouldn't have placed a bet on it, that's for sure. Yet, here he was, getting his hands dirty again, for the love of Steve Blake-who-is-Smith, walking into an underground car park in Switzerbloodyland carrying two shopping bags full of explosives and flowers.

Presuming you are being watched, recorded on video, for every step, every hand to nose tic, every look around, whilst you place a bomb and whilst you walk away, is still enough to make even the most confident, self-deluded robber sweat from the palms inside his gloves. Remembering to limp, remembering the plan of the car park, where the doors are that lead to the rear entrance of the bank, keeping his head down and then some bleeding foreigner speaking to him in German – all add to the heart rate. The foreigner in question, a ragged but clean looking drinker who crushes beer cans under a big boot shod foot before filing them in the handy recycling bins by the lift entrance, is only asking if the flowers are for him.

But Abe's mind is concentrated on the pistol in his belt, under his jacket. Luckily for the alcoholic who is used to being ignored Abe doesn't look interesting enough to pester further.

The CCTV later shows Abe emerging out of the car park, on the other side, via some concrete stairs that take him on to a wide pedestrian precinct off the Bankstrasse, with only one bag. It follows him with a relay of cameras, limping, stocky, face obscured, electronically noting the second bag being placed against one of the wide bank windows, and then on, until he disappears into a park, where he is not recorded, swapping his baseball cap for a woolly hat and then uncomfortably getting on to a bicycle, on which he rides across the park and out through an obscure exit to a road that isn't covered by cameras.

By now, though, there is plenty of action for the cameras back at the bank.

First, an explosion at the rear entrance that reverberates up from the car park and into the buildings, followed by alarms and screams and the surreal sight of a cloud of petals fluttering through a grill in the plaza like tiny butterflies. Then the second explosion, shattering the glass and scattering paper across the concrete.

A large man and, what looks like, a tall woman enter, carrying automatic rifles, both in balaclavas and Swiss militia jump suits, and press the attack on Winterthur's biggest bank by spraying the ceiling with several rounds of nine millimetre bullets and urging everyone to the ground with movements of the rifle barrels, including the armed guard who is quickly divested of his gun. The big man then plugs a device into a wall socket near the main door. It starts to chug out puffs of white smoke.

Enjoying the sensation of power, the delicious recoil, even, (she realises later), the smell of the gunpowder, Ann grins beneath her balaclava. She takes a quick look at her husband – is that a hard on? She doesn't have time to check although, later that night, the memory returns to spice up some energetic sex.

Too busy counting down in elephants. Two elephant. One elephant. Another spray around the tattered ceiling, more screams, the dry ice machine filling the room, they both turn and run out.

Waiting in Guy Christeler's car is a balaclava'd Dean, gently revving the engine. Not even a minute later and the car is already leaving the city centre, with Ann and Peter in the back seat. On an empty stretch of road, they remove the balaclavas and Dean brings the car within the speed limit.

Parking in a side street, next to the empty wreck of an old factory, they abandon the SAAB and Peter and Ann get into a waiting hire car, un-ironically rented to them by De Luxe Rent as Dean uses his ghetto training to fire the petrol tank of the SAAB, which is soon consumed by flames, sending signal smoke into the sky as they head back in the direction of the bank, just in time for the arrival of the first police cars. Forced to take a detour they see only a few spare wisps of dry ice and a hurrying, shocked looking female pedestrian who's hair is decorated like a bride's with tiny white petals as evidence of their performance.

But it's enough to gladden their hearts. Now, they hope, all is ready for the airport.

Although, to be clearer, this spot is across the busy Flughaffenstrasse running alongside Zurich Airport, about ten miles away from all the fun in Winterthur.

In the end, this kind of banditry is as elemental as a street mugging.

A Mercedes estate car arrives at the car park of an anonymous looking building in a small industrial sector right next to the main road flyover and parks near the corner of the building. Three figures, dressed in Swiss army militia jumpsuits (one of which is far too small and another of which is far too big) and balaclavas, carrying Swiss army issue automatic rifles, jump out of the car and run round the back where an armoured van is being loaded with cardboard boxes full of Euros of different value. The loading is a regular, weekly occurrence and takes place at a leisurely pace with the guards and workers aware that, once loaded, the van only has to cross the motorway through a clandestine slip road that runs beneath, where it will be unloaded once more and put in a secure container to await its eventual journey to Germany by plane.

Judging by the ease of access, presumably, security is dependent on the secrecy of location, although, with its doors shut, the building becomes a formidable fortress. Smith has long wondered about this minor honey pot, which he has kept in his pocket for several years now, since receiving the details from an unhappy Basque fixer for Euskadi Ta Askatasuna (Homeland and Liberation), who had spoken fluidly for ten minutes before passing out at the sight of his own blood. ETA had somehow never got round to exploiting the information, possibly because it looked too good to be true and, thankfully for Smith, the United Credit Lausanne bank has obviously grown complacent.

Like a shopkeeper making a regular journey to the bank with his takings, or a pensioner popping to the Post Office for her pension, the most vulnerable moment is when they leave their front door. All it needs is a potentially violent and determined mugger, or three, for the money to change hands.

Six men instantly raise their hands at the instructions from one of the robbers, shouted in German, in an accent they can't place, they testify later, when interrogated by the police. Any bravery is dissuaded by a blast of bullets from the gun held by the largest robber destroying the two cameras positioned on the roof of the building.

Guns are removed from holsters. Men are urged to lay face down on the concrete. The rear doors of the van are shut, with one of the robbers inside. The other two get in the cab and drive off, at speed, into the residential zone adjacent to the depot. The Mercedes blows up, apparently after one of the raiders chucked a Swiss Army issue grenade through the window. No one is hurt.

It's all over in a couple of minutes. There are still boxes of money left on the forklift carrier. All six men take the opportunity to help themselves to a bundle of the largest denominations, a few thousands that disappear into the thirty million or so already in the van.

Later, the armoured van is found, burnt out, on the outskirts of the small burgh of Nurensdorf, a couple of miles from the city of Winterthur, where the police were still busy trying to find out whether there had been a terrorist attack or just a botched bank heist. The boxes of Euros were gone, along with the three bandits, although, shortly afterwards, and unknown to the Swiss cops, the same boxes could be found in a container, buried in bigger boxes of travel brochures, awaiting shipment to the UK at Zurich Airport, near where they would have wound up if the robbery had never happened.

7

Chapter 7: Half Full

At some point, two freight trains pass, creaking metal brush friction between bushes newly budding, between Heathrow and Chatham.

Miriam recognises a cryptic message when she sees one. This invitation to take a look at some radical artwork, guerrilla poetry on a grand scale, delivered on hand stencilled card: 'railway yard, Chatham.1.2.2 FHH 6D77'.

Her few weeks as an arts journalist have seen her freezing her arse off in various warehouses watching minutely changing video projections; under a river bridge in Glasgow (listening to the sound of a bridge over a river in Paris as part of a sound installation); actually up an oak tree in a wooden box that was assaulted on the outside by automated beaters (baby bird under attack from magpies...) and walking nervously through rings of fire in a huge car park that was normally home to a Saturday afternoon boot sale. So a trip to a rail yard doesn't seem so outlandish. Nor does the invite, which is tame compared to the homing pigeon in a basket around who's leg was wrapped the invite (following instructions, she took the basket outside and freed the pigeon, who promptly fluttered to a perch above the door where it dribbled shit over the newspaper sign for ten minutes.)

The rail yard manager is not pleased with the request, so he doesn't smile as he takes a hard-hatted Miriam across the stock yard to where the 8.30, 6D77 freight train has just arrived and is now ready to be unloaded. And he doesn't smile as he reads, written in blocks of white gloss three feet high:

'we do what we do what comes next find out who guides the concrete where I'

And, on the other side of the train, half way along: 'walk'.

Not perhaps the message Sherriff had intended, after a slight re-organising by the train operators, but inevitable given the days between execution and delivery of the invitation to Miriam. Who is also less than impressed. She makes a note of the lines, takes a few photos on her mobile phone, thanks the manager and leaves him to delegate the clean up, which manages to miss the 'walk', subsequently mistaken for an eco-message as it travels about on its reluctant metal canvas for the next few weeks.

Surprised, Miriam is enjoying herself. After sulking for a week and determining to develop such a cynical viewpoint that Bill would have to move her back to the news desk, she found herself warming to the arts editor, a quietly manic woman in her 50s who everyone calls Pet, which is an ancient play on her Scouse roots, her real name being Shirley.

Pet introduces Miriam to a seemingly endless convoy of artists, musicians, performers and writers in a trial-by-opening, five days at galleries, theatres and venues, ending up, late on Saturday night in a Hoxton dive with the two journalists being entertained by three gorgeous young men who collectively operate under the title Elude Sexy Perception, hilarious, sharp tongued operators ready to give any politician a run for their expenses.

Instead of a cynical viewpoint, Miriam quickly develops a knack of value assessment and Pet gives her the more literary assignments where Miriam's dusty knowledge of the classics plus her obvious love of words are best applied.

Bumping into Bill in the revolving door on her way out to interview an author she gives him a quick thumbs up as they spin round each other, which is met with an approving nod from the older hack. She is pleased he is pleased. Her father's death remains put to one side. There are no more visits from that dark world.

Her father's will, to Miriam's relief, proved to be a simple, moving document with no surprises or shocks beyond her discovery that her father had bought an acre of woodland not far from where he had last lived which was left to a local conservation society. There were no secret files buried in a Swiss bank vault. No strange instructions to visit an address in Budapest. And his ten year-old PC proved to have been wiped clean in a manner probably too thorough for her father, who professed to know as much about computers as he did about pop music.

Whether Bill saves her life during this time, by re-assigning her and removing the temptation to investigate her father's death and look any deeper into the whole Smith affair depends. Did Bill know the death was a warning? Did he know, if it was, that Miriam is just the kind of pig-headed journalist on whom it wouldn't work? Bill stays quiet. It's a knack he's taught himself during the years of rubbing up against the more psychotic beasts of power.

Quiet Bill Freeman is at his desk, in his office, looking out through the venetian blinds at his kingdom, the ranged homesteads of computers and desks that are the newspaper prairie. In front of him is the photo he hopes Miriam will not notice. Why should she? OK, it was a big robbery, over thirty million Euros. Worth a whistle. But it was Switzerland and there are apparently no direct links to the UK. He can't keep asking Pet to send her new journalist on special assignments involving expenses paid to Dublin or New York. Besides, there are TVs in Dublin and New York. As long as she doesn't see this photo, or the CCTV footage it was taken from. There's Smith, obviously him. Same rangy walk from the Smoothy robbery footage of a year ago. Same build. Same mad, full scale antics. God knows who he's got helping him now. A man, a woman. And probably more: the explosions in nearby Winterthur, although credited to some un-named terrorist group looked like a distraction tactic, to keep the cops busy.

If Smith is getting busy, so will the forces who made him. So will the forces who need to bring him down at any cost. Miriam is too involved. Knows too much.

In the tenth weary hour he has spent that day in his office he realises he can no longer find a speck of himself to admire, apart from the desire to help Miriam.

His suit jacket, hanging on the back of his chair belongs to one of four suits he owns, one replaced every year for the past fifteen. At home he has all fifteen of the old suits, uncleaned, rolled up in separate plastic bags, chucked into the loft of his house. Each suit retains the stains of his career, from moving up to editorship and on, until now. Blood, puke, sweat, semen, ten types of alcoholic spirit. Representing lies and distortions and suppressed news and weighted news and sackings and libels and licketyspit ass licking of the tycoons he has served.

Crumpled Bill, the newspaper legend, needs to do something good for the balance of his cynical soul, or whatever it is that used to make him feel glad to be alive.

A knock on the glass and one of his hacks with that special look they all reserve for a scoop peers through the slats then lets himself in. When he speaks to Bill there is the slightest tremor of excitement in his vowels

'Bill, you might want to see this. You've heard of magic bullets, right?'

A ballistics report, marked 'secret'. Concerning the murder of General 'Sticks' Hemmings at Stedmans School in Hertfordshire. Bill pushes the world aside and concentrates his newspaper mind on the important thing – the story.

Miriam's new flat, a maisonette in happening Stoke Newington, taken against her better instincts because she decided she wanted some fun in her life.

Despite the feeling of being a bit too far away from the centre, Miriam appreciates the tree lined road on which she lives; it's quiet and there are enough neighbours willing to say hello to make her feel a part of something, or somewhere. As she approaches she notices, outside her front door, a newly pinned sign, wrapped in a clear plastic bag like the posters for lost cats that pop up forlornly sometimes on London trees. The skinny branch of a trunk on which this is pinned is just beginning to bud, despite the diet of dog piss and scummy pavement water at its roots. The sign catches her eye because, written in felt tip in black at the top is the word 'Miriam'.

She stops to read it. Below the title, in black biro:
'Where I walk
The concrete fresh
The snow untrod
The sand unimpressed
To where I go
Or what comes next
Come with
Find out
Who guides our steps.
We do what we do from love.'

Her first thought is: 'ah, now that's better.'

Then she wonders how the poem came to be left here, outside her home, with her name on it.

Watching, a few yards down the road, taking in the late afternoon Spring sunshine, Sherriff takes the frown of fear on Miriam's face as a criticism, but shrugs it off. What does she know? Anyway, finally, the message is delivered.

Miriam rips the poem from the tree and walks quickly to her front door. Then, hesitating, she turns around and walks back the way she came.

That was unexpected, for her and for Sherriff, who was about to walk away. Instead, he decides to follow her a few yards behind.

She sits in a corner of the pub, which is already beginning to fill with early evening drinkers, the kind of pub, off the busy High Street where men and women who's roots are generations mixed with hundreds of miles can do battle over Guinness and whisky safely, where a son can drink with his father, where a woman can look another woman lovingly in the eyes, where children can be chaperoned to eat chips and fish-fingers at the back. A small slice of alcoholic paradise as long as you watch your mouth.

Miriam has been here before a few times and prefers it to the cleaner bars filled with graduates and slummers on pretty Church Street. In the corner, in a booth, safe. She thinks about the poem and fiddles with her mobile. Who would she call? It's something and nothing but it feels like, smells like, tastes like Stephen Smith. The name is plucked from her fore-thoughts.

'Steve described you well. He has a poetic heart.'

Sherriff Clarke slips into the seat opposite her as her own heart-beat increases.

'He told me: 'she will have a frown that makes a V when

she's puzzled and a U when she's vexed' - he didn't say 'vexed', but you get my meaning. Annoyed. Or worried. Don't be. It's alright. He's fine, I'm fine. You're fine.'

Looking at the freckles on his face. The horn rim glasses. The short afro. He looks very fashionably eccentric. There is no threat in his tone. His expression is benign. But what he represents is a bloody memory.

'I'm not interested. Tell Stephen Smith I'm not interested. And I'm going to call the police. So leave, now.'

Sherriff looks genuinely puzzled.

'No, it's Blake. Steve Blake. You must have forgotten. There's no need to call the police. What will you say? A man left a poem on a tree for you? They'll think it's a late valentine's prezzie. Or something.'

Still sitting there. Pinned to the seat by her curiosity.

'Why... what does he want?'

'He wants you to know what's going on. It's art. It's a happening.'

'You do know he's a killer, don't you? You know he kills people?'

Sherriff is amused.

'He's a lady killer. I haven't seen him actually stab anyone yet. Or shoot anyone. But it's early days. Don't you think...' He leans closer to her, smelling of baby lotion and fruit, '... don't you think he's, special? Got something, special?'

Backs off. They both back off.

'No. He's just fucked up. Wanted by the police.'

'Is he? What for?'

'I told you. Murder.'

'You didn't tell me. Is he? Oh. But I don't believe it. They just want to lie, to get him, because they know what he can do.'

'What can he do? What's your name?'

'Sherriff. Come to the new place...' he gets up, reaching

into his pocket.

'…you know what he can do. You've seen it.'

'What do you mean, 'sherriff'? Like a policeman?'

'My name. Two Rs, two Fs.' From his schoolbook, Sherriff rips half a page containing an internet address scrawled in pencil. He floats the page to the table, next to Miriam's glass.

'See you soon, Miriam. Come to the new place, it's in Wales, apparently.'

She watches him leave. He high fives an elderly black man in a battered pork pie hat on the way out. The man doesn't look after him, nursing his half of Guinness, looking in Miriam's direction with a watery gaze. He calls to her.

'That man a poet, y' know? He's a poet.'

She reads the poem again. It tells her only that she's been found and that she was stupid to think it would never happen. The internet address: http://birdcagewalk.wordpress.com/. She looks it up immediately on her phone and sees a picture of a gated track leading to a dark hill and a Google map reference. That's all.

*   *   *

Five filled beer cans, emptying the water through quarter inch holes in their base on to the wall below, holes that appeared each time, immediately after he squeezes the trigger of the specially adapted, Swiss army SIG sniper's rifle, part of the booty that travelled, together with around 30 million Euros in a metal container from Zurich to Chatham and on, to a secure compound on the outskirts of Cardiff, from where it was transported by a furtive Wolfy and cautious Abe to the middle of nowhere.

Another five cans are lined up on top of the stone wall, weighted with water. A sound distracts him as he puts his eye once more to the rifle's sights. He looks around, from where he lays full length in rough grass a hundred yards away from the wall. It's Ann. Good. He wriggles his crotch into the damp earth and sights along the barrel, feeling his cock stiffen. But before he can take his shot:

'Cover your ears!'

Ann takes aim with the pearl handled pistol and lets loose a series of bullets in the general direction of the tin cans, succeeding only in knocking one of them over and damaging the mud and grass of the hill beyond. She laughs as the hollow point bullets explode the ground. Then watches as Toby methodically pots the rest of the cans, making the water flow and, for a finale, bounces several rounds into the earth below the can she had knocked to the floor, making it jump into the air. Ann is delighted.

'Teach me to shoot!'

The moment is still and the wisps of gunsmoke mingle with precocious seeds and mites, hanging in thin sunlight over the boggy field. They watch each other, Toby leaning back on an elbow in order to gaze up, Ann taking in the full length of the young man's outstretched body, from the floppy hair to the price tags, still stuck to the soles of his walking boots. Drinking the seconds. Savouring stalled time.

She throws herself down next to Toby on the grass. If it means keeping the side of her body next to his for a while, he is more than happy. He passes the rifle over and positions her hands and arms correctly. She aims and the trigger clicks.

'Empty. You need another magazine.'

Toby helps slot a new magazine. She catches his eye.

'Steve really admires you Toby. He calls you a natural.'

She touches the tip of her tongue to her top lip.

'That should be my cue to trot out some old clichés that would end up with a fuck. Do I need to?'

Happily for him, Toby avoids blushing, although his fringe does conveniently fall over his brow as he fumbles with the magazine.

'Clichés?'

Ann pushes the butt of the rifle into her shoulder and squints.

'Yes. Clichés'

'Don't close your eye. Open both your eyes.'

'Are you sure? They always do this in the films...'

The trigger, the explosion and the jagged scream come in a flam, separated by micro seconds. Toby has his mouth open, frozen on a syllable as Ann rolls away from him holding her face, her eye, which should have been shut. Would the thin layer of eyelid have given her any more protection from the shrapnel of the misfired round? Probably not enough to save her sight, if her eyeball had received the pointy end. Toby acts, pressing his palms into the earth to lever himself up, his right hand finds the sharp end of the still hot piece of metal, which imbeds into his skin, although he hardly notices.

'You were bloody lucky, darling.' Peter has finished examining her eye and addresses her via the bathroom mirror. It's a big bathroom, but the presence of the bulky solicitor and a rangy teenage boy crowds Ann against the sink as she sits on the edge of the bath.

'Well, I don't feel bloody lucky, darling. I've just had a bloody great bullet nearly take my eye out.'

'Poor darling.'

Peter stands and observes a moment. The eager beaver concern on the young man's face, his wife's pouting bottom lip, their shoulders, touching. OK.

'Look after her, Toby.'

With that, Ann's husband leaves the two of them. Ann considers the swelling and the plaster across her eyebrow as she listens to him step heavily down the stairs. A moment later and she can hear him explaining to the others that she's alright, just a scratch really. Toby still looks touchingly concerned, sitting next to her on the side of the bath, a smidgeon of her blood dashingly smeared on his chin.

'Well, that was nice.'

Toby doesn't understand.

'Peter. He gave us his blessing. What a lovely chap my husband is, lets me shag whoever I want and still loves me. Ouch.'

She turns to the boy and pulls another poor me face, whilst examining him. There is a shine in his eyes, an old fashioned glint.

'What were you going to say before…'

'Before I blew up your rifle? So sorry about that, Toby. I'm sure Steve will get you a new one.'

She has a hand on his thigh, casually stroking.

'No, it's my fault. I didn't check the position of the magazine, it wasn't loaded properly, didn't click in. The rifle is OK, actually. I'm sorry you're not.'

'You'll have to make it up to me then, won't you.'

Her hand has moved up to his crotch.

'Yes… so what…'

'What was I going to say? Oh, some slaggy things like, I hope you can shoot straight when you get excited and, I really can't remember anymore.'

There are more comfortable places to have sex than a utilitarian bathroom, but it says a lot about the comfortable relationship Steve's little army have developed to note that Ann and Toby don't bother to shut the door.

If there are glances upwards from the others, spread out around the several rooms on the ground floor below then they are hardly shocked, just an acknowledgement that they are all, truly special people, existing in a bubble of love, well chosen by their leader.

*   *   *

The man they call Steve is happy to have found a name at last. He closes the book and texts a message to Sherriff, who should be on a train heading towards Wales at that moment. It reads:

'See what you can do with 4th Unit. It's our name. Write us a song.'

*   *   *

Tonight, finally, they celebrate. The country house, low beamed with flickering candles resounds to a selection of MP3 choices as they take it in turn to plug them into Peter's macho stereo system.

Everyone leaps around at some point, apart from a poised Sherriff, smiling shyly as he leans on an upright supporting beam, loosely holding a thin joint (which is snatched from his fingers by a shirtless Dean, mid-pogo), and Abe, who sits comfortably enclosed by the huge cushions of the over-sized sofa, grinning, watching his new good friends, rolling spliff after spliff on an old Observer magazine.

As he and Wolfy and Steve loaded up a shopping trolley with some very fine booze, indeed, he blessed the coming night:

'It's what you do. A job like that – you have a knees up. Only right. No one needs to know what it's all about but us, because we deserve it, right?' Slapping the wide shoulder blade of the big Irish man who smiles benignly down.

'Right. Make sure we get some nibbles. Ah, there's mine.'

Spotting the stacked cans of Red Stripe. He loads several four-packs and takes a quick look at Steve, who is suddenly there, piling them in, laughing until the cart is full.

'I've got mine. I'll see you two mugs outside!'

And he cheerfully shunts the beer down the aisle. Paid in cash, all of them. More money than can be spent without buying mansions or yachts. Laundered in small amounts through banks in cities in the west of Britain and in Eire. It's coming up to the Easter break; of course there are more Euros around than normal. Perhaps the region is on the up. Who cares. There's no alarm raised, the numbers on the notes are safe. It's proper money and some thirty new bank accounts make some thirty bank managers very happy, for a minute or two. How easy is it to open a bank account in a fake name? It's fake utility easy (Photoshop!). It's fake passport easy (Abe's connections). It's harassed tellers on a busy Saturday easy. Post Office easy. And it's even easier in Eire, where Wolfy makes several flying visits to Dublin accompanied by Abe, in and out in a day each time, a few beers on the return journey whilst guarding two rucksacks stuffed with Great British pounds.

Everyone's celebrating.

Whooping, Wolfy spins Tedi around and around, clearing the temporary dance floor, scattering robbers and terrorists, knocking drinks over. Abe approves.

'If you want a good time, go out with an Irish, I always say. They know how to have fun, if you know what I mean.' And several friendly faces catch his eye and know what he means, even if they can't hear what he's saying.

At some point, Peter does his Maori dance and is joined grimace to grimace by Steve, both with their legs bent, splayed apart, grunting, waggling tongues to the delight of all attending.

At some point, Tedi is behind Ann, both in the classic female nightclub pose, one arm aloft, the other teasing around waist and thigh, grinding to some bass heavy thing that Tedi danced to in less happy times, days, weeks ago.

At some point, hands grab Abe from his safe spot and pull him into a kicking circle of Greek dance, Jewish wedding hops, connected at the hips, drinks above their heads, spinning, somehow sensing that it wouldn't be right to include the serene Sherriff, now sitting on the edge of the big table happily recording this circle of love in his memory, for a future, in words.

Then, with the candles winking to puffs, the only light coming from cracks of dawn through the drawn curtains, Smith gets up from the table where he and Wolfy had been toasting each other quietly with whiskey, Abe blissfully unconscious in the corner of the sofa next to Dean and Peter who provide a warm, massaging bed for Tedi, who is supine across them, Peter enjoying her feet at one end and Dean exploring her neck and breasts as she hovers between drunken, stoned sleep and erotic charge.

Sitting on a large, soft chair, Ann has the fingers of one hand entwined in Sherriff's soft hair, as he sits between her legs with his back leaning on the chair, stoned, stoned, stoned, muttering words to himself, answering voices. Meanwhile the barrister's lips are busy with the lips of someone who is, technically, a child, but, as from a few days ago, counts himself very much a man.

As Ann's ambidextrous fingers free Toby's prick one more time from his flies, his head swims with the love of it all. As she pulls the spunk so easily, one more time, on to the sitting room floor, and he sees Peter nod slightly and hears Wolfy's roar and the day breaks he is peaking and everything will be downhill from here on in, if he only knew.

'You dirty bastards!' Wolfy laughs, chucking more brown liquid down his throat.

Observing from a long way away, Stephen Smith, once again, decides he hates the taste of whisky. His fading reflection in the window glass is haggard, energy drained, skull shadowed eyes, empty. He wonders, perhaps, why he is the only one who sees it and suppresses a laugh.

8

Chapter 8: It's Good To Be Honest For A Change

In fluorescent jackets, hard hats, walking boots, under the normal gunshot grey Welsh skies, Smith and the others set out around Peter and Ann's Welsh country house and make a note of every hiding place, every escape route they can find. Under the cover of a tripod, builder's level and measuring staff they map the two acres of land belonging to the house and the area around. The rough track, which leads to the house leads from a road to nowhere else. The nearest farm is several miles west, in another valley. The nearest village is over fifteen miles away, at the end of the winding, single lane, tarmac road which meets the track. They are as isolated as it's possible to be in Britain, south of the Scottish border.

By himself, Smith pauses on the hill overlooking the house, which is surrounded by a low stone wall, scrubby hedgerows and crumpled oak trees. Below, Ann and Peter are standing together, looking at the plans, conferring. He sees Ann look up and knows she is looking right at him, considering him. Closer to the house, Toby and Dean are at the beck of Wolfy, who has his head beneath the bonnet of a Nissan Pathfinder. Even at this distance, Smith can tell Toby is bored, whereas Dean is following Wolfy intently. Toby would never make the grade with Smith's previous employer, the Cambridge brother – too flighty. Smart, yes, a natural with a rifle, but too lazy, even taking into account the natural reluctance of any teenaged boy-man to follow the boring rules of secrecy. Horatio would use him up on one or two jobs and then he would be disappeared. The Oxford brother, though, Cornelius, would brutalise him until he bowed to the discipline. But this would inevitably mean Toby's talents would be squeezed out and he would become just another drone, about as useful as an ex-soldier. What else would a Toby do with his life? Who knows? Too late now.

Holding the tripod in one hand, leaning on it, Blake becomes Smith and assesses himself, as he was taught to do.

He concludes: very fit, for his age. Strong. Senses all in tip top condition. Cognitive and hyper-aware, super-intuitive. A great well of patience and fortitude contained within an abundance of intelligence. Empathetic and very open minded. Quite mad. He smiles to himself and wonders who will spot it first and whether it will become important. Will they still love him? After all, what has he really done, except to put them in danger, lead them to crime, ruin their lives? And they're only just getting started.

Down by the house, he sees Tedi and Abe join Wolfy and 'the boys' by the car. Ann and Peter have made their way across, too. A window opens on the top floor and Sherriff pokes his head out, gazing around. Suddenly, Smith realises they are all looking in the same direction, towards him. He waves. Most of them smile, all wave back. Except Dean who is wiping his hands on a cloth and who ducks his head back under the bonnet well before the others have disengaged. Dean.

In the midst of pipes and wires and valves and micro-chipped motoring technology, wiped and lovingly tightened by Wolfy, Dean is remembering how he came to understand the beauty of engines and oil in the first place, in the prison workshop over-seen by Dan. A tiny drip of pale brown oil from an immaculate tube. He remembers the blood and the flesh and the taste of Dan White's mouth, the lank flesh of the dead cops inside the bin liner polythene, the smell of the pub, of all the pubs, and is transported to a land of tea time telly, Grand Theft Auto with a spliff and a bottle of Bucky, all as it was before meeting Smith. As he looks back, he reviews and places everything in order. Grateful or hateful, or just plain bored. Grateful to Dan, to Smith. Hateful to his mum, his brothers, his school, most of his mates. Bored, all the time, apart from now. But, knowing now, really knowing, with a prison knowledge, that he is hooked up to a big time maniac in a crazy situation that will only get crazier. So the battle, he realises, is between boredom and self preservation. He wants to see how far he will go, for himself, for the fun of it. But he doesn't want to go down like a mug. Like the rest of these mugs. At some point he will get out, before it gets impossible. If it's not impossible already.

Peter, Abe and Smith are gathered round the laptop. Peter logs out of the shared account and closes the lid of the computer. Finally, all three men are able to look away from the rectangle, which has engrossed them for a couple of hours. Peter speaks.

'That's the last one, then.'

Abe is quietly amazed. So much money shifting around, money he will never touch or smell. That's the biggest bet he's ever placed. Or, the biggest series of bets, to be precise.

'You don't mess around Steve, do you?! Ten mill! So what happens now?'

Smith is already getting ready to move, getting up from the big sofa to stretch.

'Now we reinforce the message. Thank you Peter, you're doing a stirling job. Abe, will you come with me? I need to pop into town to pick someone up.'

Peter watches the other two leave the room, hears the front door shut and a car start up outside. That's a lot of money to invest in a company which will shortly be imploding. Instinctively, it feels like a waste. But he's aware there is a bigger picture, even if Smith hasn't told him everything yet. Peter rubs his left forearm then rolls up the sleeve of his fleece, uncovering a series of welts, red and raw, freshly minted wounds in neat three inch stripes at one inch intervals from his watch strap, almost to his elbow. One of them is weeping an almost translucent puss in tear drops, caught in his arm hairs.

'Are you going to put something on those?'

It's Ann, entering quietly. She stands in front of him and holds out her hands. He lets his own hands be taken, held at fingertip. She moves one hand up and traces the welts gently, with her fingertips.

'You didn't have to do this. I know you love me.'

Peter looks up into her eyes. She is assessing him. He is loving her.

'Does it hurt?' He nods.

'Is it a good hurt?' He smiles and nods again. When he talks, his voice is thick.

'It was going to be a surprise. You weren't meant to see until they were healed. I was going to let you discover them in the dark. Let you count them.'

She counts the stripes. Sixteen.

'Then I was going to fuck you sixteen times, one for each year.'

She smiles, although there are tears in her eyes.

'Were you really a virgin, on that first night, when we met?'

A tear drips on to the back of his hand. It's a gift, a reciprocal love gift and he accepts it with an open heart.

'Thank you. Thank you for helping me, for showing me the way. I will always belong to you, Ann. Whatever, wherever. I'll be there.'

'I know you will, Peter. I know it's true. You're my rock. And Steve loves you, too. You know that, don't you?'

He nods once more.

'Steve is going to take us to places we've only dreamed about. We have a glorious future. With our new family. Of course, it might not last very long… do you mind?'

'Minutes, hours, years… it's all the same to me. Are you in pain? Does it hurt yet?'

He gently raises a hand to her left breast and strokes it through the soft cloth of her cardigan. Ann shakes her head.

'Not yet. But I know it's there. I can feel it. It makes me feel… imbalanced.'

'Perhaps, when we are in a calmer situation, we can use some of the money to get you to a specialist, in Germany. There are new drugs…'

Ann sits down next to her husband.

'No, I don't want that. I don't want to be cut, or drugged. I want to go out as I am, in all my glorious beauty. Perhaps with a bullet in the brain. Or a huge explosion. It's the sort of thing I'm sure Steve can arrange for me.'

'For us!'

'For us, if you want it too.'

'I do. That's what I want. But before that I want to have a proper go at some of these bastards. The killer bastards. They think they are… unassailable. But we are a formidable force. You, you could take them out single handed, given half a chance.'

They hold each other, him being careful not to squeeze too tight. She has her head on his shoulder. Through the wet haze

Ann notices, outside, watching from the window, a curious Toby. Peter notices too and they both look round at the young man, now poised between embarrassed departure and frozen in the act. Toby is relieved to receive a smile from the husband and wife. Peter gestures for him to come in and join them. Ann wipes her nose with a finger.

'You are such a good man. Such a kind man.'

'Toby's a nice lad. We could adopt him. Always wanted a boy.'

'His mother's a bit kinky, though.'

They laugh and Toby walks in awkwardly, only to be grabbed and roughed up, pulled on to the sofa by Peter and tickled by his erstwhile adoptive mother. Soon, this will smoothly morph into a frantic half hour of sex, on the sofa, on the carpet, that tails off with the arrival of Dean, shirtless, rubbing his hair dry from a shower.

'Don't mind me.' Ann, straddling her husband, freeing her mouth gives him a wicked look.

'Join us. Peter's very open minded. Toby, you don't mind, do you?'

Toby's face, darkened. Torn. Dean steps closer, frankly weighing up the possibilities of pleasure.

'Another time. I don't think it's really Toby's scene, is it la?'

Dean is looking directly at Toby. A moment. Dean grins. The threesome are suddenly aware of splayed limbs, of the damp of sweat and fluid and the ungainly angles of arousal. Toby is the last to smile, but, in the end, there they are, laughing, breaking down the conventions and keeping it together for a little while longer. Dean flicks his towel at Toby then penguins out the room, which, although lanced of passion is still a positive nest of human loving. Love love love. It permeates the big stone house where rifles lean against walls in every room, where grenades rest on work tops and fuses and silencers sit in a bucket by the stairs.

* * *

From their vantage point near the entrance to Cardiff Yacht Club Abe and Smith watch the empty car park. Spits of rain dot the windscreen of the Pathfinder, distending the greys of tarmac and concrete, sky and harbour water. The faint metallic ting of ropes and fittings slapping the masts of various yachts parked on trailers near the harbour walls filters through the windows of the car. The atmosphere is quiet in the front seats, Abe, for once, silent, as they scour the open space for, what was it? Medium height, white, slim, probably nervous. Name of Whitmore, from Eire. Another Irish. Bleeding dentist.

Smith is distracted by movement in the rear view mirror, a fast moving car approaching from behind them. It's enough. There's no need for anyone to be driving like that on a road like this at four o'clock in the afternoon.

'Abe, get ready. Have them ready'

Abe hears the urgency in his voice and does as he's told, hands sweatily finding two grenades hidden in the depths of his waterproof, undoing his seat belt buckle. Smith puts the car into first gear as the approaching car speeds past them and on, through the entrance of the car park, squealing to a halt in the middle of the tarmac. Smith eases the Nissan forward, moving very slowly, his eyes on the parked car. Two men are suddenly out, rear doors flung wide open. They are walking quickly towards the water. Even from here Smith and Abe can see they are holding pistols. The two men break into a run and Smith slams his foot on the pedal. The Nissan zooms across the junction and through the gates of the car park.

It's a big car but the acceleration is impressive and it's only seconds before they are past the parked car. Abe catches a glimpse of a shocked, white face, the driver, following them as they flash past then almost coming to a stop as Smith spins the wheel, turning them round to face the way they came from. Smith speaks, loudly, firmly.

'Abe, get ready, Take the pin out and hold it in place.'

Abe realises the passenger window is sliding down. Smith holding the button down on his side.

'When I draw alongside chuck it in. Don't miss. We won't have a second chance.'

And then, it seems almost instantaneously, they are by the car and the same white face, mouth open is looking over his shoulder at the looming four by four. Abe is leaning out the window, the wind, the fresh salty sea air, the taste and he is amazing himself. The grenade held aloft, then his best cricket lob, popping it on to the comfortable leather of the back seats, still depressed with the impression of two muscular butts. Howzatt! Smith and Abe are spinning once more, turning in time to see the open doors drop like fly wings from the orange and yellow frothing body of the exploding car. Does Abe see that white face, once more, detached, beheaded in the front seat before the blast obscures the humanity? Sure enough for the image to haunt a dream or two in coming nights, if he survives this afternoon.

Abe feels a tension he hadn't noticed being released: Smith's grip on his jacket, preventing him from tumbling out the window, now pushing him back into the seat as the car, yet again fights horizontal gravity, as it moves at speed towards the parked yachts. Smith sounds even calmer.

'Abe, stay in the car, keep your head down. Listen out for me. If you see either of the two guys who were in the car, roll the grenade towards them. Don't throw it. Roll it. Then duck.'

The car is suddenly motionless and Smith is suddenly gone, one of the Swiss semi-automatics squeezed into his stomach as he crouch-runs across the few yards to the nearest trailer.

* * *

Smith, on the move, looks at his watch. Two minutes. He hears the shouts, two men, trying to decide what to do. Climbing on to a trailer and into the yacht perched on top, peeking through rope - he can see one of them, dark suited, short hair, Oxford style, hiding behind a stack of plastic crates containing small floats, the dark blue of his suit contrasting nicely with the vivid reds and greens and yellows of the globes. And offering no protection at all from a high velocity bullet tearing through the plastic, into his shoulder and only coming to rest at his neck, perforations of melted plastic around the wound like a ruff. Ninety seconds. He dies, slowly, blood boiling from the hole, adding shadow to the suit, gathering like an oil spill around his collapsed legs. One hand grabbing at the space, inches from the wound, oblivious to Smith, who has jumped down and is running towards the main jetty, a bridgehead to the various vessels moored in the water. He can see a small motorboat negotiating the parked boats at the farthest end. Whitmore is standing precariously, waiting to get close enough to leap from the boat, unaware of the man taking aim, standing blatantly, legs apart, full length in the middle of the jetty, his pistol raised and bucking slightly before the sound of two cracks followed by invisible bullets which prod Whitmore first in one side of his chest then in the other, two fingers of dark red from the strike points and then Whitmore tumbling, splashing. Mrs. Whitmore's face a semi-transparent apparition between Smith and the shooter. Whitmore's killer clumsily staggers back, his white shirt striped with red, as Smith acknowledges the deadly efficiency of the SIG, but that will be no compensation for Mrs Whitmore. Well, there'll be no illicit fuck there, then.

Across the water, in Weston-Super-Mare, a fisherman digging for worm bait looks up briefly.

Less than a minute. Walking quickly to the edge of the

jetty, seeing Whitmore suspended in a cloud of red in the water, watching the motor boat, engine smoking, bouncing away from him as fast as its tiny engine could manage, the bald head of the unfortunate skipper squeezed between his shoulders in what would have been a vain attempt to dodge a bullet from Smith's gun. Or anyone's gun.

Then running back to the car park, aware of eyes from the boat house, eyes from the apartments and houses near the club staring in wonder and awe at the still flaming car. Leaping into the Nissan. Driving towards the water. Towards it! Abe can't help himself.

'Steve! Steve! What the fuck are you doing?'

Thirty seconds.

'Abe, throw the grenade at the fuel tank. The fuel tank, Abe. It's the big green metal thing.'

The Nissan is almost on the causeway, ready to slope into the water. Abe sees the metal container. Smith shouts: 'Now!' Abe lobs the bomb and the Nissan is suddenly in reverse, which allows Abe a fantastic view of the diesel container exploding, a proper Hollywood style smoke and flames spectacular only marred by the appearance of an elderly man from one side of it, aflame himself, desperately trying to beat the flames out of his head and torso, the beige of his shirt, the green of his cardigan; the yellow of the flames. Abe is screaming:

'Stop! There's someone! Steve, there's someone! He's on fire! We've got to help him! Steve! Steve! Steve!'

Time out. And the big car is facing the right direction, away from the carnage. Driving inland, Smith punching buttons on the satnav, Abe, head in hands, curled over in his seat. Smith affords him a glance then a look around the sky, above the roofs. Lazy Cardiff cops. There should have been sirens by now. Smith slows down and turns off the main road, threading his way through domestic streets until they hit the outskirts, a small wood. After another five minutes or so, a mud track leading to a gravel car park. A picnicking spot.

The spliff appears in front of Abe's squinting eyes and he takes it, sucking greedily, exhaling, shortening it by a quarter in a couple of puffs. Smith is watching him, concerned.

'Abe, we couldn't stop. That guy, it wasn't your fault. It was only because they were there, waiting. They killed Whitmore, Abe. Shot him in cold blood. And they would have killed me... and you. You're fundamentally a nice guy Abe, but we can't afford to fuck around. The explosion was a distraction, so that we could get away. They take their time when they think there might be bombs. I'm sorry you saw that guy go up. He didn't deserve it'

'Who are 'they', Steve? The cops?'

'They're all the same, Abe. One and the same. The guys in suits, they were private. But they were probably police, too. They often are. But Abe...'

Steve Blake-who-is-Smith, soft eyed, full of love for the frightened, angry little man in the passenger seat.

'..Abe, you were bloody marvellous. Thank you. Thanks Abe.'

Behind the smoke screen, Abe nods, acknowledges and, for the moment, the love of Steve Blake is enough, even if he trembles and waits for the grass to numb him into a safe place. Fuck! Wasn't expecting that. Were you, Abe?

*   *   *

Once again, small but violent moments in history are regarded in pixelated state on computer screens, by a select party of men, sitting in an office in Finchley situated above a dry cleaners. If you took a deep breath the residue of poison fumes from below would tickle a cough from the back of your throat.

One brother is clearing his throat, loudly, sarcastically,

looking from screen to other brother, pointedly, as the camera on the mobile phone lurches to the flames puking from the diesel tank. The tinny soundtrack of gasps and expletives becomes a distorted scream as the camera picks up a man, head and torso on fire, staggering towards the harbour. The laptop speaker broadcasts the captured moment from the club house:

''My god! That's Davey! That's Davey! He's on fire…'

There the footage ends. Four men lean back into their chairs. One brother sighs. The other one starts, with a malicious smile:

'Very efficient! Veeeerrry efficient! Well done! Four dead, and where's our man? He's off, on holiday probably, with thirty million Euros. With that kind of finance he could be anywhere. You must be proud, brother.'

The dragged Belfast syllables of the MI6 man are hardly mollifying.

'Well, we can safely say that was an unmitigated disaster, gentlemen. Have we got any idea where he is now? John?'

John, an unlikely spy, from MI5, has an idea.

'We're hoping, guessing really, that he's still in Wales, in the Brecons. This is our last chance to nail him before it all goes ballistic. At the moment the word to the media is an innocent man getting caught up in gangland, drugs stuff. But the grenades, the explosions, they make this far too interesting. It's as if he wants to be noticed. He was your boy…' turning to the smug brother '…what's going on? What's he thinking?'

Hands folded on ample girth, the brown dome cocked to one side.

'The boy is a mystery to me. We gave him everything - everything! He joined our family but now he has turned on us.'

The annoyed brother snorts.

146

'Rubbish! He's a typical Cambridge punk! No discipline. What do you expect? You let a kiddy in a sweet shop, you let a bull in a china shop, of course there's a mess! At least we found him.'

'By accident.'

'Gentlemen...' MI5 is determined to be back in his office within the hour. He's a busy man, with secrets to tend, terrorists to monitor, a career to maintain.

'...bickering doesn't help. I suggest we scour the nearest open country to Cardiff, send a helicopter over the Black Mountains, involve the local army, just to have a look around for anything unusual. We won't tell them why, exactly, perhaps mention terrorists, the Irish. If nothing comes up, we'll have to wait.'

He shakes his head at the dark screen of the laptop.

'Last chance. In the meanwhile, prepare the ground. Decide what we can afford to rake up about him. Let's keep this strictly criminal. He's just a very violent, rather successful villain and nothing more. Agreed?'

Apparently so. The brothers are soon left on their own, listening to the morning traffic on Finchley High Street.

The suspicious brother is regarding the other who seems to be engrossed in a dead moth, caught in a dusty broken web dangling in a corner of the room.

'Is there something you're not telling me? This is rather serious. I do hope you're not playing a long game. Smith is too unpredictable to depend on. He needs to be dead.'

The beatific brother shushes with a finger to his lips.

'Walls and ears, brother. Walls and ears.'

*   *   *

In a room protected from electronic surveillance by the latest devices, a conversation is being recorded, surreptitiously, on a simple mobile phone by Sarah

Cumberland, civil servant, officer of the Crown and agent.

Another table, another laptop. This time the eyes are on a blown up image of a mangled bullet, the magnified streaks of General 'Sticks' Hemmings' dried blood making it look like a modern art exhibit.

Straight to the point, Ms. Cumberland:

'So, does it work?'

'As a bullet? It works fine. Apparently. Does it fly...?'

A man with no title, as secretive as a British policeman on holiday in Spain, calls himself 'Dutch' with which ridiculous moniker he thinks obscures with showbiz pzazz the reality of his grubby existence. The link between the agents of state and those who use their protection to build and sell bombs and guns and tasers and chains to dictators and plutocracies and thus enrich the economy. Dutch brings with him a sense of excitement, passed on from engineers and high-ranking managers.

His fingers making quote marks around 'fly'.

'...we think, probably, it does!'

'How easy to manufacture?'

'Very easy. We've already cloned what we can salvage. Enough to pick up a signal. What's crucial, of course, is the controlling hardware... and software. Whatever it is they use to direct it. We suspect it's similar to the drone technology the Yanks use, in miniature, using tiny weights.'

'Should we be excited?'

'Well, it's a highly unusual way to get our attention. Indicates a maverick. If it works. If. It will transform the battleground. Whoever has it will win any small scale wars that take place on the ground. You could arm, whoever, and they would win. Simple as. Africa... Asia...You control the technology: you're in charge.'

'So, has anyone contacted you yet?'

'Unless you include the message via the sadly departed

general – no.'

A moment, as the unofficial head of security at Markham Austin Engineering (Plc) allows Ms. Cumberland to take in the possibilities. When she speaks, he can hear the excitement has been transferred. He is a bulky man who can still play tennis. He could be another councillor, politician, self made Yorkshire business man or the owner of a mid-sized football club. An ex-cop. A white man in his late fifties who likes it when power stirs his dick. He keeps a pack of condoms in his pocket, with a bubble pack of Cialis, for occasions like this. He is staring intently at Sarah Cumberland. He will never use her name. In his head she is a 'Ms.' It's sexier that way. He is going to take this woman, dominate her, on the table, right there. Throw the laptop on the floor. He's going to fuck her for five minutes until they climax together, adjust their clothing then head out into the impersonal streams of London traffic.

And Sarah Cumberland is excited. But repelled by the coffee breath of the grubby ex-assistant commissioner sitting far too close. Excited by the prospect of the delivery of the message. For a few minutes she will own this power, until it is distributed amongst superiors and politicians. During the journey from this meeting to the moment when she explains – they have magic bullets! - she will find a way to make this work for her. Stay on the case, baby-sit through until first use, on a battleground somewhere hot. She is up on her feet, picturing herself in khaki blouse, watching broken footage from a miniature camera on the end of someone's gun. As she grimaces a goodbye smile to the fallen face of the man who likes to call himself 'Dutch' as he half stands in feeble gallantry.

And she is gone, the door closing as Dutch thinks through the Rolodex in his mind, locating Ukranian beauties, who don't charge much, not really, for the excellent service they provide.

Taking the tube. Sarah Cumberland checks the recording of her meeting with the man from MAE, then makes a quick decision. Changing lines and heading in another direction. Using some basic spy-craft, stolen from movies, TV programmes and a two week company course in Cheam: taking a taxi, a bus, walking a few yards then deciding, sod it! - another taxi. Ending up near Moorgate station, in the heart of the financial district known as the City of London. Only then does she make a phone call.

The net of CCTV could easily have featured Sarah Cumberland's face on twenty different screens, twenty different cameras, as she greets an energetic man in a suit, who enjoys an Espresso from a coffee kiosk in the square where he sits and listens to a fairy story about magic bullets. The cameras would have recorded that her face, on departing the square alone, looked quietly satisfied, as if she had just made a very good investment. The man in a suit, after some basic checking up will discover that someone else agrees with Ms Cumberland's predictions, to the tune of ten million pounds and decides to have a little flutter himself.

9

Chapter 9: Controlled Movement

Cardiff City in the sunshine. Sherriff is enjoying the light, sipping a lemon tea in a small café, which is, apart from him, exclusively the preserve of women over the age of sixty. His mobile sits before him, next to his ever-present schoolbook, opened on a page on which are written the words 'I found him by the skirting board/then I found my brooch/right there, right by his head/I thought he'd knocked himself out/I didn't realise he was dead.' The mobile beeps, an alien sound in this place of chatter and china and he gets some looks. A message. Someone has left a comment. To be honest, he'd forgotten all about the website after it was set up. It was Steve's idea, to have a place where others could contact them but who else knew? Apart from Miriam…

He opens the message. It reads 'I want to come to Wales. Call me…' and a number. Exciting.

The door to the café rattles a bell and another imposter sticks his face round the side of the door. Sherriff looks up to see Wolfy, who, once he's sure Sherriff has taken in his presence, promptly leaves. Now knowing Wolfy well enough not to tarry, Sherriff quickly packs away his book and mobile and heads out into the sunny street.

Waiting on a corner, parked half on the pavement, a Ford Ranger, squatting like an over-muscled guard dog, panting diesel fumes into the street. Wolfy waits, tapping the steering wheel while Sherriff negotiates the door, then nips off smart in front of a van before Sherriff can get his seat belt on.

'Fiftenen grand. Fuckin bargain.' Wolfy sounds proud.

'I'm very pleased for you Wolfy.

'I've been around and seen a few things, Stevie.' Wolfy is the only person Smith has ever met who could get away with calling him 'Stevie'. Not that he's bothered, but to anyone else it would seem preposterous to address him so. Wolfy is projecting. The kind of man he wishes Blake-who-is-Smith to be, the kind of man who can be and is of the people.

He can identify with Blake-who-is-Smith. A man of action. A man who knows what he wants and doesn't deviate. Doesn't do small talk. A tough man. Not afraid of hurting someone else, if it's necessary, but a man with a heart, a good heart.

He doesn't know Blake very well at all. He doesn't know Smith.

They are sitting at another table, with another drink. If it wasn't for the tension, the nervy restlessness of living in a house full of guns, being on the run, Wolfy would be developing a booze gut by now. As it is, he feels like he can drink all night and the hangover will disappear with his first morning piss. There are cans of assorted lagers on the table, all empty, crumpled, some crushed under his boot heel, ready for the recycling. He's got the recycling habit: Eire in Europe, who would have thought?

Smith is watching Wolfy, listening. Wolfy continues.

'...we've got to move on. If we stay here they'll find us. The weather's improving. We'll have walkers and ramblers and all kinds of eejits wandering around soon. Let's go.

Tomorrow. We've got the transport. Split up. Get back together somewhere else. Scotland. Ireland. Denmark.'

He pauses and nothing is said. Smith looks on at his wide eyes under the nest of brow, the brillo beard, the dark, pitted skin.

'Steve. Stevie. Whatd'ya say?'

Smith smiles. He smiles a lot. Genuine smiles that take in the eyes, the whole face, even the body shape. Practised, effective, inclusive smiling. An important element in every manager's arsenal. He smiles out his answer.

'Soon, Wolfy. We're expecting a visitor. I'd like to be here to greet her. But, you are right. Let's organise it now. We'll choose somewhere. Somewhere in London.'

'London?! But Steve... London. There's filt' everywhere. Cameras. Why London?'

'You know why, Wolfy. Nine million needles in a haystack. We can buy three houses, all near each other. Somewhere nice, like Crouch End. You can pop along to County Holloway, pick us up some new passports.'

'Well, I suppose it makes sense...'

'I knew you'd see it, Wolfy.' And Wolfy thought about it and he did see it. That's why Steve is the man. He would have gone to Scotland. Smith leans closer, brings him in with a crooked finger, whispering.

'Wolfy, keep an eye on Dean will you? Keep him close. I need to have a proper chat with him at some point but there's no time just now. I need to go and organise one or two things. He's very young, a bit impatient. If he looks like he's popping off anywhere just remind him we're all leaving, together, very soon. Tell him to wait. He'll have some money and he can do what he wants later. Not just now, though. He might get us all into trouble. Is that OK?'

'Sure. Sure, Stevie. I'll keep an eye out.'

'Thanks Wolfy. I'm just off, to, you know, work some stuff

out.'

Smith gives his co-conspirator a firm shake on one of his wide shoulders and then scrapes his chair back, leaves the room. Wolfy is wondering where Dean is. He gets up to have a look.

At the top of the house is a boarded loft, used for storage but big enough in the central part to stand. A skylight on either side provides light during the day and a bare bulb suffices at night. It gives off a fuzzy yellow light that casts the room in grey and shadow. Dean opens the trap door gently. He feels a little nervous. After what Wolfy had said to him a few minutes ago he had thought hard for a few minutes more before deciding that he wasn't quite ready to go against the wishes of a man he has seen kill far too easily and here he is, to tell the good news to the man himself. The trapdoor was shut but opens up easily, quietly. His bare feet are perched on their balls, on the steps, the top of his head lifting the door, his eyes just above the frame, adjusting to the light at floor height. Looking along the straight lines of the floorboards, the perspective of the narrowing width leading his vision to... two eyes, open, staring. Smith, on the floor, his head on its side, resting, still, one ear squashed against the wood. Listening? Resting? Sleeping? Dead? The eyes are wet and Dean can see darkened ovals in the dust on the planks. Tears. Dean stops moving, almost stops breathing. He waits. Smith blinks. There is a white, silver stream of snot trailing from one nostril to his top lip. Smith's mouth opens and he takes a deep breath. Dean sees particles of dust sucked between his teeth. Then a sob, from the chest and a spasm in the face, the head jerking. Crying. Steve is crying. Silently, but thoroughly, exhaling sorrow into the dim light, his body contracting, his knees to his chest, his hands between his thighs. Dean very slowly, lowers his head, the trap door almost shut when he hears:

'Dean.' Not the voice of a crying man. There is sadness in the tone. None of the desperation he has just seen on his face. Dean pushes the lid open again and looks. And sees. Blake is sitting on a wooden box looking at a book, his face in profile.

'Come up.' Dean isn't sure of himself. He has just seen a transformation worthy of a late night horror movie. The distraught, finished looking man on the floor a few seconds ago is, once again, the vital leader he has come to admire and fear, standing, waving a London A to Z in his direction. Dean pulls himself up and into the loft.

'Here, take this. I've marked the pages. Look them up on Google street view, memorise the route. You'll be the main car. We'll get you something cool. What would be your ideal motor? Of choice?'

Smith is smiling at him, turning his head. There are no red eyes, there's no moisture on cheek or lip, the hair is the normal fashionably disheveled mess. Had Dean imagined it? Then he sees Smith's right cheek, the shadow of dust in its hollow. Smith sees him seeing. He smiles more, warmly, handing the young man the book.

'Don't worry, mate. Nothing will happen to you. I'll be looking out. So will Wolfy. You'll get the chance to make a difference and make a buck at the same time. You're already rich, if you want to be. We've hardly touched the Swiss money. Have I let you down yet? Have I lied?'

How would Dean know this man's been lying since he met him. The truth, his words and their actions have all been coincidences. So he nods, then shakes his head.

'Alright Steve. I won't let you down.'

Steve pats his shoulder. Steve Blake, father figure. Rubbing the dust from his cheek whilst looking fondly at his Liverpool son.

'Now, run along, Dean, if you would. I've still got some

crying to do. If I don't do it now I might do it later, when it's not convenient. What can I say...' this fine joke, a shrug of the shoulders, arms outspread '...I'm an emotional guy!' A self-deprecating smile, this time. A join me, you've got to love me smile. Dean finds himself smiling too, laughing in fact. Then embraced in a bear hug and then happily cast away and down the steps, walking along the corridor, wondering why he would ever want to leave a man like that. Fast car? London? He's ready.

Sharp-eyed Toby, lying in the grass once more, looking through the telescopic sights once more, but without the rifle this time. Just casting around the open countryside, checking the birds and the rabbits, the bush and the bog. There's a fresh wind blowing from the east. Which is why he sees the helicopter before hearing it, approaching from the west. An insect dot, even in the sights, far enough away for him to think he can jump up and run to the house at full teenage pelt without being spotted. Three cars parked in the loosely gravelled space by the front door. He wrenches open the door of one and presses the horn repeatedly. Moments later he is joined by various members of the family, including Smith, who is calmly holding a pistol. And soon thereafter they are all shielding their eyes, looking to the west. Smith issues the orders.

'Wolfy, get the bonnet up on the Ranger. Get your head under it and keep it there. Dean, open the boot of the Peugot and get inside the house. Everyone else – inside, apart from Ann. Ann, you're watching Wolfy. He's a mechanic, come to fix your car. Come on, chop chop.'

Inside the house, Smith urges everyone away from the windows apart from Toby, who he sends upstairs with the SIG sharpshooter's rifle, into the loft, with strict instructions not to shoot unless Smith commands him to. The sound of the helicopter is suddenly upon them. Peeking from the side of a window, Smith watches as the old Lynx hovers sixty or seventy feet above and slightly to one side. He can see a man in helmet, khaki, ear protectors, scanning the area. Ann plays her part well, looking up, her hair catching the wind from the blades giving her an excuse to partially obscure her face as she holds it in place, waving to the soldier above who does not wave back.

Smith is aware that, at that moment, he is sacrificing the excitement-loving barrister for the sake of a few hours borrowed time. He sees the cameras attached to the side of the helicopter and knows she is doomed.

The helicopter moves over the house, taking its time.

Unfortunately for the 4th Unit family this is its last sortie before heading back to refuel, at which point the images from the cameras' memory cards are uploaded into a computer at the 160 (Wales) Army Base which is linked, via a secure network, to another computer in a room somewhere in Cardiff. The footage is then examined by a bored man and a woman who soon whizz through the endless green and brown of empty countryside to have a good look at the remote house where, after viewing Ann waving next to her mechanic without comment, they both exhale and coincide on a muttered 'fuck!' as the camera on the left side of the helicopter pans across the roof of the house and there, clearly, is a person pointing a rifle with a telescopic lens through a skylight straight toward the lens.

*   *   *

The men from the more official secret armies of the State prefer the military option. A small unit of commandoes surround and attack the house. Pass it all off later as an anti-terrorist op. Leave it to the pro's. A conference call, interrupted by the clatter of kitchen utensils. One brother is making himself a light lunch in the kitchen of a house, somewhere. The other brother is battling the noise of a busy café in Islington. To the men from Military Intelligence it sounds as if a small, old fashioned war is being monitored on their speaker-phones, with the clangs of cutlasses and the shouts of men engaged in mortal combat being somehow conjured from the oaths and jollity of the old fashioned café and the aggressive sandwich making in the unknown kitchen. Neither of Her Majesty's officials would have been surprised at the sources of the sounds and neither of them remark on the psychedelic sound bed – it's what they expect when dealing with the brothers.

The arguments are brief and almost arbitrary. The one thing all four men can agree on is that the maintenance of secrecy is the single most crucial element of their operations. The brothers get their way. Their people are, in the end, completely deniable, after all. And it is agreed that a combined force of under-managers who are already situated in the city of Cardiff be dropped a couple of miles from the house. Thence, to move in and make the problems disappear, with bullets and explosions and flames and smoke.

Is there a palpable sense of excitement coming from the food corner? There is. Accompanied by a palpable sense of unease, the normal state when having to deal with these maniacs, emanating from two men who have to, ultimately, in some way, explain all this mess to a politician.

*   *   *

Whenever she drove, she drove like a Londoner: aggressively maximising every inch she could take between bumpers and pavement. So the countryside phases her into slow motion. Without the competition she is forced to realise the speed she travels at, the bends, the sudden tractors and the blind dips and summits can be lethal. Accentuating this countrified alienation is a sharp headache at her left temple. Nevertheless, Miriam makes good, steady progress. Once on the main road in the right direction through the hills there weren't a lot of choices or mistakes to be made. Earlier, at a roundabout on the outskirts of Merther Tydfil, just before the sky opened up over the rising slopes of grass and rocks that signal the National Park Miriam had caught a glimpse of a familiar face, a passenger in a car being driven in the opposite direction. It took her a few minutes afterwards to work out what it was about the glimpsed head and shoulders that made her think of London, initially thinking it was just the sight of a darker face in this out of the way place. Then, with a small shock, realising she had just seen the poet-stalker, who provided the initial connection that brought her on this trip, the improbably named Sherriff, who had initially responded to her comment, giving her directions to add to the map reference, already sure she was going to come. So, she must be moving in the right direction, she surmises, even if he isn't. After about forty-five minutes of careful accelerating and sudden braking she turns off on to a smaller A road. Drive on until you see a lightning blasted tree (picture). Turn left. Drive on until you reach a ruined farmhouse and stockade (picture). Take the next left. Carry straight on until the road turns into a track. Follow the track to the very end, going up, up, up until you can't go any further. There's the house (picture). And there will be Stephen Smith with his merry gang.

Miriam isn't sure if she's ever done anything as foolish as this in her life before. The motivation has proved irresistible, though. The unfinished business of their affair. The questions, the hints at depthless secrecy. And, finally, the clincher: she is a journalist and this is a story, a huge story. She is in a unique position to find out the truth and write it up.

As the stones begin to rattle the undercarriage of the car

she acknowledges her heart is in her mouth. She seeks reassurance in the minimal information she has gleaned from the website. If Smith is a crazy killer he seems remarkably sane in the comment he left for her. There is a fondness implied in his apparent eagerness for her to just 'come and see, it's all very boring really but it would be great to see you again. I think I owe you an explanation.' You bet, buster. The suspension of the little hire car complains about the bumps and ruts. Her head hurts. It's the same spot that received the blow, where she was knocked unconscious by the fake MI5 man, the violent man who murdered his colleague in her flat, who's blood dripped horror through carpet and ceiling into the flat below. Almost a year ago, it happened to a different Miriam.

Now she must acknowledge she is afraid and, if the track had been wide enough, she might well turn the car around there and then and run away. Hemmed in by a low stone wall on one side and a thick line of bushes on the other, though, she is forced to push the car onwards, uphill, until, suddenly, she is there. A large stone cottage amongst threadbare, wind blown trees and bush, with a shed and chopped wood, a large four-by-four parked outside and the front door of the house open.

From a hundred yards away Smith watches Miriam leave her car, engine running, and take two steps towards the house, then stop. She stands, angling her body back, in the direction of her open car door. Smith urges her silently to get back in, drive away, quickly! Then it looks as if she is going to do exactly that, but she's just reaching in, turning off the engine, slamming the car door and has, moments later, disappeared into the house. Next to him, Toby nudges his arm urgently and nods away from the house. Crouched low, two men dressed in camo jackets, heading down the hill with long strides. There will be more, he knows. How many? Probably six. There is movement on the ridge of the hill and Smith uses a small, very powerful pair of binoculars to pinpoint another two men, one carrying what looks like a grenade launcher - which makes this very serious indeed. Watching as the man kneels and aims the launcher at the house. Deciding. Very casually:

'Toby, the feller up there, with the grenade launcher. What do you think?'

Toby grins. Of course! Wasn't this the whole point? He takes aim with the SIG. The single crack ricochets around the hills like an errant clap, but the bullet strikes the grenade on the end of the launcher, which explodes. From their low vantage point the sudden primary coloured splat looks like a flat bonfire in mid air, flaming slowly out and obscuring the two ant-men in its blast. The sound comes a second later, a unique disturbance that soldiers would never mistake for a car backfiring. The smoke wisps away on the wind and the two men have disappeared. Smith is impressed.

'Good lord, Toby! Come on, let's go.'

They wriggle along the indent, keeping their heads low. Smith is assuming: that the grenade took out both men on the ridge; that the two men they had previously spotted will be at the house in a few seconds; and that there are another two operatives out there somewhere. He hears gun fire from the other side of the house. Anyone approaching via the track would have had to negotiate a triangulated Tedi, Dean and Wolfy. Hopefully that's all of them. They always operate in twos. He decides.

'I'm going to the house. Keep your head down and don't take chances.'

Then he's up and legging it over the rough grass, zig zagging, head hunched in shoulders, aware that someone is probably aiming bullets at him as the ground pings and blats and the air feels alive with invisible motion. Toby watching him, is reminded suddenly of interminable cricket matches on the fields of Stedmans School where he always tried to find himself a spot to field as far away from the wickets as possible, sometimes managing to disappear completely for an hour or more, to lay in the grass, chewing on a stalk, until, one hot summer day he heard his name being called and sat up in time to see the ball approaching in his direction from on high. He reached out with cupped hand and the ball fell into it, all energy spent. To celebrate, he had zig zagged over the grass, roaring, ball held high, all the way back to the pitch, where he discovered he had just caught the sports master out. Life could be sweet, he thinks as he cradles his rifle in crooked arms, worming his way to a spot covered by a stone wall where he might have some more fun with gunpowder and lead.

Underneath a table in the kitchen of the house, Miriam is cursing herself, trying to squeeze herself into as small a shape as possible. Outside, the sounds of gunfire erupt then quieten, with no other human sounds to accompany the violent noise. She checks her mobile – no signal. There seems to be nothing for her to do except hide and await whatever madness she has driven into. Then a window smashes, somewhere in the house. She clearly hears something metallic strike something like a vase or a plate. Then an explosion. She screams. Smoke gently enters the kitchen, the sound of crackling fire follows. The kitchen door is suddenly kicked open and she pushes herself against the table leg. She can see a pair of combat boots, green trousers tucked in, followed by another pair. The boots step towards the table, both pairs. Someone speaks, RP accent.

'This is a fucking disaster. Where are the others? '

There's no answer. Miriam holds her breath. The same

voice.

'Set the charges, go through, I'll cover. I think they're all outside. Classic.'

Both boots walked quickly towards the smoke.

On a darkened street, a junction with the alley that leads to the back yards of a row of small terraced houses, built in the 1930s. There are street lamps along the length of the alley, but none of them work, all have had their bulbs smashed. The street itself only has two working street lights out of the six that are on the block. All the work of Kings Firm Chiverz, or KFC one of whom, Dean, is panting, leaning on a wall, smiling, almost laughing – obviously having just completed some energetic exercise. He is wearing black, from head to ankles. Only his Pumas are a pristine white, with black stripes. Another figure hares round the corner and literally bumps against the wall next to Dean. He, too is laughing. When he talks, his accent is broad Scouse.

'Did you see him? Fuck. Did you? See his face when he saw the blade. Shit himself. He actually sat down. On the ground. I almost got me knob out.'

They both laugh. Both boys, faces buried in hoods, peaks of caps poking out like a plague doctor's beak. The late arrival examines his hand. There's blood on the palm. Dean takes the hand. Licks the blood. He looks into the shadows where his friend's face resides.

'You should've.'

'Should've what, la?'

'Got your knob out.'

Dean's hand is at the boy's groin, rubbing, unzipping. The movements are frantic, getting it done before... being noticed, beaten, chivved... before the moment passes and they are suddenly back in the bodies of those who would chiv them. Dean can taste the salt of the boy's sperm once more as his breaths slow and the blood that was pumping from his arteries on to the mud and grass of Wales tips the balance against the blood still in his body. For some reason, that moment with the apparently straight fellow gang member had always been a holy minute for him in his short life and he chose it now as his last electronic pulses of memory, as you would with a TV remote, looking for something cool to send you to bed.

On the other side of the track, Tedi's face, muscles tensed, teeth clenched to prevent the sob, the howl that's building deep inside her, as she watches Dean's crooked hand and wrist relax into death. It's all she can see of him, the rest obscured by bush and wall. But it's enough. She holds a hand grenade, the pin already removed. She knows where it's going. As the under manager closes in on his kill she waits. As he arrives at Dean's body she lobs the grenade across the track and ducks down. Dean and the secret man, the hired gun, the groomed agent, member of a gang infinitely more powerful than the KFC has a moment before death when he realises he will be mingled forever with this stranger about whom he knows nothing beyond that he had to die. A mess of violence, to fertilise the bushes and grass. Peace at last.

The table goes over with one kick. For a superannuated second Miriam confronts a tall, fit looking man, probably in his late twenties, smart hair cut very short around the sides, in a combat jacket, open at the top button to reveal, incongruously, a tie between a white collar. He is tanned, shaved, there is a hint of after shave lotion floating past the smell of smoke to her nostrils. She notes the small stress lines gathered around the corners of his eyes. She just has time to think several thoughts in quick succession: 'he doesn't want to kill me/same haircut as the man who killed his colleague in my flat/he's handsome' before the man's face explodes in

164

red and flesh and he topples like a felled statue, on to a table leg where he lies, propped, head drooping, in a war pose, seen in photos from the American Civil War to the present day. And blocking the light, in the same space as the now dead soldier, here is Stephen Smith, with a worried look on his face, examining Miriam with his eyes, nodding, putting his finger to his lips then striding into the house, leaving her with the dripping modern sculpture of his victim. Miriam stays put.

There is more gunfire. Smith is suddenly back, rifle in one hand, moving fast. He grabs her wrist, pulls her up. She is dead weight and he drags her to her feet, barging out the door, pulling her like a reluctant child, into the drive, behind one of the cars, covering her with his body. As the house explodes. More like a messy demolition than a war. Another house on fire.

Smith is speaking into his mobile phone. What magical network does he use? Why can't she get a signal? Her own phone is slippy with sweat from her palm. He sees her trying to will the phone to make a connection and smiles sadly at her whilst he talks.

'Peter, where are you? No, I'm fine... Who? Dean? Damn. OK, wait there, I'm coming.'

He puts the phone in his pocket. For the first time she notices that he, too is wearing a camouflage jacket, splattered with dots of dark liquid. How do they tell the difference, who to shoot? He looks at her again. That's all. Just stares for a few seconds then leaves her.

Near the track. Sat on the floor, arms on heads. It's a puzzle for the two men. They try to figure out which one of the eccentric, wild-eyed group dressed in an assortment of international camouflage and khaki surrounding them is the Rogue. None of them fit the brief, until the arrival of a tall, lithe man in his forties who is immediately in charge. It takes a moment. He pulls a pistol from his jacket and shoots them both, quickly, in the head. The dead men would have been even more puzzled, if they could have watched, as the pistol is passed around the group, giving everyone a chance to pump a round into one or the other of their bodies.

Blake-who-is-Smith opens his arms wide, wide enough to take all of them in. Tedi, eyes still watered; Toby, in a fire of excitement; Peter, frowning, examining Smith but giving way to the hug; and Wolfy, who seems much the same as ever, allowing the boss to slap his back manfully. Where's Abe? Smith looks round. They all look. The sound of a car, revving the engine, gravel slipping under wheel. Smith steps into the middle of the track. The Ranger appears from the side of the house, moving erratically. Abe's head is just above the steering wheel as he tries to drive with the seat in position for the much longer Wolfy. The Ranger comes to a diagonal stop before Blake, who takes out the pistol once more, but this time, throws it to one side. Opens his arms once more and cocks his head to one side, smiling, palms upwards, urging Abe out of the car where the little man, at his very smallest since he was a kid, falls to his knees and sobs in terror and relief.

'I can't do this! I can't do this! I want to go home!'

Smith is with him, kneeling next to him, holding him.

'That's alright Abe – we're going home. Back to London.'

Stroking his head. Holding him until Abe is still. Looking up. There's Miriam, watching him from a few yards down the track. Smith stands up, resting one hand on Abe's head.

'This is Miriam everyone. She's a journalist. She's going to write about us, aren't you Miriam?'

10

Chapter 10: It's A Domestic

One hour. Britain is a small island really. A small island with one, big place, London. Diving into the pool of nine million from one hundred and fifty odd miles away takes some organising, though.

Setting out in Miriam's hire car is the unlikely family unit of Peter, wedged behind the wheel of the little Fiat, a stony faced Tedi and their erstwhile son, Toby, already dozing in a teenage haze after fifteen minutes, sat next to his uncle Abe, who ducks at every approaching car until Tedi turns in her seat to glare at him. Make it to the A470 inside an hour and they're safe.

Miriam finds herself walking past the now blazing house with a silent giant on one side and Smith on the other. In an outhouse she struggles to stand on one leg to slide the other into a pair of waterproof trousers several sizes too big for her. Luckily, Tedi's walking boots are a perfect fit and the city woman in her noted archly that the foreign woman managed to turn her own combination of green cargo pants and Miriam's heels into the season's new look. Emerging wrapped in khaki, bare feet uncomfortably acknowledging another human's sweat, the men are waiting for her. Nothing is said. They march, in the direction of a burnt patch at the top of the nearest crest. Miriam notes that Wolfy is now carrying a large rucksack, almost as big as her, as if it contained nothing heavier than butterflies. Whilst her former lover totes a rifle and soon ranges out ahead by about a hundred yards. As they near the top of the ridge, Smith is suddenly by her side again.

'I wanted you to see this. I want you to see everything. If no one documents it then it hasn't happened, because *they* won't be telling anyone.'

Miriam's not sure if he means the shadowy forces to whom he has alluded in the past or the bits and pieces of human bodies that must have made up at least one whole person at some point. She is sick. The smell seems to come from the earth itself, coating the inside of her nostrils, then refusing to leave, as if she had walked past the open window of a hellish restaurant, where the same piece of meat is cooked and sold and eaten and the meat belongs to the flesh of the diners themselves. The stench of revolving, endless misery. What people do to each other. She is helped away from the scene, bends, pukes again, then refuses to move.

'No! I'm not moving until you tell me… what the fuck? I get out of my car and then, and then…'

Smith consults his watch. His voice is as reasonable as ever, although he is scanning the sky whilst he talks.

'Not now. Later. First we need to get into cover. In about half an hour a helicopter full of SAS will arrive and they will shoot first and then decide we're terrorists later. Even if they don't kill you now, you'll get passed on to someone else who will see you end up next to your dear father. I really didn't mean this to happen, but, if you're going to chronicle the truth, at least you've seen it first hand. So come, Miriam, please, or Wolfy will have to pick you up. It will be far more comfortable for you to walk. Please?'

Wolfy is behind her as they walk on. The pace is soon set at a brisk half trot, half quick march. No longer going up, but around the small mountain, the rest of which the ridge had hidden from view when they were lower. Not even an hour later and Miriam hears the familiar but muted sound of a helicopter. Wolfy licks a finger all around and points upwards. Smith acknowledges the wind direction. But he talks to Miriam.

'Don't worry, they're miles away. They'll secure the house first before doing anything else. They're expecting to find us in it, blown to smithereens.'

They start heading down hill, towards the dark, greeny-brown of a small wood. Even from several miles away it's clear there is some kind of road running through it. Another hour and they are walking in the shade of Oak and Ash trees, sweet new leaves looking fresh against the bark. In the middle of the wood a small gulley lined with granite and moss descends unexpectedly into the soil and mulch. Several feet below, a fayrie's waterfall indicates an underground stream magically appearing above ground before pooling and then coursing away the other side of the gulley. It's irresistibly pretty. Miriam immediately takes her boots off and rather carelessly clambers down to scoop up icy water, to splash her face, to sip, to spit, to clean the carnage from her pallet. Returning she finds the two men sprawled on the soft bed of dry old leaves and twigs, watching her. She sits down, away from them. Then, in a sudden fever she talks.

'You. Smith. Blake. Whatever you're called. Whatever your real name is. Talk. Tell me. You got me into this nightmare. You owe me an explanation.'

Whatever she had been expecting to feel at being reunited with her lover, the tint of warmth that distance and time had given her feelings, is now just a combination of rage and fear and bewilderment. He sees what she needs.

'My name is Stephen Smith, Miriam. That's my real name. But I've used many names over the years.'

He turns to Wolfy who is sat, listening, looking down at the earth.

'Did I ever tell you that Wolfy? I forget.'

When Wolfy speaks Miriam is not surprised to hear he has an Irish accent.

'No, you never did Steve. But I always presumed it wasn't your real name, Blake, I mean. And I don't care. You are what you are, whatever you call yourself.'

'This is Wolfy, Miriam. He's a tower of strength and a very intelligent man, too. He could probably tell you what we're doing better than me. Tell her, Wolfy.'

Wolfy looks at Miriam. What does she expect? Some kind of revolutionary spiel, Marxism distilled into romantic declarations via Hollywood. Allegiance to the struggles of the Zapatistas, the IRA, the Maoist guerrillas of the UCP in Nepal. Some kind of half-baked throwback to an era of car bombs and police murders in the name of some kind of a revolution.

Wolfy enunciates:

'We're raising hell. We're having a good time. And along the way, we're doing some good. You know, the kind of good you read about. Getting rid of bad guys. Telling the truth. We're the knights of the round table. With fucking semi-automatic rifles and thirty million quid in the bank.'

When Wolfy falls silent it's as if a thunderstorm has broken and passed, all in a few seconds. How do you argue with such a definitive statement?

Miriam doesn't try. She addresses Smith.

'What, and that's it? That's what you're doing? And that's why these people are trying to kill you? That's why the army – the fucking SAS! – is trying to kill you? Actually, I don't blame them. You're all crazy!'

The end of the day is sliding through the branches, the air is damp. Wolfy and Smith both stir and soon Wolfy is clearing a space in a thick clump of hedge with a machete he has pulled from the rucksack and Smith is walking to the edge of the woods, carrying his binoculars. He calls over his shoulder.

'Miriam, I'll tell you everything later tonight, when we're settled. See if you can help Wolfy will you? I'm just going for a scoot around.'

Which part of herself is watching as Miriam helps Wolfy set up a tarpaulin under the branches of the hedge? As she fills a kettle with pure mountain water from the pool, as she rolls out three sleeping bags on a ground sheet under the tarpaulin? Not the part that likes to think of itself as representing her independence, her inner strength. No, that is buried way below the weary resignation of coming, once more under Smith's spell and the gleeful enthusiasm for a genuine scoop which, this time, this time! She will exploit to its fullest. She's out on the range with the James Gang. In a Model T Ford with Bonnie and Clyde. Hiding in a Berlin squat with Ulrike Meinhof. Supping tea with Bin Laden. Determined to survive at least until she sees her headline appear, she enthusiastically embraces whatever might come. After all, it couldn't get any worse, could it?

Silently watching her as she pulls her trousers down and squats to pee a short distance from the camp, Smith relaxes a little. Just the SAS to worry about then, for one night. Good.

*   *   *

On the pavement outside Cardiff Central train station Sherriff turns to wave to Ann who is still sitting where she pulled up several yards away in the car park. She doesn't notice as her head is down, apparently checking her mobile. Unperturbed, Sherriff heads for the ticket office.

In the car, Ann is digesting the text message she has just

received from Blake: 'under attack. Do not return. Plan B'.

She checks the large shoulder bag on the passenger seat. Inside, under a supermarket plastic bag containing an unopened pack of sanitary towels, are several wads of fifty, twenty and ten pound notes. Underneath those there is a Swiss army issue Pistole 49, the ex-personal property of Hauptman Christeler, who had kept it despite being issued with a newer version. He told his sons he had once shot an apple from the head of his best friend when he was 'their age' one drunken night in Rekrutenschule with this very pistol, so he trusts its accuracy. To Ann, its weight adds to the other securities in the bag, which include a box of nine mill bullets.

'Under attack'. Plan B means leaving the car where it is and walking to the nearest car hire firm, where she will rent a vehicle with her fake bank card and her fake passport and take her fake self to London ASAP. She has a look around. It's not a busy station and the people she sees all seem intent on arriving or leaving. Acutely aware of the CCTV, however, she makes a point of calming herself, using tricks she has taught herself for the moments before a court appearance. She becomes conscious of her breathing, slowing it down, taking a full diaphragm full of air and allowing it out slowly through her nostrils. She smiles and the physical action induces a change in her temperament. Actors and barristers: not to be trusted, she agrees. Reinforced she clambers confidently out of the car, for all the world a well paid and successful lawyer on her way to a meeting.

The train pulls in to the platform on to which Sherriff has just established himself, one foot raised and resting on the wall on which he leans, as if he is waiting for the Texas and Pacific from Fort Worth and not the 10.25 from London Victoria, which will magically become the 13.35 in the opposite direction after a clean. The train has been standing for a good minute before a figure appears, negotiating an open door sideways from the first class carriage whilst brushing the crumbs of a second breakfast from his well wrapped tummy. Stepping on to the platform, pausing, looking round as if he has just stepped into a Welsh wonderland. Sherriff feels himself being raked, his senses particularly sensitive every time he travels and enlivened today by a skinny joint in the car on the way to the station. Time being a little slower for him he manages to have a very good look at the man whilst pretending not to see him.

Later, watching the reflections of other passengers appear and disappear in the train windows during periods in tunnels or shadow, he remembers Steve telling them all the story of the Poisonous Pumpkin Brothers...

It's earlier than it seems, but an overcast night has taken all the light from the sky outside. The curtains are open and the window reflects the embers of the fire, which is nicely set, with two huge logs burning from the inside out and adding a visual warmth to the central heating. Everyone is there, spread around the room, sprawled, touching, comfortable, some drunk, some stoned, some just happy to be. Steve is sitting backwards on one of the dining chairs, leaning his arms on the back, his chin lightly on his forearms. As usual, everyone is listening as he talks. It's always good to hear his voice, but Sherriff particularly likes it when he steers from the practical to the legendary. The fable tonight concerns two ambitiously venal brothers who are so bad their mother refused to name them. They live together in a cave at the end of a long canyon in the darkest and stinkiest part of a dark and stinky city. They are huge, round blobs of fat, pasty snowballs of grease and rotten skin, so huge, in fact, that they never wash, because it would just take too long. When they shit they can't wipe their asses because their arms won't reach, but they prefer to stink, anyway, because it adds to their power.

The two brothers started a career in evil when they were young, bullying other children who lived near them, making them steal from their parents, setting them up to commit sexual acts and be caught by adults, playing awful pranks on the eldest and most frail of the grown ups in the neighbourhood and never being caught.

One day, one of the brothers, finding himself, unusually, alone, decided to convince a young boy to rob a cake from a cake shop. In return, the boy wouldn't get beaten up for another week. The boy, who was tiny and had no mum, did as he was asked, managing to filch a tasty pile of cream and sponge and caramelised fruits the size of which surprised even the brother. Dismissing the boy to the other side of the street, the brother sat down on the kerb and began to demolish the lot, his enjoyment greatly enhanced by the drools of the watching boy. With his face streaked with white and his great appetite temporarily assuaged, the brother leaned back and expressed his satisfaction with a burp. Into the sensual cloud of which the other brother arrived, having spent several hours evacuating his bowels and now feeling a great void in his intestines which he needed to fill urgently. The smell of the hardly digested cake teased the brother into a jealous craze. He questioned his sibling who lied through his teeth even whilst licking his lips. Putting two and two together the hungry brother called the poor little boy over and questioned him brutally. Torn between punishments the boy broke down and told and then retracted all several times until both brothers laid him out cold on the pavement, bleeding from his ears.

Not a word was said between the brothers about the incident. But from that moment on they ceased to work together, preferring to gather around them groups of boys and girls who they trained to be almost as violent and

174

ambitious and selfish as themselves. As the years passed, the two gangs often fought, although the brothers would stand away from the fists and feet and sticks and bricks and bet on the outcome. They stayed together in their cave but each plotted and connived to make their gang superior.

More years passed and the two gangs had become organised and effective, disciplined and semi-legal. The brothers enjoyed hiring their underlings out to people with money; companies and governments who, for one unaccountable reason or another, didn't want to be involved in a kidnap or a torture or a robbery or a coup. They kept their prices reasonable and they spent very little money on themselves, apart from food and drink, which they both continued to enjoy to excess, as they grew huger and huger until they had to have the front entrance to their cave enlarged and a special, wide door hinged to the walls.

Sometimes the brothers found they had been hired to do the same job. Sometimes they were in opposition. Whatever their gangs were concerned with, however, the brothers stayed together, the best of enemies. Although the gangs were occasionally depleted with a war or an arrest or a murder or two, the brothers always managed to find new recruits. They looked around and decided to model themselves on the most successful organisations in the ancient kingdom of Britain. They saw how the institutions of learning bred rulers and chiefs and bosses and managers from the schools, which traditionally fed young people into their academic funnel. They realised they had their own feeder schools and so they rummaged around in the nether regions of the armed services, the cheaper universities, the emergency services, the police and, of course, the criminal underworld. They encouraged their new recruits to indulge their own greedy passions and so tied them up tight, with blackmail and desire and the smidgeons of power their allegiance brought. One brother called his thing 'Oxford', in mocking homage to the traditionally more right wing and straight-laced college. The other brother, of course, called his thing 'Cambridge', because he preferred the looser, more chaotic feel of the fens establishment which bred traitors like swamps breed mosquitos. They played with their minions, dressed them up in this and that until a uniform of sorts was established, one which could be worn on civilian streets without too much comment, but distinctive enough, nevertheless, so that, when they met, they could do battle and know who to kill. Oxford wore stiff, dark suits, with dark, knitted ties. They wore severe haircuts: if male, then shaved around the sides to a number two on the clippers, with a bowl of longer hair around the top; if female, then cut an inch off the shoulder, then scraped back into a bun or pony tail at the back. Cambridge were more relaxed, in worn Tweed jackets bearing elbow patches, corduroy trousers, smock dresses, unruly hair straight from the pillow. They affected pipes and roll-ups and locally brewed ales.

At this point, Steve had paused and asked them which was he? Oxford or Cambridge? Without a doubt, amid laughter, he was Cambridge. When they had settled once more Steve simply said:

'If you see the brothers you will know them.'

Peter guffawed and said:

'I think we will!'

'No, Peter, you don't understand. You will know them. They will be as familiar to you as a favourite uncle and somehow seem just as kind. But if you do see them, be very careful. And if you see them together – get away, as fast you can!'

As the train got away as fast as it could Sherriff knows he has seen one of the brothers. He sends a text to Ann. 'Watch out. I just saw a brother. Be careful'.

* * *

At the sight of the lovely woman locking her car in the car park, hoisting her shoulder bag and smiling at the world, the jovial fat man could be forgiven for looking yet more jovial. The fact that he is walking in the same direction as her is, of course, entirely coincidental, as he obviously prefers food to women, however svelte they may be. She walks along at a brisk pace, which he manages to match whilst seeming to stroll at half the speed. The sweat that runs down his spine to the crack of his backside is all part of the thrill of a chase.

Following along, not too far away, he tracks her as she walks past shops, undistracted by banks, ignoring office entrances and travel agents until she turns off the shopping thoroughfare and into a side street that leads past a car park, towards a car rental sign attached to the back of a large block, indicating the rear entrance. Close enough to hear the tune from her mobile phone, that bloody nuisance instrument. Stopping whilst she stops and fishes it out of her bag. Imagining the text she is reading, quite accurately, actually. Using the moment to gain the several feet that separate them. Three paces away, calling her name. Just to be sure.

'Ann?'

Seeing in her eyes as she joins the information from the text to the sight before her and shooting her between those eyes, in the middle of her forehead (how could he miss from this distance?), catching her body, one of her hands clasped uselessly on the butt of the pistol in her bag. Dragging her to the doorway of an emergency exit. Taking the phone. Sauntering on, to the car hire firm and on, because he doesn't really need to hire a car – there's one waiting for him at the other end of the street, engine running, windows darkened, rear door opened, ready to whisk him away on leather seats to an important meeting. During the journey he indulges himself by replying to Sherriff's text: 'who shot Ann? I'm your man!'

His stubby fingers mean several tries at the punctuation until it's perfect and he presses send, by which time he's bored again and the joy has left his demeanour. He feels hungry.

* * *

The combined resources of a popular national newspaper in the United Kingdom can put a small dictatorship to shame. Burglary, of different types: obvious, surreptitious, aggressive. Phone tapping, bugging, hacking; blackmail, extortion, bribery; stalking, stunts, instigating violence and incessant harassment. Then there are the basic resources: finances, people, database, address book and ultimate, world weary cynicism.

This army of power at Bill Freeman's fingertips has failed, dismally, to come up with anything on the magic bullets. For several weeks he has gradually reduced the task force from the whole of the news team to one, young, hardly paid new recruit, with the ink still drying on his HND qualification, who is charged with hunting through the cyber world looking for any mention of a new, small arms invention that is about to transform the battlefield.

So it is with the tiniest quickening of heart beats that Bill eventually finishes reading the short poem on a website, the link forwarded by his surprisingly thorough apprentice, that features, amongst other things, an ode to the 'Digi Swarm, guided by electric to the hearts of evil' wherein the rather bold statement that 'we have the bullets and the software to control them' seems rather incontrovertible. A quick conversation with his web expert confirms that the ISP is untraceable and the website could have been set up on Easter Island for all they know, but, trusting his own judgment in respect of the standard of English and philosophy taught at

British schools, he's fairly certain the writer is somewhere on the island, and probably a Londoner. So, a dead general; a ballistics report condemned as false by the coroner's office in Hertfordshire; an internet rumour. And a hunch.

He looks at the poetry site again. There's not much. There's a kind of confused revolutionary feel to the three pieces, between heroic romance and schoolboy Maoism, circa 1969. But there seems to be a message. A sense of anticipation. '... We do what we do from love.'

And what the hell is a '4th Unit'? A quick google brings up a hip hop dance troop, a Sea Scouts group in the West Midlands (is there any sea in the West Midlands?), a video game...

Surprisingly adept at surfing and controlling his virtual environments, Bill sets his default browser page to http:// 4thunit.wordpress.com/ and determines to follow his hunch. Something's happening, he can feel it. Every morning he will wake up his computer to the site and watch and wait until it does.

*   *   *

The version of the story of the Poisonous Pumpkin Brothers received by Miriam isn't quite as Grimms as that received by the rapidly depleting family, a few dark nights ago. At their impromptu campsite she gets a potted version and more, besides. In fact, Wolfy is surprised to learn he is part of a new, uncategorised type of terrorism, designed for a never-ending series of single issues. The range of possibilities, from attacking banks and huge companies to undermining the stock market and infiltrating the media is so wide it will be impossible for the Establishment to know where they will strike next. And the Establishment, it is, that is established as the Enemy. Smith lists the regiments of corruption: the monarchy and all her brood and all their relations and all those who are inducted with honours and titles; the armaments firms and their government stooges; the small f fascists who rot the insides of the police and the armed forces; all the secret people – the M.I's, the SAS's, the Specials, the whole range who dwell beneath acronyms the public are hardly aware of; the media liars and distorters, owners of communications companies and their lackeys, the journalists, the talking heads, the pundits and all the politicians who go on to a lucrative career examining the world and elegantly avoiding its evils; the institutions of class: the schools, the colleges, the clubs, the tailors and the restaurants; those who breed the horses ridden by weekend hunters and cops on horses with extra long clubs who are only ever brought out to quell the unarmed masses; the governments, local and national, the tin pot rulers of departments who shrink care budgets but increase the hospitality fund, the leaders and heads who declare war with impunity for whatever commercial interest has gained their ear and all their supporters; the expensive criminals who have established themselves as legitimate business men and women, who provide political leaders with the unaccountable muscle necessary to maintain power. And it doesn't stop at the borders. This anger, this recrimination, this retribution can travel anywhere an airplane goes, anywhere a million dollars can buy passes and keys and access and arms in order to attack the enemy. The Establishment, who are established across the globe, who would rather deal with each other, in their exclusivity than be minutely accountable to the ordinary, pissed on, fucked over proles.

With this impassioned speech, Smith achieves several things. He binds Wolfy to him with his almost ineffable logic. He drops Miriam's jaw to a gape, which she self-consciously shuts with a snap. He brings her to him and then loses her as he achieves, finally, to bring it on home just how crazy he is.

But, even with this realisation, Miriam can't help but want to be, somehow, in on the whole thing. It's got to be the best excuse for blowing things up she's ever heard. It's the basis of a novel, a film, a TV series and a groundbreaking magazine article. Smith is a hero. It's her job to paint him and show him to the world.

In the woods, they are just dark shadows to each other. Smith's words, quietly spoken, flattened out of resonance by the organics of the leaves and the mud and the tree trunks, sound reasonable and his proposed actions sound like the only response from a man trained in violence and subterfuge, torture and death. Because Smith doesn't stop there. He goes on to tell his story, how he came to be and how he came to his opinions, ready to act on them. It's a dark, intense night in the woods, the children hiding from the baddies in balaclavas, the wicked witches flying overhead nearby in an ugly, clattering monster bird. When he's done, he's hoarse. Wolfy is asleep, sitting upright, back against a tree. Miriam is curled on her side, her back to Smith's, but the back of her legs acknowledging the warmth from his thighs which are next to her. Rousing in the grey light she sees the face of a priest who has confessed all the confessions he's ever heard. Exhausted, now. Eyes in hollows of dark. He sees her and smiles. Does she understand? Sympathise? Agree? Certainly, a lot of what has been spoken makes absolute sense to a journalist, anyone, in fact, who reads the Guardian and has marched for peace or against fascism. But the end result… that's the problem. The logical conclusion. The actions. The deaths. The basic, uncivilised, warlike shit that someone like Miriam can't abide being done in her name, let alone do herself.

On the tense walk to the farm down the road, scanning the tops of the hills, listening hard – Miriam asks herself if she is a coward for wanting to just step back and observe, knowing what she knows? Watching the Landrover roll quietly from the farmyard, the trailer still attached ('perfect' says Wolfy), watching as Smith buries himself below empty fertiliser sacks, as Wolfy carelessly throws a rake and a shovel across the pile, she tries to place herself in this mess: if they're caught, is she one of them? An observer? A spy? Part of her knows, as the Landrover bumps along the track, that, it's true, her bullet-ridden corpse wouldn't be trying to excuse its involvement. And her mother would probably be finished off with the startling news that her daughter was a terrorist. But, surely, she is being inveigled, hogtied by the coincidences of the past year, this isn't something she chose – was it? Who bought the train ticket?

At one point in the relatively short journey away from the hills a helicopter joins them. Wolfy ignores its presence. Until it's gone, when it is then blessed with a 'shit-heads!' and his foot on the accelerator.

At the end of a long single lane road on the edge of Merthyr Tydfil, in a disused quarry, they swap vehicles. The Landrover is hidden under the branches of a large oak, replacing a pre-positioned BMW Estate, which they now travel in. The trailer was tucked away behind a large shed. Wolfy is still driving. Both he and Smith changed out of their camo gear and into jeans and fleeces, kept in the boot of the BMW. Miriam is bare foot, back in her visiting outfit, with which she was possibly going to seduce? Tempt? Show how clear headed and independent she is? Either way, she's aware of how crumpled and creased and possibly smelly she is but her fatigue beats her vanity and soon she is sleeping as the car takes them east. Her dreams are soundtracked by the radio, flicking through news stations and talk shows and at some point she drowsily thinks she hears about a mysterious gunfight in the Welsh mountains, with two people dead and a house on fire. Police are investigating, of course. Will the police find the other bodies? What's left of them... Will it really be the police? According to Smith there are many organisations who would be suitable enough to track down an ad hoc anarchist terrorist group.

As they pass Swindon Miriam finally falls into a deep sleep. Stephen Smith looks over his shoulder fondly at her as she quietly snores.

'Good fuck was she?' Crude and to the point, Wolfy.

'Very nice.' Smith leans his seat back and enjoys the sun on the side of his face.

'You know where you're going, right Wolfy?'

'Up shit creek. Right?'

'Right.'

11

Chapter 11: Yes, Really

'The last time we met you were about to spend some time on holiday, I believe.'

Two big cops, could be father and son, sitting and standing, respectively, either side of an anonymous desk in the informally disciplined way cops do. If there is a more rigid stance to the one standing it's perhaps because he has spent the past four years as a policeman in the Ministry of Defence force, as the seated cop is reading. Out loud.

'Apparently you've excelled and all is forgiven Don. Do they call you 'Hippo' over there?'

Don Hipkin. A big man, fifty-fifty muscle and fat. Of course they call him 'Hippo'.

'No sir. I left that name behind in Manchester.'

That's the accent: the gruff, old-fashioned Mancunian of British war films, 1960s British TV, Z cars. There's nothing Madchester about Hippo, even if he is exactly the right age to have spent his Friday nights at the Hacienda, waking back up into a depressed teenager on the Monday after six eccies and innumerable spliffs. That was for others. Hippo's body was a sacred tool being developed for one thing only, at that time: pound the living shit out of another human being in the boxing ring. He was brutal and very strong, taller than most of the undernourished scallies he faced. He slaughtered them and then there was nowhere for him to go. Lacking the finesse or the desire to train day and night it was almost inevitable that he would end up in the police force, like his dad. So the sparring and the monthly bouts were soon replaced with Saturday afternoon outside Old Trafford followed by Saturday night outside the Embassy or any other of the fly-trap discos in town which were booming thanks to the flood of pills and machine music and the national press going on and on about bloody Manchester. Up for it. Up for it, every weekend, on the end of his fists and size twelve's were mainly scrawny students and the odd party of beer-bellied older guys, still steaming the lager. Every now and then he would have a real challenger, one of the bouncers getting out of order, an errant gang member needing a bit of discipline. That's when his real skills would come into play.

But Hugh 'Harry' Beard hasn't brought him to his special team because the man is a brute. Harry knows that, at some point, Hippo got bored. Bored with the violence, bored mashing his knuckles, sweating in his uniform. Bored and soft. The truncheon started to be brought out more often, he started to act like the female cops who were all known as 'Doris', not out of fear, more from boredom. He became a big fat Doris. Backing off from the up for it lairy lads. Hanging back until he got a chance to bring the wood down on a shoulder, jab it into the kidneys. He stopped exercising and the percentages shifted to eighty-twenty, fat to muscle. He started to get a reputation for being a big fat pansy. Taken off face-to-face details, no longer the first choice on a raid – he didn't give a monkey's. Hippo had the chance to bask in the offices, pick up some tips from the detectives taking a rest from something... more interesting. His superiors discovered, even before he did, that Hippo was actually a smart cop, a natural. Given the chance he could apply his brain muscle in the same way he had applied his bulk. He rose. Went on training courses. Was recommended, made it to Detective Constable then... nearly punched a suspect to death. The jibes had begun to get annoying, to get to him, and so he'd gone back to training and taking part in inter-area police boxing bouts. He easily became heavyweight champ within six months, his strength returned, but with even more tonnage behind his hands. Even Hippo was surprised, which is why a bit of 'routine' roughing up nearly turned deadly, watching his meaty, gloved fists pulp the man's intestines with three blows. One, two, three: haemorrhage! Taking a short cut was how he excused himself at the time. The short cut led to an attempted murder charge. Somehow, everything was sorted by a sideways move into the Ministry of Defence Police, the MDP, where Hippo became plain Don and started all over again, determined this time to keep his knuckles inside his pockets. It doesn't do to have a police champion, of anything, being sent down... for anything. He has done well. His ex-boss, Superintendent Beard is impressed. He was impressed before Hipkin's arrival, when he read through his file, even more so now. He's perfect in every way. Between them, they might track these bastards down. If they don't, then Harry Beard has got himself a fall guy and a clear route to an honourable retirement with full pension.

'You'll be working directly under me, Don. Technically it's a combined operation, in reality, we'll be making the most of your colleagues' special training and technical knowhow. We've got a good budget and permission to stick our noses in anywhere we choose. Sit down.

'What do you know about this lot, Don?'

'Rumours, chat – I've been told they're Dutch gangsters. I've also been told they're our own – secret squirrels, going round stirring it up, to increase the defence budget or something like that.'

'The fact is, Don, these rumours could be true. We know very little about them and what we do know we're not sure about. What we're going to do is this: we treat them like criminals. They've broken the law, we go after them just like we would any tin pot gangster from Moss Side. Got it? We do old-fashioned police work, get the evidence, track 'em down. Nail 'em. Alright, they've got guns. So have we. They've got money – but we've got the national resources. Military Intelligence is with us and some other useful friends.'

'Which friends, sir? The Americans?'

'No, Don, not the Americans. This is our own problem. We'll sort it out. First, I want you down in The Smoke. You'll be based in a building in Clerkenwell, all fitted out, lovely new computers – you'll love it. Go there tomorrow. Take this…'

Beard hands him a laptop in a soft case.

'…it's all on there. Take the train, you can carry on working then. I'll see you there. That's all.'

Hipkins is still there a moment later. Beard raises his eyebrows.

'Sir – why me? Why have you chosen me? I've got no experience hunting terrorists.'

'These aren't terrorists, Hipkins. I told you, they're villains. And I chose you because you're the right man for the job.'

'Thank you sir. Thank you for giving me this chance. I won't let you down.'

Now he leaves. And the chair seems grateful. Pathetic bastard. Well, he'll either do it or he won't.

The well-fed boss cop considers his lunch options. For a couple of hours, at least, he'll give the superintending a rest.

Hipkins has been around long enough to know he wasn't chosen on his merits. He can also smell one of them weirdos a mile off. They all can. It's not like the masons, who are part of the fabric – even his dad went through the old one trouser leg up, blindfold business. No, this lot permeated the force like a taxi driver's air freshener. They smelt sweet, smug and false. Beard is definitely one of them. Alright, there's not much hair on top so the give away cut doesn't look right – hard to do with just a couple of strands to fold over the crown. But the rest of it. The solid situation of his career. The rumours of his dinners, the kinds of people he's been seen sitting down with. What's a police superintendent doing hanging about with the army? Spotted having a posh nosh-up with a general, no less, staff car parked outside the restaurant, blatant. Councillors. Property developer. Villains – top rated, untouchable villains. It's hard to hide things amongst nosy coppers. But then, he doesn't hide. That's the whole point. Almost showing off. Or warning off. No one knows how he made it up through the ranks, he was a totally undistinguished rank and file who had magic feet, tippy tapping up the golden stairway and then, apparently, quite happy to stick at super. Hippo's dad had served with him, in the early years. All he could remember was that Beard had a nasty streak, even for those days of more basic policing. Perhaps that's why he had chosen Hippo: they had a common bond of violence.

Whatever the reason, Don Hipkins is going to be very careful. He's going to make copies – in triplicate. He's going to document every order or suggestion, he's going to record every conversation (kitted out with a great little pen gizmo from the spy shop in Prestwich – twenty nine pounds!) and he's not going to take a step until the ground has been mine-swept and tested. Steady and slow, that's the way to go on this job.

The circumstances of his hiring obscure the nature of the job itself. It's not until he's sat on the train (first class!) taking up two seats, with the laptop open in front of him that he begins to get a proper idea of what's required. Bloody 'ell! How did he miss this? There's been murder and mayhem and I haven't been told. The parts of the story that have sifted through the various filters of various secret people plus some added details are a front page of shock. It's like the IRA all over again. The IRA and the Krays. Why haven't they all been looking for this mental case, this Stephen Smith? Why isn't the country on high alert?

Reading on, he discovers why. There are 'sensitive' aspects to this case. The public mustn't be alarmed. In other words, he used to be one of ours – who's? – now he's gone off the rails, gone barmy and collected a gang of psycho-politicos to help him. He can't find details about who he worked for exactly – why not? He's cleared, isn't he? (Signed the OSA just like all coppers. So why can't they tell him?) And he's loaded. A serious amount of cash from Switzerland, laundered and sequestered who knows where. A highly funded commando unit who are after... what? The report calls them 'anarchist'. What do anarchists want? Blow everything up? Well they're not doing much of that and when they are, it's the strangest places: a fuel container in a boat yard in Cardiff? So they're eco terrorists, right? Their own house – not even a squat, but one they actually owned – in the middle of bloody nowhere, Wales?

Then there's the deaths: one corpse (an Irish man – significant?) found in the waters of Cardiff Bay – shot. The bits of another one, apparently blown up inside the house. A woman, shot in the head, execution style in a car park in Cardiff. Why are they killing their own? Are they Welsh nationalists? Then there are several suspected violent incidents, including one armed robbery and one attempted armed robbery from around a year or so ago which were probably the work of Smith, but with another gang, this time seasoned villains, all old enough to know better. Lots of supposition and theory. Too much mystery. He'll need to start establishing facts. Step one. Nothing happens until he knows what's happening.

Closing the lid of the laptop, checking his watch. Just enough time for a light snack before Kings Cross. He has the inherited ability to divorce the needs of his stomach from all police requirements.

*　　*　　*

'Weirdy Beardy Weirdy.'

'He's our cover?'

'He's got a basic plod. They call him 'Hippo', amusingly.'

The two brothers decide not to acknowledge the irony. They are basking in the sunlight, a happy coincidence of half an hour amongst the day's gloom when they happened to take their constitutional in a small park conveniently near the Fryingdon Fish Bar on Farringdon Road, Clerkenwell, London. Of course, they couldn't sit in the park without a little snack to keep them company. One brother is enjoying the savoury delights of a chicken sandwich, with all the trimmings that don't include salad. The other is nibbling his way through the second of a large slice of coffee and walnut sponge cake, a choice he now regrets. Too much coffee. They are surrounded by a small flock of pigeons who trot in ever bolder figures of eight, closer and closer to the brothers' dainty feet, tucked beneath the bench.

'What does he know?'

'He 's been told about their deaths, but not about ours.'

'Is he any good?'

'He's quite violent. Not that bright. But he has help. With him involved we can bring it all out into the open. Ask the public, to a certain extent You know how they like to help.'

'Ah, the public. Very useful to have concerned citizens on our side.'

'And who do we have on your side, brother?'

'You'll be pleased to know I've taken personal responsibility, brother. There will be no more shilly-shallying on our part, I can assure you.'

'It's about time, if you don't mind me saying so…'

'Well, he was one of yours. If you'd kept an eye on him…'

'My most brilliant pupil… he flew the nest. Who could stop him?'

'Not you, obviously.'

Unusually, the second piece of cake really is unwanted. The brother looks at the pigeons milling around. Trying to take the food from his mouth. He stands, squashing the cake in the cardboard box.

'Fuck off!' He kicks out, the birds flutter then settle and he swings his arms around.

'Fuck, fuck off. Shitty birds. Scavenging bastards. Fuck off!!'

But these are London pigeons, used to the worse actions of insane citizens. They have been shot and crushed, poisoned and chased by falcons. They live on the diet of the city and their little lives run on the accelerated heartbeats caused by chemicals and fumes that finish them off early. An angry fat man in a park is small beer. How frightfully frustrating for a big man, so used to having his cake and eating it.

*   *   *

If the flattened corpses of pigeons are skeletal angels on the tarmac, and the fresh globules of spit on the pavements are the ephemeral silver pennies expected by arriving future mayors of London and the dots of gum are the buttons which can undo the concrete and take you to a secret world beneath the city, then you know you are in the company of a poet.

Because he has no soul, Neil Cooke is unaware of the poet's alternate world and Sherriff keeps it to himself. Neil

Cooke is also unaware of Sherriff, who has blended his stick insect frame into the contours of a large tree overlooking the main course of South Herts Golf Club, in the outer reaches of the city. Watching the lean Personal Security Detail stride purposefully out on to the open green Sherriff talks quietly into a mobile phone.

'That's not him.'

Even from the yards away where he hides, Sherriff can hear Cooke's own mobile ringing, with the main riff from John Barry's James Bond theme. He allows himself a snigger.

Cooke doesn't speak when he answers. He listens for a moment.

'OK. It looks all clear. I'll back off to the trees and watch from there. Any funny business and I'll be there in seconds.'

Cooke starts walking towards Sherriff. Too fast for Sherriff to move without being seen. He freezes. Cooke gets closer. Sherriff feels his mobile vibrate in his hand he answers carefully, whispering.

'He's coming. What should I do? ...I can't ...OK, I will, I remember.'

The pistol had seemed too long, comical, even with the silencer on the end. Sherriff had struggled with a place to hide it: every piece of his clothing is chosen to show how slim his body is, there's no waste, no flaps of material to drape over a bulge. In the end he had decided to use a leather shoulder bag, strapped beneath his jacket. He just has time to unbutton the bag before Cooke is suddenly, efficiently there. Already talking into his mobile.

'OK. I'm in place. Come out. Keep your phone on.'

For a moment Cooke is engrossed with putting his ear-piece in, constantly watching out across the green. Sherriff is close enough to smell the cigarette smoke still hanging on Cooke's leather jacket. His hand is on the grip of the pistol, which is still in the bag. The barrel is pointing, pushing the side of his jacket upwards obscenely, straight at Cooke. Sherriff breathes very quietly, very slowly. The branches are dappling his vision, a grey-blue sky bright enough to dazzle, spreading a pretty light. He's in a wooden glade, a magical place, facing a monster with the sword of truth. He should think of an epitaph. For the monster. Who is talking once more.

'That's it. Walk straight out. We wait two minutes. If nothing happens, then we get the fuck out. Sorry. We leave.'

Whilst Neil Cooke is being told off for swearing, Abe is on his strangest mission yet. A golf cart he can handle, but wearing a prosthetic face and a wig, let alone the unnatural constriction of a suit is putting him out of sorts. Beneath the wig, his ear piece, his mobile on, hearing the secondary conversation of Smith and Sherriff (he presumes it's Sherriff) and then Steve – Smith... Blake... well, he knew it was probably a false name, but still, you come to trust someone, get used to a name... what's a name, anyway? He should know better. Should've known better. He hears Smith tell Sherriff to kill someone. Shit! It never stops. He knew it was iffy, but the blood! More death. What should he do? He's already doing it.

The golf cart bumps out over the green, towards a man in a Mackintosh. The wind suddenly gusts. Abe knows this green, played it once as a guest of an acquaintance, a keen golfer who moved to be close to the club. Not much of a course. The wind would have made him take out something heavier than normal to tee off. He's just a few yards away from the man in the Mackintosh. The coat tails are swirling around a leather hold-all bag. The man's face is grim. Smith's voice in his ear:

'Let us know as soon as you've got the bag Abe. Don't look back.'

Abe has stopped. From inside his suit jacket he takes out a padded envelope. Mackintosh man doesn't move. Abe stretches out his hand, offering the envelope. The man appears to be listening to something, puts his hand to his ear. Steps to the buggy and offers the bag with outstretched arm. Not quite close enough. Abe can't help himself.

'Come closer you stupid cunt!'

The man looks startled. Abe hears Smith, warning:

'Abe!'

But the man takes the extra step and the exchange is made and Abe is turning the cart. He hears Smith speak urgently, but not to him.

'Now!'

Abe doesn't look back.

In the glade, the monster has noticed Sherriff. It was inevitable, once his attention relaxed from his Personal Detail, who is now striding back across the golf course in the direction from which he had arrived. Cooke was even feeling a little more relaxed. Used as he was to unusual situations which demanded all kinds of responses from him, which involved bending his body into unusual shapes to fit in awkward hiding places, there was something about the mundane location of this assignment that had annoyed him. He would never usually agree to any kind of meeting on his detail's behalf that was in such open space, without back-up, without at least something more powerful than the small, illegal Beretta he is reaching for now whilst he takes in the site of an elegant, long legged trendy-Wendy detaching himself from a perfectly normal looking tree. As Sherriff's jacket spits painful needles into different parts of his body he is still feeling relaxed. This is, of course, all wrong. The show was over. The exchange had been made. A million quid, for a padded envelope of possibility. They've got the cash. So why kill him? The combination of silencer, leather and cloth is so effective the shots sound like a mouse's cough. In fact, it's all so quiet in the glade that Cooke can hear the mouse calling, for some reason, 'Sherriff! Sherriff!'.Perhaps he's calling for help, to rescue him from this sleepy eyed insect-man, who is killing him with magic bullets. How many more? He hears the mouse again:

'Stop! That's enough!' He'll never set a mousetrap again. Eyes now level with the mud, the leaves, the patchy grass, Neil Cooke, Personal Security Detail, expects to see the mouse, crying perhaps, running towards him. He looks and looks as his body stills.

The voices in Sherriff's head distill into one, single voice, that of Smith's, as Sherriff realises his finger is still squeezing the trigger but the gun no longer responds. He stares at the dead man on the ground. Dots of darker black decorate his black leather jacket, his black trousers. There's a chance Sherriff has made the man more pretty, although he certainly won't appreciate it.

'Sherriff! Get the fuck out of there. Now! Come on! Run!'

He takes the earpiece out and hears Smith from afar. Bending, looking into the man's staring eyes. He sees the reflection of the sky, through the foliage and branches in the glistening of the eyeballs. How beautiful. Transfixed, he doesn't notice the fast steps, the crunching, scuffling sound of Smith reaching him through the winds, not until he talks, gently now, a hand resting on Sherriff's back.

'Sherriff. Come on. It's time to go. Leave him there.'

Sherriff looks up, into Smith's concern.

'You made me do it. I know I had to, for Ann, for Dean, but I never ever wanted to kill someone. Not really. Are you pleased now, Steve? Is this OK? Did I do it right?'

Smith has taken him by the elbow, lifted him, has his arm around his shoulders, is guiding him away through the woods.

'Yes, you did it well. If you've got to kill a man, that's the best way to do it.'

Is he pleased? Who can tell. Some part of Stephen Smith is pleased to be here, in the woods with this extraordinary, talented poet, this fine wordsmith, helping him away from a difficult situation. Another part of him is wondering if he shouldn't return with a can of petrol, to burn any evidence, melt the bullets...

12

Chapter 12: Eastern Knight From The North

Everything smells funny. It's a clean room, top floor of a stubby office block overlooking a council estate, incongruously placed between the outskirts of the City of London and Exmouth Market, now less of a market and more of an address for media content companies and savvy professional couples who want to be able to walk to Soho as well as live in Islington. The computers are unpacked and the bubble wrap and boxes are piled in one corner of the room. All laptops. One networked printer. One dusty fax machine, for some reason. New kettle. New microwave. New projector, very powerful, making a clear picture on the wall, even as the afternoon sun battles the swampy London clouds through the south facing windows.

Everyone's in civvies. Everyone's got a southern accent, nearly all turned out of the MDP training school in Essex with an Essex accent. They seem like a nice crew, mostly young. He scans the room, noting the members of 'his' team he has already introduced himself to. An asexual body wrapped in baggy cargo trousers and wooly jumper, topped by a frown and a fluff of hair named Flo is his 'assistant'. She is chatting with two men who could be brothers, twins, even, small and trim, Dicky Drew and Mark 'Zorro' Jones, both bantam weight wrestlers, often found taking part in the MDP's enthusiastically supported competitions. There's a stiff backed Scot called Jim – looks like he's got a pole rammed up his arse all the way to his head, when he turns to look at Hippo, his whole body moves round with his eyes. And the jolly, loud man at the back of the room, prematurely balding, wearing a loud polo shirt with the words 'Orginal Gangster' stencilled on the chest – that's 'Dodgy' Tranent, who's Christian name is lost in the mists of his second christening, the story of which he has promised to tell 'over a pint'. Hipkins has decided this will probably never happen. The only seniority he holds in this room is his age and years of experience. Otherwise, they're all detectives, like him. They're all Military plods, like him. He can't figure out why he's here. That's what smells. And there's more. Even on their first day, compiling data, anything related, anything to do with guns, anything to do with unexplained deaths of anyone to do with anything... he's already turned up two dead cops in Liverpool, beaten and shot. Another dead cop in London a year ago, shot, female, apparently by another policeman who went mental and then shot himself, days later. Three dead villains killed in an attempted armed heist. Two more armed cops, killed in a motor accident. It's been an unusually busy year. An average annum of death, nationally, in the whole force, might bring in one or two by gunshot wounds, the odd stabbing or beating, but the majority are normally road accidents of one sort or another, mostly collisions due to high speed chases. Here are six hardly explained gun deaths, apparently unrelated to gangs or robberies. And they've only just begun. So far, Smith has turned up just once, at the attempted armed robbery where he made a daring escape and disappeared, despite half the Home Counties and the Met looking for him. One survivor from his gang, a Victor

Hill. Hipkins is looking at his file on the laptop screen, his eyebrows are raised. Not much time for an armed robber, caught red handed, even if he did turn grass. He'll be out in a couple of years. Make a note to pay a visit.

The atmosphere in the office is that of an exam room. He senses there won't be the normal time off in the local boozer, the changing room camaraderie. These boys and girls have their eyes on the prize. They'll be bossing him about in five year's time. Why has he been given this job? He catches the eye of an efficient looking brunette, she smiles at him and then returns to her laptop – slide, slide, click-click. On the white wall the projector hums a quiet picture of Stephen Smith, a mug shot from his passport, taken several years ago. How does a multi-lingual boffin like Smith become a terrorist armed robber? Why wasn't he noticed before? Well, the Hippo's in charge and he's due to make a decision about something soon, so it might as well be now.

'Boys and girls! Ladies and gentlemen! Your attention, please!'

Fifteen expectant, newly washed, uncreased faces give him their undivided attention.

'We won't bother introducing ourselves, I've met some of you but you all know who I am and we'll get to know each other over the coming days.'

He pauses, takes another look at the minefield and decides to blunder in.

'Something stinks. There's something about this whole situation that's not right. None of it fits. You all know it. I know it. But our job is to find and catch the criminals. Nothing else is important here. We are going to get this bastard (pointing to Smith's picture projected on the wall behind him) using old-fashioned police work. We're going to get him and his friends and accomplices and then we'll worry about anything unusual going on. So. I want a life story, I want photos and certificates and family and references. I want to know the colour of his underpants and the smell of his farts. And I want it all by the end of the day. Anyone who hasn't been allocated a part of Stephen Smith come to me and I'll give you something to do. Thank you.'

Who's in charge here? He is, for today, anyway. He takes the temperature, there is renewed vigour, people are talking to each other, no one is even looking at him, apart from… that one, there. In a suit, admittedly, a casual, modern looking suit, but a suit and a tie and that haircut. Sitting at the back next to Dodgy Tranent. Hipkins starts the walk, down the middle of the room, straight to the desk, leaning over, in his face.

'What's your name, son?'

The young man doesn't flinch. He answers, quietly, firmly.

'Detective Constable Cargill, boss.'

'Don't call me 'boss', son. I don't outrank you. How did you come to be part of this strange situation, son?'

'Assigned, from South East Div. Most of us were. What shall I call you, then? Don? DC Hipkins? Hippo?'

'DC Cargill, why do you get your hair cut in that particular way?'

Cargill stares at him. Is that a wink? There's definitely the look of, what? Two Man United fans in a pub full of City boys, one giving the other the secret signal. A Masonic wink. A gay-boy wink. The shared secret.

'You know why, DC Hipkins.'

"No, son, honestly, I don't. Why are you here? Are you watching me?'

Hipkins is aware that they have company, he glances to his left. One of his team, a woman, holding her laptop, wanting to show him something, like an eager student with a question for the history teacher. He ignores her and returns his attention to Cargill.

'Unfortunately, your haircut doesn't fit, DC Cargill. Please take yourself and your haircut back to Division HQ where you will be reassigned. Nothing personal, son.'

Cargill doesn't move. He's smiling.

'You're not serious…'

Hipkins ignores him and stands, giving his attention to the woman still waiting, now looking a bit shocked.

'Yes. Love. What can I do for you?' He can't help himself, playing to cliché. Before she has a chance to answer he is staring once more at Cargill, still sitting, still smiling.

'Are you still here, DC Cargill? Leave the laptop behind. Stand up. Walk out the door. Fuck off. Now.'

Thankful that he doesn't need to pick the little bastard up by the scruff of the neck. Thankful that the smile has gone from the little bastard's face. Aware that he might have damaged his career prospects somehow, as the little bastard walks quickly out of the room. Aware that his brand new team might think their colleague is a little bit crazy as he examines the desk, sweeps his hand beneath the edge of the top, checks the contents of the bin, opens drawers and generally makes like a paranoid spy.

Hippo's been around long enough. He knows the score. His dad set him right when he started, when he was still the station's go-to man for a spot of instant thuggery. 'Don't trust any bastard, son,' he'd told him. 'Specially a copper.'

* * *

Abe and Wolfy are two relatively well off builders, looking for a lock-up to store some substantial amounts of scaffolding that has come their way from, probably, Fenchurch Street station, where it was used to hold up great lengths of corrugated sheets of steel beneath the canopy of glass, newly installed at great expense. They don't mention this to anyone, the backstory exists in their minds as an accoutrement to the jeans and fleeces and baseball caps they wear, admittedly, probably what they would be wearing anyway, if they weren't play-acting in Stephen Smith's little drama. Abe is particularly happy with the latest task: he's back in Tottenham, where the streets are sort of familiar and the constant wash of human souls beyond the van windows cleanse him of the horrors of the countryside, although this particular spot happens to be pretty much devoid of anything two legged apart from themselves.

'This is perfect.' Is only the third sentence spoken by Wolfy to Abe since setting out to look for somewhere suitable for their next enterprise. The 'perfect' place is a locked and gated yard, fronted by a tall metal fence, overgrown with bramble and nettle. Beyond the fence is a two story building, utilitarian and far from pretty, red brick, with mean little windows on the top floor and just two doors on the ground. One door is faced with a rusted metal panel on which is a sign stating 'office', the other is a large corrugated roller-door guarding a space big enough to drive a large van right through. Above the roller-door is a large, wooden board, paint faded and cracked declaring 'N.S. Metals'. The building and the concrete yard benefit from clumps of weed and the place has the air of long disuse. Abe follows Wolfy round the side of the yard. There's a narrow, muddy alley that leads to the rear where a steep bank of scrappy grass overshadows the building. They scramble up to the top through a gap in another security fence, stretching around the large expanse of reservoir bound by the bank. Unbelievably, a few yards away, they spot sheep and goats grazing on the slope. Beyond the water, traffic moves slowly in a haze of exhaust and pylons are the treetops in this clash of bucolic peace and super industry. Looking in the opposite direction they can see the spread of part of London's ignored industrial heritage, the north-eastern swamplands given over to numerous chemical, metal, storage and transport facilities, a place where a white van with a cab full of blokes in work gear is as normal as a pigeon in Trafalgar Square. And they are on the edge of this edge-land, overlooked by no one, with no other place for traffic to pass by on the way to. Perfect.

*   *   *

'There. That's done. They've made undeclared investments. The rumour mill is in full swing and their stock has never been higher. In two weeks, we pull all our stock and let the shareholders know what's been going on. We also contact Folgate Forensic Solutions to investigate possible fraud. Their share price will collapse and then the shares will be suspended on the stockmarket and an extraordinary general meeting will be called. The directors will be out within the year and, as long as Miriam does her job, there will be a police investigation, too. Heads will roll, the armaments industry will piss itself for five minutes and I'm going to get drunk.'

Peter closes the lid of the laptop. Dressed just in a pair of boxer shorts his loose skin and sallow face are evidence of intense mourning. His left arm still striped with healed scars, his right arm is decorated with long strips of sticking plaster, evidence of more self-abuse. Tedi watches him swig straight from the whisky bottle. He grimaces, dribbles some on his chin but doesn't stop. She reaches over and removes the bottle from his mouth, mid gulp. He splutters. She takes the bottle out of the room. Peter doesn't attempt to wipe the liquor from his face. It's a pleasant room, bare, varnished floorboards with several rugs dotted around, at one end a table big enough for the whole family to sit round and eat, although they are yet to enjoy their first communal meal at number 53 Northumberland Grove, a house that enjoys a façade which mixes pebble dash with mock Tudor beams and cladding – all the suburban architectural misdemeanours in one – five bedrooms, two bathrooms and a good sized basement. The curtains are pulled, even though it's mid-morning. Nothing unusual in this area, where people are happy not to know their neighbours. Beyond the curtains, across the road is the edge of a small council housing estate, known locally simply as The Grove. There's an almost constant police presence here: support vehicles, one with a CCTV camera on top and even two policemen on mountain bikes roaming in and around the estate day and night. The back windows and door of number 53 are strengthened by inelegant, black iron bars and every house on the small terrace has a burglar alarm. A classic London locational set up, as Smith had described it, the fortified homes of the not so poor under siege from the inhabitants of the slum across the road, although The Grove looks more like a socialist planner's idea of a worker's paradise, with its low rise flats, leafy play areas and open plan, communal space and car parks.

Peter hasn't noticed. Since hearing of Ann's death in Cardiff he has been in an almost constant fug of alcohol, hardly talking, hardly eating. Now, a week later, he remains unwashed and willing himself to extinction. Having just completed the one task urged on him by the single minded Smith he now feels free to disappear into oblivion, even if Tedi has other ideas. Returning without the bottle she stands in front of Peter. Somehow it has fallen to her to nursemaid him through his grief. They are alone in the house. Now is the time. She slaps him across the face, once, twice, three times, hard. He looks up at her, cheeks reddening, eyes swimming with tears. In her neat T-shirt and jeans, dressed for housework, hair in a scarf at the back of her head, minimal make up. She has a job to do. Grabbing a fist full of Peter's strong dark hair, wrenching his head back and then, slapping, again, with her other hand, until, finally he puts a hand up and grabs her wrist.

'Stop it! What do you think you're doing? Just fucking stop it!'

Tedi still has his hair.

'Not until you wash your dirty body. You stink, Peter. You killing yourself. Go wash and brush your teeth – your mouth stinks too.'

Pulling until he starts to stand, then letting go as he collapses into her arms, sobbing.

'They killed her! The bastards killed her! What am I going to do? I can't live without her! I can't Tedi. I don't know how. She was dying but they killed her. Too soon, too soon…'

She comforts him on her tip toes until she can't keep her balance, then, gently but firmly, pushes him towards the door.

'Go. Clean up. Wash it all off. Put some fresh clothes on. When you come back down we'll see how we get revenge – for Ann, for Dean. Go, now.'

Sensing the little boy who occupies the carcass of a big man, knowing what he needs. Absolved, occupied, spaces filled with tasks and work. Later, perhaps, she will fuck him, gently, with the lights off, in the dark, remind him of life and love and hold him as he sobs once again. She goes to the kitchen as she hears the taps turned on upstairs. A big man needs meat. It's what her mother would have done for her father, she's sure, if he had stayed alive long enough. In the fridge are several steaks. Wolfy lays in supplies of them and eats them for breakfast and dinner and puts them between bread for lunch. She takes two and slaps them into a sizzling pan of oil. On the stairs, the burning beef and oil meets lavender and steam in an aromatic clash of sensations that tell of unusual life continuing.

*   *   *

The front door of a flat near the city centre of Liverpool gives way to a strong smell of curry. Stephen Smith examines the young woman standing there, surprised and distracted and swallowing.

'Miss White?' he asks, but already knows by the resemblance that it must be. He is careful to stand well back and smiles at the teenager. 'I knew your dad. He left some... things with me and I just wanted to return them. They belong to you, now, the whole family.'

In his hands a strong plastic bag. He passes it to her and starts moving off. She calls over her shoulder:

'Mum!' Then, as a stern faced woman appears, looking over her shoulder at the departing Smith, already disappearing into the stairwell.

'What's your name? Who are you?'

The same questions asked by a skinny woman managing a baby's bottle and an ashed dog-end in the doorway of another flat, in another part of the 'Pool. She looks nothing like her son, but he was, apparently, the spit of his dad, who looks just like his dad, Dean's Grandad, so his looks came from the male side, obviously and his mother never stood a chance. She doesn't know he's dead. Smith works that out and adjusts his excuse:

'He told me to pass this on to you. It's all legal. He got very lucky with the horses...'

'My Dean never does the gee gees. Where is he, anyway? I haven't seen him for weeks.'

'It was a one off, I think. Ask him, next time you see him. I'm sure he'll explain it all. He said to tell you...' as Smith walks quickly away, half turning '...use it for a holiday. He sends his love...'

Which is something Dean had signally failed to do ever since he had been old enough to get into trouble, which wasn't very old. Nevertheless, words to gladden a mother's heart. As will the bundles of twenties and fifties in the envelopes in the plastic bags at both Liverpool houses which come to one hundred thousand pounds between them. Months later, when these same notes turn up in the system, tracked from the briefcase handed over on a golf course in north London (scene of another mysterious murder) there will be puzzlement as to how two apparently unconnected Liverpool housewives come by murky money from a terrorist sting. Investigations will come to nought. The right answers need the right questions.

*   *   *

Whilst Smith is spreading alms in the northwest, Sherriff is enjoying himself at his regular clinic on the south coast. Added to his normal choir of voices is the sound of the puzzled Personal Security Detail still wondering how he came to be in the ether as opposed to driving his Markham Austin Engineering company big shot back to head office. Sherriff has him placed as surprisingly friendly for a man he shot to death and, if they were ever to meet, would probably get on fine with the other personalities who are crowding his head, one by one in succession as he sits in Haloperidolic stasis by a window. The nurses and doctors recognise this is probably as bad as he's been but Sherriff's world is currently not accepting the usual diagnosis. His school notebook remains open and unused beside him for the days he is 'away'. On the open page is just the one sentence, manic gibberish as far as the doctors are concerned: '4th Unit murdera/a-comin to get ya'.

Sherriff is aiming to be away for some time. He needs the holiday, he reasons. After all, hasn't he been working hard, making the world a better place? One of the more consistent voices, sounding a lot like Steve Smith, no, Blake, no, Smith – one of the voices, very insistent, reminding him, take as long as you want, Sherriff, I'll still love you just as much. Come back to me when you're ready and write us a song. But in the meanwhile he sighs deeply and shifts in the seat. Behind him, through the window, the sky goes on through blue and grey and white clouds into space, but Sherriff is gazing further away still, looking and listening for inspiration.

13

Chapter 13: Of Course

The circular relationship between London's drinking water and the stuff that gets flushed down the toilet is well documented. But it still amazes Eddy that anyone would situate a large Sewage Treatment Works on the doorstep of a reservoir. Admittedly, there's little chance of an overspill, so the prospect of human turds floating in the lake are remote, unless they belong to some of the sub-human junky life who occasionally have a midnight ramble in the rough patches by the water. Eddy has seen the evidence, picked up the syringes to save the sheep and goats from catching aids. For a man who works with the filth from our bowels, Eddy is pretty fastidious.

On his walk to work every weekday morning he looks to his left, in order to keep the industrial parks and the city mass from his vision. On the way back, if it's still light, he looks to his right, for the same reason. The water is healing. The way the light bounces off the ripples when the wind blusters and gusts on a sunny day delights him. It's his country walk and his Wellington boots stay on until he has reached the doorstep of his parent's house a mile away from the treatment works in one of London's many suburban dormitories, neither in nor out of the city.

So the fact that he notices the big, wild haired man on the roof of the otherwise disused factory next to the reservoir is unusual. Not used to being observed on his solitary walks, Eddy stares back at him. It's a stand off. Eddy's a big man, a beanbag of flesh and fat in button up overalls, striding along in size twelve boots. The man on the roof appears to agree that he has met his match and disappears from view quickly and suddenly. There appears to be no sign of life in the factory other than the wild man on the roof. Gyppos, after the lead and copper, probably, Eddy's thoughts echoing his father's words, although what lead or copper exists in a corrugated iron roof who can say? But it's not like he's going to call the police. Anything that happens away from the water is no concern of his, besides, his one brush with the law has put him off them for life. A couple of years back, coming upon fluttering yellow tape blocking his way, suspended between the fence and a metal post sunk into the bank, he was soon on his way to the police station in Edmonton, the prime suspect in the murder of a young woman, who's body had been found next to the water. His size twelve's matched the footprints in mud nearby. His bulk and obvious strength soon had the detectives comparing him to the fabled gentle giant killers of One Flew Over The Cuckoo's Nest and Of Mice And Men, even if they weren't sure who had been killed, or why, in these films and they treated him accordingly, trying to bully out a confession until his mother had confirmed an alibi later that day, after which he went to his work place.

Mud sticks, as Eddy knows, so when the news went round of his arrest he had several days in which he had to convince one or two mouthy individuals that "Eddy the Nonce' was not a nice way to be addressed. These individuals, finding themselves flat on their backs on concrete or tarmac did their best to renounce their sins and soon the remarks ceased, although the graffiti continued in the gents and Eddy's reputation remained as someone with a dark and violent other life, which generally suited him as he was left alone to get on with his work and was no longer pestered to come down the pub for a Friday evening piss up. Naturally solitary, Eddy has his mum and dad and his hobbies and, once a year, a boating holiday on the Broads and he intends his life to keep on this steady and even keel for the foreseeable future.

*   *   *

Friday night finds a young man on his uppers but determined to go out. What are the chances of bumping into someone who knows someone you knew who is willing to buy you a drink or two? He's been stretching that pint out until all that's left is his own spit at the bottom of the glass, seriously thinking of heading out into the night to find a pisshead, unsteady on their feet, holding some weekend ackers they might be willing to share with a little persuasion, when another pint turns up, followed by a shot glass brimming with voddy. Courtesy, apparently, of Mr. White. Officer White, late of Her Majesty's Prison Service, as represented, in this instance by 'Steve', a colleague and friend of Mr. White who doesn't look like a pouf, but who can tell these days? Who begins to talk.

'So, Will, Dan - Mr. White - saw a lot of promise in you. He thought you were one of his brighter lads. Was he right?'

Will appreciates the drink but he knows when he's being interrogated. One sentence is enough.

'I've done nothing wrong, yeah? You can stop pretending to be my mate. Thanks for the drink and all that but I'm not a grass and I'm not a villain, so you can just leave me alone, alright?'

It's a busy pub, the chat competing with increasingly

louder party music. Smith cups his hands over one of Will's ears.

'Hold out your hand. Then follow me outside.'

Left staring at a bundle of money as he watches his new friend push through the drinkers. Fuck! Two hundred. He heads in the opposite direction, the other exit, past the bouncer, round the corner and face to face with the mystery benefactor. Who is holding a fan of fifty pound notes out in front of him a like a magician preparing a card trick.

'You're hard fellow to give money to, Will. Don't you like money?'

It's one of life's lottery moments for Will, ex-offender, no-hoper, queer in denial. He could run off and be two hundred pounds better off or he could stick around and listen to some more chat and head towards disaster. The fan of cash waves and he can swear his nostrils fill with the smell. It smells like a thousand, at least. For a moment he considers having a go at the tall, fit looking guy who is obviously tempting him but the steady stance and the look in this guy's eyes… reminds him of the one or two you get to meet in nick who you don't even look at, let alone talk to.

'Alright, you want to give me money. Why? Because you knew my P.O.?'

'That's the best question you could've asked, Will. I want to give you a taste, that's all. Like a heroin dealer. You get this one for free, if you want more, you come and work for me, have fun, earn a lot of money… Now, you want to know what you'll be doing.'

Will notices the 'you'll' – not 'might', then, not 'if you fancy it, lad'. OK.

'What, then?'

'Take it first. Take the cash then I'll tell you.'

A middle-aged couple walk past on their way to the pub, knowing enough not to notice an obvious bit of drugs bother taking place in front of them. Will takes the money, scrunches it up, stuffs it in his trouser pocket. Now he's ready to run. Smith watches him.

'It's alright, run off if you want. I wont follow. I'm not interested if you're not into the idea. But why not hear me out? Over there?'

Across the road, another pub, dim lights in the window, no bouncers on the door. A quiet place.

Smith insists that Will gets a round in. At the bar Will does a surreptitious count of the screwed up notes. It's enough to cheer him up considerably, even if the night is getting weirder by the minute. Back at the table in an alcove Will checks the venue – a place the weekend avoids – as he sits down and takes a pull on his lager. Smith begins again.

'I don't have a lot of time. I need someone fit and smart and not from London to help me in some criminal enterprises. Dan reckoned you were both and I think he had reason to know.' An appraising look, Will surprises himself by blushing. Smith continues.

'Don't worry, I'm not interested, I don't care whether you like men, women or donkeys, or what you got up to with Mr. White. I need a fast driver who's not afraid of using a weapon. I need you for a month, then we never meet again and you're richer by one hundred thousand pounds.' His voice is urgent but not desperate, the tone of a prospective employer making an offer that can't be refused.

'It's a kidnap, extortion and a bit of robbery. You stay in the car, you wear a disguise, if anyone shoots at you then you shoot back. But that's unlikely. Say yes and we leave tonight, right now. Say no and you can leave the pub with the wad in your pocket and it ends here. I'll give you a minute to think it over while I have a piss.'

Even though Will knows it's a test, he can't help but admire the man's style. Proper, old fashioned gangster style, leaving him with the money like that. Even the way the man's dressed – no trackies or trainers, a smart jacket, clean, expensive jeans, could be a civil servant, a politician. He finishes his lager. Twenty-one years old. He looks at the customers at the bar, two old men, bulbous nosed, hairy ears, hard balloon bellies: his dad, before the drink killed him. He looks outside through the window, across the road, at people turning up at the pub drunk already, too poor to get pissed at the pub. The bouncers, bored, tired, scared…

…It's a Merc. Of course it's a Merc! Smith gets in the passenger seat. Will gets behind the wheel.

'Let's see what you can do, then. I need to be in London by four AM.'

'What about the bizzies?'

'Fuck the bizzies. Drive.'

Watching the young man's eyes, bright and bought, Smith muses on his genuine usefulness – was he always going to make use of Dan White's prison love angel? Is this fun, putting his life in the hands of a half cut boy-racer, risking getting pulled by the police, risking it all for a whim? Probably, but let's find out. As the speedo hits one hundred and twenty he smiles and then begins to talk about things.

'Money is power.'

'Right, Steve.'

'Guns are power.'

'Yes, Steve.'

'Information is power. We've got all three. We've got power.'

'Yes, Steve.'

'If you go to the cops I'll rip your throat out.'

'I know.'

It's the short version, but it will do. He turns on the radio and suddenly feels weary.

'Wake me when we get to the M25.'

*   *   *

Smith looks weary. He told Miriam he had just returned from Liverpool, handing out guilt money to the family of the boy killed in Wales. Not that she saw the boy, not the whole boy, anyway. Now she sits and listens to him talk at her in her Stoke Newington flat. He seems to think he saved her life.

She has been listening in the usual semi-numb state she falls into in his presence, examining his face for traces of truth, always wondering how he came to be, here, again and why. Then he hands her a floppy disk.

'What's this?'

'It was a copy made by your father.'

'A copy of what?'

'A copy of the original file, something he had put together over a number of years before he retired.'

'And how did you get it?'

'I stole it.'

'Who from?'

'Your father was an honourable man in a nasty business, Miriam. In the end, he wanted to do something about it. He spoke to some people, passed this on to them. He thought they might help, might do something. They decided not to help. In fact, they had a quiet word with him and persuaded your father that the best way he could enjoy his retirement, enjoy being with his family would be if he didn't rock the boat and various other clichés that served as veiled threats. In the end, he agreed with them. He didn't want to put you or your mother at risk'

Holding the disk between thumb and finger like a slow burning match. Old technology, it already looks absurdly kitsch. The information it contains a pin prick of what fits into a USB stick the size of a large fingernail. Words and numbers, no room for audio, or moving image. Very old school. Worth killing her father for, perhaps?

'What's on this Steve? I don't even have a computer I can use it on...'

'Your dad's old computer – is it still at your mum's house?'

'I think she threw it out. It was ancient.'

'You'd better use this, then.'

He hands her a CD from the small rucksack he has brought with him, no markings, no case.

'It has all the same info. You can check it against the floppy when you get a chance but I managed to transfer it a few months back. Check it, for your own peace of mind.'

From the same rucksack, Smith hands her a padded envelope.

'Then have a look at these. The footage is of the head of Markham Austin Engineering making an unauthorised cash payment for software he believes will enable them to produce remote controllable small arms ordnance – magic bullets. There's a million pounds in the bag. It was witnessed by one of his company's security men, who was found murdered nearby. On a golf course.'

He gets up. Wanders to the window overlooking the street and watches for a moment. Something causes him to smile.

'I doubt if we'll meet again after this Miriam. Please accept my sincerest apologies for any upset or hurt I've caused you. You might find it difficult to get anyone interested at the paper in these facts – at first. Persevere! I'm sure the truth will find its way eventually.'

He's at the door.

'After I've left, call the police. Tell them you were too scared to do anything while I was here. Call this number, not nine nine nine. Ask for Detective Constable Hipkins. Tell him everything. Cheerio!' He places a slip of paper next to her on the arm of her chair and she catches a hint of the smell, or the trigger of some other unknown sense, or a combination, of him. For some reason she feels instantly very sad.

Inches away from her eyes, the grey of the floppy disk, still held, suspended, out of focus, her whole body ready for cramp, Miriam realises she hasn't moved, is hardly breathing. She listens to footsteps on the street, walking away from her. Once again, that man has burgled his way into her life, leaving her feeling violated. And excited. It's as if he's writing the drama for her – all she has to do is review it. This is a bloody piece of political theatre, staged by an avant garde troupe specialising in Dada-esque symbolism (painted trains?) and Situationist acts of violence, would be the first paragraph, in the arts section, next to the opera and the pop music. And then she feels sad, again

*   *   *

A haircut for mourning. Toby, scrubbed head, shaved, an ocean of baby stubble from ear to shining ear. In the basement of the Tottenham house surrounded by various, well built tools of death and mayhem, the SIG sniper's rifle in bits before him on the floor where he sits, naked apart from a pair of underpants, taking each screw, each sculpted slice of metal and plastic, checking it, if necessary, rubbing it with a piece of muslin dabbed in clean oil. Re-assembling, slowly, enjoying the fit, the wind, the torque, the click. This is the third time since Ann's death. His finger rubs the groove near the bolt where a small chunk of metal had broken off when the rifle had backfired in Wales. The blue mark in his left palm the place where it had pierced his skin after nearly blinding Ann. Better than a tattoo. As the rifle takes shape in his hands he promises her blood, minute adjustments of human life to make a better world; one less baddy here, one less baddy there.

Since Steve Blake became Stephen Smith, to Toby's mind a

subtle transformation which has coincided with his own, maturing darkness of the soul, the two of them have reached a new agreement. Without consulting the others, they have decided that Toby must become a lone wolf, a separate cell. During several long nights they have looked over faces, men in suits, most of them over the age of forty and Toby has pointed his forefinger at each of the chosen ones and – bang! Shot them, on the computer screen.

Now there is a list. A name, accompanied by either a work or home address in London. Smith has traced each name to a deed, somewhere in the world, of unnecessary evil. It's very clear. For instance, Toby conjures up a face, a man with salt and pepper hair, he enjoys a salary in excess of half a million a year, a director of a company who exploit the mineral wealth of the Congo basin in Africa. This man, coincidentally, also benefits from investments in an arms brokerage firm who have done rather well from illegal shipments of Chinese guns to all sides in the endless war fought in the same region. It benefits him that chaos reigns, women are raped, children are mutilated. It benefits his pockets, his bank balance. There is no grey area here. Smith has made it clear. This man is aware of what is done in the name of his money. He can't be sacked and blackmail takes too long, is too involved. The law will never hurt him because he exists in a tacitly accepted state of grace, enjoying the protections granted to those who maintain the timeless traditions of international trade and who bring wealth and security to the whole country, which is no excuse.

Another face, in Toby's memory, another man. And another and another. It's a project for the holidays, the climax of his internship. How many? Six weeks starting in June. He's got plenty of bullets, stacked in boxes next to him. The rifle takes shape as a rifle, sliding the last piece, the bolt pinging into place. Then the long range scope – he examines both ends, squinting down it, pointing it at the blank white wall. A speck of dust. Using a photographer's blower brush, he removes the speck with a puff of air.

* * *

There's only so much he can do, decides Bill Freeman, as an old fashioned part of him bristles against a female journalist insisting on tackling something more serious than knitting or mime. But the evidence is compulsive. And the headline is beautiful. Magic Bullets! How can he convince Miriam that this is a step too far, that there are people who would see them both as puny flames in an intense darkness, easily snuffed, made to disappear, much like her father? He tries.

'It won't go. It will look like we're taking sides. Attacking the industry. Partial. Besides...'

The look on Miriam's face, resigned, closed, she's nodding, prepared for his answer.

'...it will probably get us shot. Or blown up. Drowned. Ran over. The owner dines with these people, has investments with their companies. I really would love to, Miriam. But this is one step too far. We're not The Guardian – in fact, even they probably wouldn't. We'll cover the fraud in the financial section – someone else can pick up the implications. The magic bullets we leave alone.'

Outside his office, the eco-system of tittle-tattle and influence maintained by his beloved workers, swimming behind glass smeared with breath and temperature fluctuation. Miriam, calm, still nodding.

'OK, Bill. I'd better be off – I've got an interview with a life style guru. Another one.' And she's gone, leaving the door open.

What just happened there? Has he just witnessed the final spark of another disillusioned journalist peter out? The beginning of the new, cynical, bitter Miriam? Welcome, then, fellow hack. Welcome to the real world. Where freedom is the space between high walls.

*   *   *

A mosaic of neatly scissored printed pictures and information written in Arial type has already engulfed the pin board on the wall at one end of Hippo's pool, as it has already unofficially been christened by its occupants. Slices of sunlight highlight every other three inches of the board in stripes from top to bottom. Hipkins enjoys the effect – the positioning changes through the afternoon and inspires his focus, sometimes falling in unexpected places. His performance, as he sees it, has so far been well delivered, well received and largely ineffective. His colleagues seem to respect him and enjoy his unexpected orders on random aspects of the hunt. Information collated thoroughly and a pattern emerging but no closer to finding their prey; morale is good and he is hoping that, whatever happens, he will be credited with 'doing a good job under the circumstances'. And what circumstances.

It's almost as if there is a liquid wall, solid but giving, clear but obscuring. Take their main man, Stephen Smith. Yes, there's his life: born, school, university, work as a linguistics expert, translator... but, somehow, he's not there. Every company he has apparently worked for is just an element of another, larger firm, existing in the opaque world of international finance. He might as well have been a cleaner or a plumber for all they knew of his day to day activities. The connections from the information on the laptop from Superintendent Beard are cryptic clues, details of deaths but without reasoning. There have been no demands, no statements of intent, no propaganda or manifesto. The rest of the gang still haven't been identified, apart from the dead lawyer, Ann Garvey, who has a husband, who is missing. Their house in north London remains locked, empty and unused for months. He's put it under surveillance but all that's happening is a small mound of fast food packaging is building up in a bin across the road where the cops sit and watch. He's put out an old photo of Peter Garvey to the media, looking well fed and smug, wearing court dress and wig, bizarrely holding on to the collar of a friendly looking white dog, standing outside of the house in Wales that is now a gutted, burnt-out shell. Part of a liberal, left leaning, husband and wife legal team, willing to work for the big bucks, too. He's interviewed family, friends, colleagues and enemies and all he has is a story he could have written from the photo. Guns? The Garveys? Skiing, perhaps, a yacht, even – but they weren't the huntin' fishin' types, loathed the country set, apparently. But so do most of the metropolitan legal's he's ever met, the intelligent ones, anyway. It means nothing.

Apart from these three, all he has are descriptions: a big man with thick, dark hair. A small man. A young man. An apparently mixed race, or he could be an Arabic man. Another woman, possibly foreign. They could all be possibly foreign!

If these are anarchists, then they are the strangest ones he's ever bumped into, although, it must be said, apart from cracking the black hooded skulls of some Italian kids on an anti-Nazi demo once, his experience of the breed is very limited.

Picking up the phone for his twice weekly chat with Harry Beard, Hippo is casting around for some positive new info of which he can think of none. The phone is ringing in his ear when his practical female second in command hurries over with her laptop. As Beard picks up, Hippo finds he is looking at a surprisingly clear picture of a white Luton van taken from a CCTV camera. In the cab, the driver is a big, wild haired man looking to his left at a smaller, bullet-headed man with baby features, staring straight into the camera and gesticulating, as if to say, 'look, they're watching us'. There's something wrong about them. Any copper worth his salt would spot it. It's something. A van. It's a start. In London, north London, to be precise. It's worth following up, worth mentioning to Superintendent Beard. So he does.

14

Chapter 14: How To Zero

Insides scalded with hot chocolate. Slurped too soon, cooled with a bottle of water, the sugar and the adrenaline and the promise of sun combine in a heady buzz in the pure body of a teenager. It's busy in Soho and Toby is enjoying the activity. Remembering to keep his shades on (wrap around, piped in fluorescent yellow to match his lycra shirt). Remembering not to scratch the unsightly wart on the lower side of his left cheek – a present from Tedi that morning, as was the soft kiss she gave him as the adhesive dried. Remembering to affect an Irish accent, loosely modelled on Wolfy's impenetrable Cork, when ordering his drink – not a problem, he had it down pat. Watching the young Ukranian's eyes move from his, to the wart and then nevermore to linger on his face whilst she served him. A classic London mix of an Italian café staffed by eastern Europeans, featuring a restless drift of local workers – advertising, retail, management, recruitment – who don't give a resting bicycle courier a second glance as they squeeze a lunch hour into fifteen minutes.

Just around the corner, an apartment, part of a modern construction overlooking Carnaby Street, top floor, windows of the main living space floor-length, giving a clear view of Soho roof tops, pigeons and airplanes in grey sky. Where a family man enjoys some extra-marital pleasure with a woman younger than his daughter. A permanent arrangement, involving a complicated array of relationships, beautifully managed by his secretary. The girls, sourced from a Russian client, a present, in fact – but preferring a single, middle-aged pervert to the potentially endless line, given as the alternative choice. You fuck one or you fuck many. The wife, who's diary is quietly monitored so that London dates don't collide in embarrassment after, maybe, a West End show, dining at the Red Fort, or one of the other obvious places. The daughter, who works in Kensington but likes to party in Soho, virtually monitored via her mobile phone (she doesn't know), a system which has failed only once, when she left the phone in the bed of a one night stand in… Soho. A disaster, narrowly avoided by luck, the father exiting a cab as the daughter enters one across the street, each oblivious to the other. Then there are the very few clients important enough for him to drop everything for – where they are, as far as can be told – do they need to see him when they hit London? Does he need to see them? And, finally, the girl's mother, who is sent a monthly stipend, who's rent is paid, who sometimes needs help with difficult neighbours, corrupt cops and officials and who is proud of her daughter's success in London, even if she's unsure – doesn't really want to know – exactly how she earns her rubles.

Security is someone else's job. The secretary bows to superior knowledge in this department. Today, 'security' is a dark suited driver, carrying an illegal firearm, waiting in the underground garage nearby for, usually, around three hours. He amuses himself reading a paperback by the car's internal light, anything will do, whilst stretching his muscles in the sitting position, as he was taught to do by the orthopaedic specialist brought in by his employers. Always ready – cramp dealt with. Boredom dealt with. Two mobiles sit on the dashboard, one a direct line to his employer with no other numbers installed. He could be reading anything, but in this case it's a Wilbur Smith.

On the top floor. As the bullet pierces the plate glass. Toby has taken into account what happens when bullets meet glass, the slight deviation caused by the impact, however high powered the charge. But, amazingly, his aim remains true. Expecting the glass to shatter, Toby has another round lined up, but, instead, the glass cracks, slowly from the bullet hole until the kicking foot of a dying man hits it hard with a well shod heel and one whole segment falls out on to the balcony, revealing the shoe, the foot, a white ankle sock and bare leg to the top of silk underwear, now damp from piss. Through the gap in the window now, Toby watches the beautiful young woman on the sofa freeing her wrists from the neck tie binding them, bring her stockinged knees to her naked chest, her hand to her mouth, as her eyes widen and she tries not to scream. Toby wishes he could help her, instinctively knowing that the death of this man brings more trouble than freedom. But he must leave quickly, after dismantling the rifle so it fits snugly in the bottom of his courier's bag slung across his shoulder.

Down the stairs, past reception where the receptionist is still vaguely waiting to sign for the parcel he won't be delivering. On to the street, in the full glare of CCTV, to unlock his bike and hammer into the metallic streams of traffic where he blends in with shoals of motion, beating traffic lights, racing buses and escaping through side streets to the north, via the south.

It was a heart attack, which is almost true, as can be attested to by the young woman who's lap is now guarded by a cushion grabbed from the sofa, watching the blood slowing from the hole on the left side of the pervert's chest. Work stress brought it on – it doesn't get much more stressful than a bullet. Will be missed by his family and colleagues at work – which is a straight forward lie, as the different degrees of delight at the news of his demise, registered with a faint smile or a glass of champagne, demonstrate. But at least it's true to say, his mother loved him, while he was still alive.

So begins the beginning of the end of Toby's internship, his gap year climax, his apprenticeship and he is doing very very well. Ten out of ten. Well. One out of ten, but he's feeling confident.

* * *

'It's a mind your own business box.'

'OK man, I was only asking.'

Normally the beef would build to something grander, resulting in the street chaos he thrived in, but something about the lickle white man with the baby face and patchy hair dissuades the young Grover from continuing. The 'something' is a large wolf-man who joins them at the rear of the van parked outside number fifty three and who just stands there, big arms folded, waiting. Waiting for him to move on. Well there's nothing to see so he does. The cardboard boxes could be anything – PCs, money, drugs, bogroll – and the men are so obviously wrong, it's bound to incite his interest. But some small scale burglary and herb runnings is as far as he wants to go down that particular route to Strangeways, so, with a back of the teeth spit and the slightest hint of a crippled ankle he saunters off, across the road and into the estate. Wolfy slams the doors shut as Abe watches the youth disappear round the corner.

'Think we should tell Steve?'

Wolfy shakes his head.

'Don't bother him.'

To be honest, the boxes are ridiculously over-sized for what they contain, but do the job of hiding manacles, a pack of cuppasoups, a kettle, a roll of gaffa tape and sundry other useful items for a modern kidnap. The bare bones, Smith had insisted, and that's what the boxes contained. Smith had also ordered a roll of king-size bin liners and latex gloves, to be worn all the time they are inside the factory. Even when they use the bog. It seems to Abe to be a right palaver, considering they'll end up torching the place anyway, but he finds he is increasingly unable to fathom logically and goes through his days completing his chores in a dream-like fashion. Drive here. Take a picture. Drive there. Buy a car. Pick up the groceries. Pick up a package of what he is certain is plastic explosives from some bloke in a pub in Tooting. Tooting! Since he met Smith Abe has seen parts of London he's only ever heard about. That Tooting package cost a bundle, but it felt like comme ci, comme sa. He's getting used to the prosthetics now and has no qualms about walking into an afternoon bar, where his warped features look as normal to the clientele as anyone's might after several pints of Tennents on an empty stomach.

The apprentice calls from the front door of the house.

'Do I need me coat?'

The apprentice, the scallywag. Dean's twin replacement. Not as sussed, cruder and still not one of them. This new Scouse git is just your basic scally scum, thinks Abe. But they try, they reach and keep him calm. Does he need his coat? He's northern – all he needs is a little bitty T shirt in a gale or a blizzard and he's already over-heating, whips it off at the drop of a sunbeam, flexing abs and pecs and all the other bits and pieces Abe's never possessed. Will is a mistake, in Abe's humble opinion. He just makes everyone miss Dean more. Wolfy is the only one who seems to have taken the lad's arrival in his stride. As with Dean, Wolfy makes a point of keeping him busy, quietly getting his head under the bonnet and checking the schematics of the BMW estate, running over maps and routes, spotting cameras and pointing out the errors of Will's lapses into the casual racism that Dean never exhibited.

Tedi views the new arrival with obvious suspicion. Taking Smith to one side, overheard by Abe, to ask why he had brought this 'brute' into their group. Smith just smiled and murmured 'be patient'. Perhaps in an attempt to compensate for his sexuality Will had taken one look at Tedi and began a crude and sustained attempt to get her into bed, including taking every opportunity to whisper obscenities in her ear until, finally, she very deliberately punched him very hard on the nose. Ready to retaliate, but catching the ever watchful Wolfy's eye, Will fumed until Smith intervened and, to everyone's surprise, thrust Will's arm up behind his back and pushed him, face squashed, against the living room wall, all the while whispering, in a parody of the young man's own advances on Tedi, into the side of his head and continuing until he had manhandled Will out of the room, leaving Tedi beaming in the afterglow of the gallant intervention.

What the others didn't see was the next hour Smith spent teaching the apprentice the value of respect. A masterclass in dazzling linguistics, psychology and bullying, Will was transformed with tears and sobs and assurances and devotions and became an instantly nicer ex-hooligan. A sketch in progress. A watercolour ready to be washed away in the first downpour. A temporary necessity. Or just a bit of fun. Smith enjoys all of these descriptions of Will, but the most accurate is 'resource'.

*   *   *

The morning after the afternoon in Soho. Once again the yellow-streak courier takes to the tarmac, bottle of water and a lighter load at the bottom of his bag. Weaving between side mirrors and hubs, growling, snaking buses and lethal lorries, heading once more into the bowl, this time the ancient old City of London, with it's shiny fake skyscrapers placed like Leggo on a carpet of history, where the real work is done, as ever, over fortified wines and stuffed intestinal tracts at around three o'clock in the afternoon or amidst the whiff of perfume and beer in a strip joint at nine o'clock at night, just before the taxi to the station, to the suburban family. Toby whizzes past armed police at checkpoints, more interested in brown skinned bogeymen they hardly register the lithe young courier passing with a breath of teenage aftershave and with a small but lethal pistol in the bottom of his bag.

Joining his daddy at the base of a squat office block is young Mr. Heath, swarthy like his father, an unexpected arrival but no less welcome, as every powerful man likes to think they are continuing or creating a dynasty and before the young Mr. Heath's arrival, some five years ago, the older Mr. Heath was preparing to leave his considerable savings and property portfolio to a selection of various people who, he calculated, could continue doing the most damage to the things he hates. So, there was the substantial donation to the Conservative Party, with a decent sum going to the latest version of their anti-immigration rivals. A trust fund to the feisty daughter of a colleague who had drunkenly fondled his cock at a reception a few years ago and now works as a journalist for the Financial Times and enjoys a dabble on the market herself. A large portion of his money would, of course, continue throbbing through the veins of the weapons procurement company he had founded, which had negotiated all kinds of bits and pieces of machinery across the globe which, when assembled, would take the arm off a young man in Chechnya, take the eye out of a baby in Palestine, disembowel a fifteen year-old boy in Uganda. Very democratic destruction. And then there's his wife, who was going to receive, well, just enough to maintain a house in Maida Vale and the odd holiday, but certainly not enough to indulge her passion in collecting modern art, which he loathes, which is why she collects it.

But that had all changed with the unexpected arrival of Thomas, the small creature stickily holding his hand and stomping at the pigeons who have flown down to help him finish his crisps. Thomas is here to witness the changing of the terms of his daddy's will. He's going to get the lot! When he reaches eighteen, he will inherit a bachelor pad in the City and a decent sized gaff in Manhattan and fifty grand a year until at twenty-one, the whole Heath empire will fall into his lap via a manilla folder and several signatures at 'here, here and here, Mister Heath, if you would' on the contracts waiting for activation on the top floor of this building.

Unfortunately for Tommy, his daddy's journey towards the ether is hastened by the arrival of what will become 'the yellow man' who haunts little Tommy's nightmares for years to come, until therapy and time allow him to push the memories of the bustle and violent arrival of a young man on a bicycle, the sound of the brakes, the click pop sound of the gun, just inches above his head and the surprised eyes either side of the third, liquid red eye in his daddy's forehead. For years, Tommy remembers the yellow man flying away, literally flying, but eventually this is rationalised to the boy's interpretation of the sounds, the flapping courier's bag, the wind disturbed as the 'yellow man' rides off into the traffic, disappearing from CCTV view just past Aldgate tube station.

*   *   *

'Miss Tayor-Malick?'

Hippo's journey down the aisle between the sports section and the news section towards the arts was one of a grand state liner coming up the Thames. All that's missing is the bunting and water cannon and ship's fog horns. He's even got an orchestra on deck – his mobile phone ringing the theme from The Sweeney to the snorts of several journalists, which he pointedly leaves unanswered, as if the motion of walking is enough activity for a man of his size. The pilot ship of his assistant, the ever so sensible woman in ever so sensible boots and jeans is sniffing out the rocks and currents slightly ahead of him, but it's Hippo who does the talking.

'Is there somewhere we could go?'

In the meeting room, Hippo takes his time, moving around the glass walls, adjusting the slats of the blinds until they are safe from prying journo eyes and finally, thankfully, docking himself on to one of the uncomfortable seats at one end of the long glass topped table. His assistant remains standing, holding a notebook but looking at the top of Miriam's head. Miriam has to stop a hand from checking to see if there's anything there or if her hair needs tidying, distracted from DC Hipkin's questions.

'So, he hasn't been back?'

'No.'

'And you've heard nothing more from him?'

'No.'

'Take a look at these photos, please, Miss Taylor-Mallick.'

In front of her, two shots of two men in a van, one of them the taciturn Irish man who drove them from Wales. She shakes her head. Then realises she hasn't been asked to identify them yet. So she concentrates on the small, round faced man, who she suddenly places. Perhaps a slight look of connectivity enlarges her pupils. Hippo takes a guess.

'You recognise them, right? These two men? Can you tell me who they are?'

What possesses Miriam to protect Stephen Smith, even now, after witnessing the mayhem, after concluding that he's probably psychotic, mad, dangerous? Perhaps because she senses that somehow, he's more on her side than the police – the authorities – who are willing to protect and kill to protect (kill her father!) the sordid trade in guns and bombs, detailed on the floppy disk and CD given her by Smith at their last meeting. Illegal trade to crazy men who unleash legions of violence, drugged up schoolboys, religious maniacs, power hungry misogynists happy to slaughter anyone and everyone. Well, perhaps this Hipkins doesn't go round killing people but he certainly protects the status quo. That's the basic function of the police. So she is almost happy to lie.

'Never seen them before.'

'Are you sure?'

The sensible assistant is looking at her face now. Miriam smiles back.

'I'm sure. Who are they?'

'Miriam. You do understand how important it is that we get hold of Smith and stop him?'

'Stop him from doing what?'

'Killing any more people. Killing and robbing and blowing things up. Take a look at this please.'

Another photo. This one of a man she genuinely doesn't recognise.

'This man was found dead in Soho yesterday. We think his death might be connected with Smith.'

Shaking her head again at the head-and-shoulders, glossy ten-by-eight colour picture, a brochure shot, for a trade fair, perhaps. Or a politician's mug shot.

'This man was involved with the armaments industry. Like your father. Are you sure you don't know him? Where were you yesterday afternoon?'

Do they think she killed him?! Calming herself.

'I was here, DC Hipkins. All afternoon. There were many people who were here with me. Do you want to check with my boss?'

On the other side of the glass wall, through two layers of blinds and a quarter inch of glass, her boss sits, staring, wishing he had left the bugs in place. For several years he had left the hidden microphones discovered by a private security firm who were investigating leaks and gazzumped headlines. It turned out that someone on the news-desk, fairly high up, was recording their morning meetings and any other conversation held in the room and flogging the recordings to a rival newspaper. Bill had inherited the hardware and left it there until, sick of himself one day, he had smashed the receiver and torn the bugs from either end of the fluorescent light fitting hanging over the table.

Now he needed to know. He trusts Miriam to tell him the gist but she won't be able to read the cops like he can. Bill counts himself an expert on authority. He can smell rank. He can interpret threat levels. He's a newspaper man. Then his phone rings. He answers.

Seconds later he is leaving his office, just as Hipkins and his assistant leave the meeting room, Miriam following them out. Miriam goes to make introductions.

'Bill, this is…'

Instead Bill takes control, walking with the officers towards the lift, waving Miriam away.

'Bill Freeman, editor. You are? I'll go down with you, I've got to pick something up downstairs.'

In the lift, just long enough.

'So, Detective Constable – your name is familiar, did you box? I'm sure there was a promising boxer, heavy weight, called Hipkins. Was that you?'

Hippo is out of his league and he knows it. This editor is best dealt with by a Super, someone who speaks the language of power. Still, he tries.

'Can you confirm Miss Taylor-Mallick's whereabouts yesterday afternoon, sir?'

'Of course I can, she was at her desk. All day, actually. Why?'

'Does Miss Taylor-Mallick have any left wing sympathies, anarchy, things like that?'

'Anarchy? Miriam? Are you serious? She's a very hard working journalist. She hasn't got the time to eat sensibly or have a love life, let alone indulge in a spot of anarchy. She's very punctual, if that helps, most of the time.'

The lift door slides open and they are in the lobby. Pausing for a moment, Bill looks the big policeman up and down, completely ignoring the assistant.

'So, you got the short straw, Hippo. Bad luck, mate. Actually, good luck. You'll need it.'

Dismissed. Hippo watches the shirt-sleeved editor walk over to the reception desk where a woman points towards the main entrance. Sighing, deep inside himself, Hipkins is a few steps behind Bill Freeman as they head towards the revolving doors. Negotiating the doors takes some organising of his stomach and shoulders and when he is through the editor is already walking off with a tall man who is obviously a good friend as he has a hand on Freeman's shoulder and they are walking hip to hip. Hippo stands and watches. For a second it looks as if Freeman is about to run away but is kept in place by the arm – almost as if he is held there against his will. Freeman's friend is speaking into a mobile, all the while smiling at Freeman and glancing around. Suddenly, the sound of gunfire. Straight from the telly, thinks Hippo. Nothing like the muffled rounds heard at the firing range. These shots echo with the slap-back of concrete. A part of him floats into the dream of his situation: he's under attack, from automatic weapons. Looking to his side, his assistant is on the ground. Shot? There's no blood. She has her revolver drawn, but one hand is covering the top of her head. Fat lot that will do. Next to her body, chips of concrete are being dug from the pavement. One of them hits him in the face, on his forehead. There are screams and the busy street is full of motion, people running, ducking. Behind him, one of the huge plate glass windows of the newspaper offices has cracked. The gunfire continues and, finally, Hippo is in the moment, reaching for his own gun, calling out 'gun drawn!' and searching for the source of the bullets. A motorcycle is suddenly on the pavement, scattering pedestrians, then back on the road. Too quick to get the registration, just long enough for Hippo to understand that the man sitting at the front is a big man, dressed in black, a courier's antenna on the top of a full head helmet and that the figure seated on the pillion is holding a Glock, also dressed head to toe in black leather, but with the unmistakable shape of a woman. And that it is *them*. They've just attacked him. That they have tracked him down and shot at him! It's a bare minute later and his assistant is standing shakily, making calls, revolver still unholstered and Hippo is trying to make sense of it all. The motorbike is long gone. His own mobile is vibrating in a pocket and he is realising he has the answer to the question so many cops ask themselves but never find out: what would I do? If caught under fire, shot at, attacked. What would I do? Apparently the answer is, stand there like an idiot and do nothing. Nothing.

And he is still standing there as a BMW estate drives past in the opposite direction to which the motorbike had gone and he sees the baby faced man from the van in north London, sitting next to a young man with a thin face and long, Van Dyke beard. In the back he thinks he sees Bill Freeman and the tall man who might be a brother or a family friend, still hugging the editor, still smiling, catching Hippo's eye. And winking at him. A blink and the car has gone and the practical side, the northern bit, the spade's a spade bit is making him call on his mobile, describing the motorbike, the BMW, calling for back up, sending people to get the CCTV disks and stopping pedestrians from walking off, herding them, still frightened and wide eyed until he realises he still has his revolver in his hand, is using it to gesture and prod and that he still hasn't identified himself as a policeman yet. Not Hippo's finest hour. Not promising to be his best memory. Especially the bit about letting the editor of a national newspaper walk out the building arm in arm with Stephen Smith.

*   *   *

Uniforms work. Smith is admiring Tedi as she ruffles her hair out of the helmet shape. Typically, the leather trousers and jacket look more like fetish wear than practical clothing on the reluctant ex-stripper. Her figure emphasised by the high contrast of black against the blank beige walls of the near empty office. Smith isn't the only one watching. Slumped on a swivelling office chair, Wolfy, too, looks glamorous and strangely sexy in his own matching leathers. Suddenly they look like an obvious couple. Pleased, Smith turns to Bill Freeman, sitting on an upright chair at the opposite end of the room from the window looking out on to the weed strewn yard. Will stands behind him, his hands firmly planted on Freeman's shoulders. The look on Smith's face seems to say, aren't they a handsome couple, as he nods towards first Tedi, then Wolfy.

'If you do anything to make your stay with us anything less than straightforward, someone will kill you, Mr. Freeman.'

The grim Mr. Freeman just scowls in answer. Smith observes: his tight clenched fists, his feet, balanced on their balls, the muscles in his neck standing out like beading. He makes a decision.

'Can we get him secured, please?'

With a creak of leather, Wolfy is on his feet and behind Freeman, joining his wrists together with leather cuffs and stuffing his mouth with a ball gag and collar as Smith leaves the room. Will stays where he is, applying pressure to Freeman's shoulders. Bending down to look into Freeman's face, Wolfy tells Will to:

'Ease off a bit sunshine, you'll bruise him.'

Bill Freeman watches the movements, the shifts in attitude and atmosphere and examines it all with a journalist's critical faculty. The look in his eye, which Wolfy has recognised, is one of glee. One of us, Wolfy might have said, if he hadn't learnt to keep his mouth shut long ago. He likes us. I like him. Take it easy. Sitting back down on his wheeled throne, Tedi joins him, sits on his lap unexpectedly – he can feel her, hot through the double cowhide. Wolfy notes she hasn't removed her jacket. The Glock automatic lies on the desk between them and Freeman, Wolfy reaches across Tedi to take it, put it away somewhere safe, but Tedi blocks him, playfully and, instead, takes up the gun, miming a cowboy taking a shot, blowing on the barrel, which turns into something more obscene involving her tongue, all the while staring Wolfy down until his big hand closes over hers and he slips the machine pistol away from her, as she pouts theatrically.

'Come back with me.' Her voice is low, but not embarrassed.

'Later.'

Smith standing in front of Freeman, but looking at Will, who looks confidently back, confident he's doing as told, not acting up, being a good boy scout. Smith awards him a smile.

'Where's Abe?'

One leg crooked over the other, prone in the back of the van, parked in the forecourt, Abe is assessing the odds. He's coping – against the odds, doing alright, actually. Perhaps he'll come out better than he thought. In twenty years write a memoir. Or get someone to ghost it. Lot of work, lot of words, a book. Low profit margin. Talking with Peter in a sober moment, getting a few tips on investments, in the event there's something left when Steve has finished, whatever it is they're all doing. Peter reckons bricks and mortar, and gold. In times of trouble, always gold. He shifts about on the flattened cardboard boxes, trying to get comfortable as the van door opens. It's Will.

'Steve wants you. In the basement.'

Perhaps it's nostalgia. Probably not worth examining too deeply. But Abe reminds him of Bassett. If Abe could learn to shut up. Or at least, whisper, like old Bassett did. Of course, Abe possesses the fundamental cowardice of the torturer, would enjoy the feeling of power, as a little man. And yet Abe has a decent core. He loves his mum. Wouldn't hurt an animal. But would he hurt a man? This man? From basement to basement, the armoury had been transferred from the house to this space, swept of cobwebs and cleaning products, with a low ceiling criss-crossed with rusty pipes, low enough to make Smith stoop. There are boxes stacked at one end, a single fluorescent strip bringing an approximation of daylight, a familiar ambience for Smith, who has often 'worked' in similar circumstances. Bill is on the same chair, brought down with him. A lamp is positioned on the floor, pointing towards the captive's face. It's not turned on yet. Eyeing Smith and Abe, a thin line of spit escaping the side of his mouth as he tries to enunciate expletives. Smith ignores him. Abe is distracted, flicking his gaze alternately up and down between the two of them.

'Abe, if I asked you to hurt this man, do you think you could? Hurt him, not kill him.'

Abe wishes he has a stammer, some syllables and some seconds, time to think and for a desperate moment he considers faking one. Why him?

'Well Abe? What do you think?'

Smith won't let him go.

'I don't want to, Steve.'

'I know you don't, Abe. That's's why I'm asking. But do you think you could? Think. Imagine it. You. Hurting him.'

So Abe thinks and imagines and…

'Yes. Yes, I could. If you really thought it was necessary.'

Steve is pleased. It's enough.

'Great! Thanks Abe. I'll be fine, off you go – just going to have a chat with our esteemed editor. Go on, really. I'll be fine.'

Is there a part of Abe that is disappointed? Only in as far as he has gritted his teeth, prepared himself for something awful and, once ready, been left hanging. Casting a look back, seeing Smith gazing fondly after him, the bloke in the chair, tension releasing with every step up to the ground floor. Well, that's something he knows about himself, which he didn't know before. Or perhaps he did, but didn't want to know.

Releasing the ball gag, Smith is all efficient kindness as Bill draws several huge, gasping breaths.

'Do you want a drink Bill? Now there's nothing medical we need to know about, is there? Heart condition? Asthma? No? Good!'

Pulling up a box, sitting opposite, placing hands on his knees, Bill's knees.

'You're not afraid are you Bill? You don't look scared. Bill – I'm going to give you a chance to follow your heart. I'm going to tell you a story – it's a bloody good one, Bill, and it's true, all true. And you're going to print it. Tomorrow. Hold the press. And all that. Can I untie you? Can I trust you?'

Moving behind, unclipping the restraints, letting them

dangle. What came first? Bondage, or sex?

'Right Bill, talk to me, ask me anything and I will answer with the truth. Anything. Sure you don't want a sip of water?'

Bill flexes his wrists.

'Can I stand?' His voice is broken, a first thing in the morning voice, pre-coffee, not expecting to talk yet.

'No, I'd prefer it if you stay sat Bill. Do you need the toilet. No?'

'What's the plan, Smith?' Finding his editor's voice.

'Do you have one? Perhaps. Probably not. Do your friends know?'

'Know what Bill?'

'That you're mad?'

'They may have an inkling. But they're very forgiving. And there's a bit of a method in it, etcetera.'

'So. You want publicity. Why me? Why not the owner?'

'Because the owner is difficult, to be honest. Not sure if it would have been possible. Definitely in the short time frame we're committed to. Anyway, you'll do fine.'

'I can't get your story printed stuck in a basement. You must know that.'

'Of course you can. If we're quick. So far, what have we got? There's some bullets fired and you're temporarily missing. You just need to have to turn up again, that's all. The story's ready. Miriam has it written. It just needs to be subbed and printed up. You know you can rely on Miriam for good copy. We've even sorted out some photos. All verifiable. Extremely dodgy, of course, upsetting to some very powerful people you wouldn't normally want to upset. Once upon a time, that would have excited you, Bill, wouldn't it? How do you feel now? Do you have a twinge? A little buzz? Of course you do, you were born for this, I know and you know. And if they get your boss to boot you out, even if they end up knocking you off, like Miriam's dad, it'll still be worth it, won't it?'

Freeman looks around the basement, at the boxes. There's a rifle leaning in the far corner.

'Is this it, then? Where you keep all your weaponry? I know you're not afraid to use them. What else have you got? Grenades? Plastics? Nail bombs? Suicide vests?'

Getting up from his perch, Smith opens the box. He pulls out bundles of shredded paper and drops them on the floor and then a small machine pistol, handing it to Freeman by the barrel so the gun is in the journalist's hand, pointing at Smith's chest as he sits back down.

'A Glock. Famous for spraying bullets in bad American TV shows. We don't make them in the UK but we facilitate their sales, send them all around the world, mainly to poor countries where people can't afford to eat properly. Now, if you were a fascist you might see some good in a kind of eugenic solution – poor people tend to overpopulate their countries with panic reproduction, equating a large family with some kind of insurance, a pension, healthcare in old age. And if you were a fascist you might say the Glock helps even the balance, get rid of some of the extra humans. But it's not that simple. Mainly it's the young who die, not the old and infirm. It's the young men who get given the guns and they tend to use them on each other. You really don't need to be a trained marksman to hit someone with a Glock. Just plenty of bullets.'

Smith holds out his hand and Freeman hands back the gun. Freeing the clip, Smith shows it to Freeman – it's full.

'See? Bullets. A gun's no good if it's not loaded.'

Freeman takes it in and holds out his hand again for the gun. Smith laughs.

'You had your chance Bill. So. Guns, bullets, death. Hurt. Lots of hurt around the world, all in the name of commerce, sometimes not even profit, when it comes to government grants: we pay some other country enough money for them to buy our arms, which, of course, is a sick joke. For such a militaristic country, don't you think it's strange that our citizens aren't allowed to own guns? Perhaps it's just as well. Look at Northern Ireland and imagine Peckham or Glasgow... No, we don't inflict our arms economy on our own. That's a saving grace, of sorts, for these murdering bastards. They only kill the wogs and the pakis and chinks. Right?'

Freeman wants to interrupt. He knows the story. Smith holds a hand up.

'I know. Nothing new. How about though, if you got a chance to kick them where it hurts. The really nasty ones, the grade A creeps who really don't care, the moneyed psychos, the arms dealers. How about it, Bill? Would you be up for it? Of course you would, you hate them as much as we do. You're one of us, really Bill. I can tell. Here's what to do. Listen to my story, get back to the paper. Hold the front page! Call them up. Tell them, put Miriam's piece on page one then sit back and watch history happen. It'll be fun! You'll feel young and vibrant again. Alive. Vital. Doing your job. Everyone will know and then, it's not just up to us, to you and me, it's up to everyone to show how much they do or don't care. Probably nothing will happen, why should this outrage be any more effective than all the others: castrations in Kenya, phosphorous in Iran, death squads in Ecuador? But we have to try, don't we? Now. Questions? Want a few minutes to think it through?

Frank Beard is looking forward to this. If it works out as he hopes, there will be an audience too. Teach the jumped up meat head to sack his boy. He takes the stairs one by one, feeling the creases in his trousers warp and straighten. The uniform is fitted to contain him and the jacket is strengthened like a corset. It keeps him uncomfortable but in the correct posture. Feeling a dab of moisture somewhere near his armpit. We can't have that. Pausing. There is the faint sound of activity from the floor above. He takes the final flight of stairs facing two large windows that give out on to the street and the housing estate across the road. A small group of youngsters is gathered around an older boy on a bike, spilling out on to the road, fags and cans, spit and mobiles. Scum.

A buzzing in one pocket. He stands on the landing to take the call, enjoying an unexpected beam of sun bending around a dirty cloud to the south, diffused by the glass. A familiar voice. He answers.

'I'm just about to… well, I've got to say something… he's a bloody useless lump… if you think so… I'm not going to congratulate him, if that's what you mean! …yes, alright, softly softly… yes it is a nice day… yes, goodbye.'

He'll be damned if he's going to take it easy! It's a question of asserting his authority, he does have some, after all. Strange, never heard him say 'goodbye' before. Not normally that polite, not his style. The mobile is neatly packed into the pocket of his jacket, it hardly interrupts his 'silhouette'. The other side pocket is tailored for a small handgun, currently containing a pack of Marlboro Lights. A quick check, smooth down of flaps, adjust the cap low over the bridge of his nose. Beard prepares to make his entrance through the double doors, his hands outstretched to push them open with maximum saloon bar impact. Fuck the brother. Fuck the boss. He's going to enjoy himself. His arms are still outstretched as he stumbles backwards, eyes glazing already, caught and frozen in a wince of pain. Falling heavily against the rails of the landing, his head bending back unnaturally loose and cracking against the hollow metal tubes, the blood and matter from his left ear striping the white gloss of the rail so neatly that the cops who find him presume it's a random piece of decorative paintwork they've never noticed before. This time, the glass crumbles and the window disappears, replaced by a naked gap in the wall, framing the kids on the street, gaping up, a couple of them already smiling, enjoying the sound of trickling glass. Beard is outside of their line of vision, two neat holes in the side of his head on one side, the mess on the other. He stays in this position, arms relaxed by his sides, jaw slack, dead weight, for a good ten minutes, until one of Hippo's team, sneaking out for a crafty fag, walks casually through the double doors and does a comedic double take before raising the alarm.

Around the rear of the housing block opposite the last gasp of Frank Beard, the boys have found a nice looking bike, locked to a lamppost. One of them takes an experimental kick at the spokes of the front wheel. Then a harder kick, then he is joined by several of his friends and seconds later the front wheel is bent at a twenty degree angle below the hub and the boys step back to admire their footwork. Which is when Toby appears from the stairwell to the building. A result. The boys watch and wait for a reaction – this is obviously the bike's owner: cycle helmet, wrap arounds, shorts, courier bag. Toby pauses. The biggest, oldest boy is smirking.

'What's the matter mate? That's a shame. Is that your bike? Somebody kicked it mate.'

Hand inside his courier's bag, feeling the still warm barrel. Toby nods and walks away, ignoring the jeering boys, a finger checking to see if his wart is still in place, waiting until he is around the corner before breaking into a run.

It's an encounter from another age. A kind of har is floating ribbons of grey around the grass on the bank and softening the water in the reservoir. On the other side, the endless traffic is lights through a mist. Bill Freeman has streaks of grass stain and mud on the knees of his trousers after slipping on the dewy slope. Somehow he has escaped. In fact, it's no miracle. The door was unlocked, there was no one around as he came up from the basement, he could hear voices from somewhere else – he headed in the opposite direction and found another open door, a fire escape in the back of the building. A scramble over the wire fence and some scratches from the rusty barbed wire snaked along the top, a hard fall, too hard for a man his age, and here he is. Facing Eddy, who is making his deliberate way back from work after a couple of hours of overtime, unblocking a pipe, enjoying the quiet of the plant in the evening and looking forward to this very walk, where he hadn't expected to encounter anyone, let alone this desperate figure. Freeman is looking around, looking lost, a fugitive in shirtsleeves. Eddy has determined to bulldoze through whatever odd situation might be arising, but the man is already moving to block his path, talking to him. Bollocks. He comes to a stop a few feet away, regarding Freeman warily.

'Sorry, look, can you help me? I'm a bit lost. Do you have a mobile? Do you think you could call the police for me? I've been… attacked and they're still around, so don't talk too loudly…'

Eddy realises the man is talking to him in a harsh whisper. Another crazy. Asking for the police. Eddy's never owned a mobile phone, never felt the need. He exists in a world outside of instant communication. If he's late for tea, his mum gets worried. If he's late for work, his bosses know he's ill. It's simple and there's no need for the complication of miniature technology. So when Eddy reaches inside his pocket he's not getting his mobile, it's a handkerchief he's after, to rub away the dribble of snot brought on by the water's chill, the small fog creeping up his legs. Bill Freeman can see it's already too late, looking over Eddy's shoulder, holding a hand up, crying:

'No, there's no need to do that! Stop! Don't! Keep your hand in your pocket!' - talking to someone behind Eddy, then talking to Eddy, confusing him, upsetting him. He replies sternly.

'Look mister, I'm going home...'

And letting his voice trail off as a strong hand grabs his wrist and something hard pokes the small of his back. Suddenly, there are people everywhere. A tall man and a small man taking the mad man in front of him back down the bank, a woman holding something in front of his face and his arm being pulled up behind his back by something hairy and as tall as him as the woman tells him:

'Don't do anything stupid.' In an accent straight from the television. Then he's struggling, wrenching his arm free, pushing at the woman but tripping, rolling down the bank, coming to rest on his back and another face, the hairy face calmly looking down at him before... stars, bright light and pain gradually shifting in a tide to one side of his head and the ear on the undamaged side picking up and his brain understanding,

'Fucking get up or I'll kill you where you are.'

Some part of Eddy floating upwards, his body light as air as he hovers round the front of the empty factory he passes every day, looking at the big man hefting him with small grunts, seeing his profile inches away from Eddy's nose and suddenly realising and saying out loud:

'You're that diddicoy! You got the lead!'

And receiving a jab in the ribs for his observation and a muttered:

'Wherever you go, there's racism.'

Then Eddy is swallowed up by the big roller door, which comes down behind him and he is once more tripped but more gently this time, laid to the ground where he sits holding his head looking up at his new friends.

In times like these a fridge is a young man's best friend, the welcome light, shelves stacked with jolly colours of fruit and drink and veg and yoghurt. Toby is glugging orange juice straight from the carton, draining the best part of a litre with hardly a breath. Then, because he's been well trained, he is rinsing the empty carton under the tap and scrunching it up, ready for the recycling container, which carbon reducing practise is diminished somewhat by the fact that the fridge door remains open during the entire operation. It's not until he closes the door that he sees the note, attached by a magnet in the shape of Big Ben. He recognises the doctor's scrawl of Stephen Smith. It reads, simply:

'Toby, go home.'

He's not surprised. But he's shocked at his reaction. Tears well his eyes and he doesn't remember sitting down, the note crumpled on the table in front of him. Just five minutes ago he had arrived at the quiet house calling out 'hello?' to the walls and the ceilings, his adrenaline still ticking energy into his system, feet aching after a twelve mile horse shoe shaped trek on buses, trains and foot from Clerkenwell to New Cross, to Sutton and then Hammersmith and finally home to Tottenham via New Oxford Street, checking behind him, gradually divesting the cycling gear along the way, popping into charity shops to replace the shorts and top with jeans and hoody, arriving with the count in his head: three down, seven to go. Although, in truth, he's not sure if this latest one does actually count as he seemed to be added in at the last minute. Still, Smith was as accurate as ever and the fat cop had arrived on the dot and the vantage point from the empty flat opposite was perfect. Two shots, one for luck.

So, is this it, then? Summer is over early, it seems. The note makes perfect sense to Toby – the lack of information a densely packed series of instructions: go home to Potters Bar. Get on with your life. Act normal. Say nothing. Well done. Thank you. I love you. Wait for me.

There's not much to pack, in the end. It all fits in a rucksack. The courier's bag hangs on the back of the chair in the kitchen, the weight of metal and wood in the bottom bulging the shiny, dirty plastic. Toby has a twinge of nostalgia about its contents as he opens the front door, a similar feeling to when he was ten and his family had moved house and he had noticed his beaten beloved football had been left in the front garden, somehow forgotten, as they drove off. As for his friends and Smith, who knows what a young man really feels when he has climbed a mountain and has his eyes firmly set on a vista of an endless new horizon. Joy and passion and hope and a vicious yearning. Or the circumspect turning of a page, which brings him from cliché to humdrum. Either way, Tottenham has left him and tomorrow approaches just half an hour later as the train passes reservoirs and pylons and patient, staggering traffic and he fingers a brick of banknotes in the bottom of the rucksack. That's a lot of money for a seventeen year old, that is – one hundred thousand pounds – too much to contemplate but it doesn't come close to the riches he carries in his heart.

15

Chapter 15: Killing Hitler

'You always think someone knows better. Even when you get to middle age, we hold on to the assumption that the government, the police, the specialists, mountain rescue... someone knows more than we do about everything. And then, the realisation, after one too many encounters with authority, one too many stories of corruption and incompetence in the media, it comes home: it's you, not them. There's only you and what you're prepared to put up with. Some people end up refusing to put up with any more. I'm one of those. I hope that answers your question, Mr. Freeman.'

It's as straight and clean as Peter has been for weeks, since Ann's death. He makes a good case. Freeman is obviously impressed. The basement is not the most comfortable venue for socialising, but they make the best of it. More chairs have been brought down from the office, the flattened boxes from the van. The lamp, discretely pointing downwards, is the only light. There are beer bottles and wine bottles and the remains of take away kebabs and chips strewn around the floor. In the furthest corner a bemused Eddy is almost as happy as he's ever been. Untied but watched closely by Wolfy he is full and feeling slightly sleepy. The talk has been beyond his ken for the most part – he's made a point of not understanding difficult things throughout his life and he's not going to start now. One thing's certain – if these are bad people, they treat him better than the police and he likes them more. In fact, he thinks he likes them better than his work mates and possibly anyone he's ever met apart from his mum. They haven't talked to him very much, which he appreciates and most of that was Wolfy who somehow divined his attachment to fishing and who has spoken knowledgeably to him about flies and lines and rods. His eyelids are heavy and he keeps on forgetting he's been kidnapped. Kidnapped! He's not a kid, not anymore. Then he remembers his mum and starts to worry, nibbling his lower lip and looking towards the door. Freeman, warm enough against the evening chill in a donated puffa jacket is asking more questions.

'And what do you do after this?'

Tedi, leaning against the wall, still in her leathers, one arm dangling over Abe's shoulders, occasionally, to his delight, playing with his left ear. Abe staying very still, hardly daring to breath as Tedi explains.

'We carry on. We don't stop. Like Steve says, this is a new power bloc. We take them on and people join us, we get power like they got power, through force and money and violence. But we make it better. The difference is that. We only kill the bastards.'

'You know who the bastards are, don't you Bill?' Smith is sitting on his box, near the door.

'You've been dealing with them all your working life. You know all about the armourers, the royals, the secrets, the armies, the aristos. Oxford. Cambridge.'

'Have you told them about...' Bill nods towards the others. Smith shrugs.

'Of course. Why not? They deserve to know everything. I've told them everything. Lots of people know, actually, Bill. It's all a bit of a myth, the whole 'I'll slit your throat if you mention a word', just made up to frighten the peasants. It's all very corporate now. Like the Mormons. Like the Scientologists. There's quite a few people involved now. Of course, Oxford have their specialisms and so do Cambridge. But really, it's only old salts like us who still use that terminology. The youngsters just get on with it and don't ask why. They're bought into the whole power trip very early on.'

Tedi almost spits.

'Oxford! Cambridge! Is this a school or a private army! Double talk. We've got nothing to hide. You will tell our story.'

'That remains to be seen, young lady. And what about you?' Freeman is looking at Abe, who straightens up regrettably.

'Me? I'm just along for the ride, have a bit of fun. I don't pretend to know it all, but what he says makes sense.' Abe is looking at Smith. He continues.

'I'm a sporting man. I like sure things, but occasionally I'll take a wild punt. This is a bit of both. I know, for sure, that anyone with a bit of money or power has to be corrupt, has trod on some other poor cunt to get where they are. I also know that my man Stephen over there is one very bright button. And I also know this is fucking crazy and I'm liable to get shot. But it might just work. And then what? Quids in, mate. We're all quids in. Think about it. If you got a chance to kill Hitler in 1939 you would've, wouldn't you? That's what we're doing here – we're beginning to kill Hitler.' Abe sits back, apparently exhausted. Smith nods, perhaps surprised. He opens his mouth but is interrupted by a howl from the corner.

'I've got to go home! My mum's worried! It's too late!'

Eddy is half on his feet, pounding on Wolfy's head, but the Irish man has a grip on one of his legs. Very quickly, Eddy is subdued, with Wolfy and Abe literally sitting on his back as Tedi talks quietly in his ear, soothing him. But he moans into the floor and won't be calmed. Freeman looks around and sees Smith watching him closely.

'It's alright, I'm not moving. What will you do with him? He's obviously upset. Probably learning difficulties, maybe autistic.'

'Someone will go and have a chat with his mum, take him home, after he's quietened down. I'll have a little chat with him, sort him out.'

Smith is on his feet.

'Come upstairs with me Bill, let's leave them alone for a few minutes.'

The main part of the factory is a large, empty room, lit only by the spill from the street lamps across the yard through narrow windows above the roller doors. Freeman follows Smith out of the basement and discovers him talking quietly to Will, the slight young man with the Liverpool accent, who is carrying a machine pistol. Introductions had been made as he had met each of the group, convincing him that he was definitely going to be killed. Now he's not so sure. Indicating the smaller door cut into the corrugated metal of the roller door, Smith leads Freeman out into the yard.

The distant roar of the city battles subtly with the weird wild sounds of the reservoir. Owl hoots and the infinite variety of emergency sirens, the endless mechanical collisions of metal against metal, brakes, wheels, doors and the odd quack of a duck hidden in the dark, on the water; the bell around the neck of a goat, still grazing the banks. A rare star is momentarily subsumed into the patterns of lights from two aircraft, heading to and from Heathrow airport. Smith is looking across, towards the orange glow of the soda lights reflected in clouds hanging blue black and grey.

'I'm going to give you your mobile Bill. What are you going to use it for? The paper? Or the cops?'

Eyes still at the sky, Smith has Freeman's small mobile held out in one hand. Freeman doesn't take it. Not yet.

'You know they'll kill you, the brothers. They won't let this go.'

'Expose them, Bill. Set your reporters on them.'

'You know I can't.'

'In that case, run our story. It's the least you could do, really, isn't it? When you know we're giving our lives, when you know those good people in there will be dead soon. Miriam and you, between you, can write it up. One remarkable week, that's all it takes, for a chink of light. The BBC won't be able to avoid it. The internet will be on fire! It will make you and they won't touch you, not in an obvious way. They'll be too scared about what you know, what I've told you. Once the box is open they can't shut it. Do it, do it Bill! Do it!'

And then Bill's phone is in his hand and, yes he's ringing the office, the night editor and giving the immortal orders, something he's never said before and, even now, it seems so corny.

'Hold the front page. Call Miriam, tell her to mail it through, tell her to fax it and text it and bring it in person. Whatever she's written – you print. Got that? Good!' And it's done.

'I need to be there. Will you let me go now?'

'Of course, of course Bill!' Smith is beaming, his arm around Freeman's shoulders. Back inside the factory everyone shakes his hand, he gets given a bottle of beer. Even Eddy gets carried away with the excitement and forgets his mum for a moment. It doesn't take long to organise Freeman on to the back of Wolfy's motorcycle, Tedi's perfume in his nostrils. He calls through the helmet as they glide out of the yard:

'What about the lad, the one who helped me?'

But Smith just smiles and waves and closes the gates after them.

The wind tries to find his skin through gaps in his clothing but Bill Freeman doesn't feel the cold. Past the blurring lights of pubs and cars and minicab offices, fast food joints, buses and restaurants, through the millions of people caught in the concrete, aware that he is the messenger who probably won't be believed but, damn it! He's going to shout it out anyway, for the madness, for his old self, for the insane Smith and the tiny kernel of hope he has inside that has kept him from the exhaust fumes or the pills or the tidal currents that have tempted him for so many years. Alive again, for a while. Properly alive.

It's the reason why they love him. As Smith helps big Eddy up the bank, to walk him back, explain everything to his loving mum. Who else but Steve could explain away a kidnapping, guns, their crazy situation but good old Steve? Their faith in him almost complete, although he caught a look from Wolfy. Did he realise? Does it matter? Of course not. It's a fine night and the air is quite reviving by the gentle water. Eddy is happy to be returning and chats away, explaining his walks to work, about the pike he swears hides in the water, about how, one day, he'll bring his rod up here and get that big fish and, wack! Wack it on the head with the stick he uses for the fish. He never eats them, but his dad told him, the foxes take the fish away from the riverbank. He never throws them back. That's just stupid. You catch the fish, you kill it. He might eat one, but only if he went to Scotland where the water is clean. Eddy is happy the moment before he dies. It's a shame Smith can't weigh him down and leave him in the water, but he's a big boy and Smith hasn't got all night, so Eddy must make do with the bushes at the bottom of the bank, rolled down through the goat turds and the stingers and pretty well buried in the green for days whilst his mum worries and the police eventually put him on the missing person's register. It's a shame, but Eddy's no good alive. He's just too stupid. Dead, he can be forgotten and valuable energy diverted from him to more important things. Like getting ready for the reckoning, just around the corner.

The journey back takes as long as a guess, however far away Eddy lived, there and back, so Smith takes a circuitous route, doubling round through the self-replicating industrial estate. Spotlit yards, bundles of razor wire, interchangeable names for stores and industries and centres; red brick and strict lines in corrugated aluminium, sprayed in gentle pastels and vivid red, drains and tarmac, lorries parked like tank battalions; broken bushes gasping in the exhaust, strange steams emanating in the night time from thin chimneys; the low hum of constant work, fluorescent gaps in doorways and blinds; pavements unused and weedy with dandelions; light triggered by movement; prison yard cameras, some pointing out, some pointing in. Lots of cameras, all connected to screen and recorder and sleepy security, the footage, acres of digital information arranged in movies that are never watched. Passing one site, the camera following his progress, unusually, the movement indicating vigilance or boredom. Smith gives his observer a wave as he returns to the bosom of his loving family.

*   *   *

What do they know? They know they are killers, cop killers. They know they are left wing anarchist terrorists.

Since the morning papers have been digested they know there are five men and a woman and that they are trying to start some kind of a revolution. And they know they've been using a house in Tottenham.

Which is enough for Don Hipkins, for the moment. There hasn't been this much police activity on The Grove since the night after the Broadwater Farm riots, when every estate in North London that had more than ten black families living in it was locked down and invaded in a show of force by the Met and associated police forces from all around the Home Counties and beyond. But today it's all concentrated on just the one house, which has already been smoked and surrounded and invaded and occupied. Number 53 hasn't got much to say for itself, as he wanders through, careful not to touch anything apart from the floor with his polythene clad boots. Representatives from several different government and army organisations are waiting for the same opportunity. But it's his case, he gets first dibs and it's doing him no good whatsoever. Nothing. Just nothing. Clothes. Food. A bag with a gun, possibly the same one used for several murders. No prints, no prints at all. Anywhere. The neighbours know nothing on this side of the street and there's no point asking the growing crowd of curious people from the estate across the road. Hipkins was close, he knows he's close now; they're around, nearby. But they could be anywhere. He's just wishing them to be close. No, they are close. The vacillation will continue until… evidence! Something. OK, he's been up and down the stairs, every bit of everything has been looked at, bagged, shown to him and now the beige walls are mocking him. Right, back to the CCTV. It's produced gold before and it can again. Infinitely more boring than massive raids on empty houses but hopefully more useful. He's a good cop. A good policeman. A methodical man who believes in the uniform, the holy blue. Get on with it, Hippo. Track that bad man down!

*   *   *

It had been fun to be at the BBC again, good old Broadcasting House, with its indelible brown sections, its grand pretensions constructed in the Bakelite age. The party had been like a series of connections plugged into an old switchboard by very efficient female operators who measured their freedom in lipstick and listened but never told. Old faces, familiar names, handshakes as messages. Subtle rank. Lovely. The food was straight from the canteen, proper energy food, by the same universal caterer who fed MPs and Lords down by the river and the masters and prefects at Eton and Harrow. The meat, softened by liquid cabbage, makes the special shit of the ruling classes. Good quality beef or lamb, with a thin line of fat running through, like the deliberate mistakes in the carpets of Persia, but this time so's not to offend the stomachs of those who would be seen as egalitarian whilst clawing another, what? ten? twenty? years of life from the soul of the working classes.

Their stomachs playing a duet back in the house at the end of Milford Street, the brothers fed and feted chew the cud of gossip, gleaned from the evening.

'I fear we have been shrunk.'

'Whatever do you mean?'

'Apparently budget cuts galore.'

'There are always budget cuts. We are indispensable. They know that.'

'Apparently not. That's the trouble with capitalists, they can always see a saving. Give me a commie or a royal – they understand quality. We provide a service, a proper service. The Arabs understand.'

'Agreed. Unhappily, *they* don't. How can we help them? To understand...'

'It's all in hand.'

'You don't mean your blasted policeman, do you? Got his own boss shot outside his front door. Not very efficient.'

'Did you notice I had a little phone call whilst we were there?'

'I did.'

'Good news. That nasty ex-employee of yours, Smith. They've found him. In Tottenham, of all places.'

'Tittingham.'

'Tot'nam.'

'The Nam.'

'Tits up in Tittertown.'

'Good. I am pleased for you. Will you get him this time? You haven't done very well so far…'

'Of course I'll get him. There's nowhere for him to go. Take a look at this.'

One podgy hand passes another a slick sheet of glossy paper, a photo, Stephen Smith, waving on a nighttime street.

'Cheeky.'

'He's a cunt.'

'He looks happy, don't you think?'

'I reiterate…'

'Are you going?'

'I might. For the craic.'

'The foreign woman?'

'You're hilarious, brother. Will you come too?'

'I might. Will there be explosions?'

'Pretty colours? I expect so. There normally are where your boy's concerned.'

'Ah, Stephen. Could I have loved you better?'

'What will we do with the journalist bitch?'

'Nothing. I like her. She'll come around.'

'What about the editor?'

'Why ask me? What do you want to do?'

'I want to flay him alive. But he might have one or two things up his sleeve. He's old fashioned, like us. Very saucy of him to turn up tonight, I thought.'

'Indeed. Saucy bitch. We can wait. He'll probably drop dead anyway. Didn't look healthy at all tonight.'

'Not like us.'

'To us. The picture of health.'

'To us.'

A shared bottle of Irn Bru, spread between two glasses. A taste they had picked up from an old Scottish soldier a few years back. Not so old, actually. But old enough.

*   *   *

'When this place blows, it will truly blow.'

Faces flushed, Peter, Abe and Wolfy, who is being unusually loquacious, perhaps due to the Irish whiskey he is swigging from the bottle, perhaps because he can sense he is going to die soon. Excited, all three of them, a little high, because of the very good quality MDMA Smith had slipped into their drinks an hour or so ago, feeling the fellowship, sharing touches and hugs. Abe, particularly, has benefitted from the medication. Completely unreserved and finding time to compliment Peter on his accent, Wolfy on his strength, Tedi on her beauty. Tedi is enjoying the wait, sharing her attentions between all the men, reminding them that her name is Mateja Gojsalic and not to forget there is a woman, a mother, a wife waiting inside her, when all this is over. Don't forget. I might marry you, or you, or you...

Will is bemusedly sober. Smith correctly guessing he would immediately recognise the effects because he's spent several year's worth of weekends bouncing around with E and Ketamine cocktails, taking him up and down and in and out and is somewhat of an expert in the quality thereof. Getting a little impatient and not really understanding, asking Smith when the money's turning up. Smith calms him down with a big bundle of twenties and tens, magicked from somewhere in the building. Keep the boy here a bit longer. He'll enjoy firing that thing, the machine pistol swinging from a forefinger as he strides the room.

A helicopter signals the beginning. Smith remains in his seat, re-reading Miriam's article, the second one, describing the attack in Wales, describing the group, the family, injecting an element of drama into the narrative which Smith is enjoying, even if its basically untrue. He's no revolutionary hero! Peter almost waltzes by, looking over Smith's shoulder.

'Did I tell you how much I loved you, Stephen?' Then waltzing off to pledge the same to Tedi. The rattle of machine gun fire from the roof. That will be Wolfy, in his leathers, making a good shape. Returning fire. The attackers will be confusing themselves: so many strangers with guns, with only the regulation baseball cap and body armour to signify which side they're on. Smith's is in a plastic bag at his feet. He'll put them on later, when there's a bit more smoke. He hears Will from the other side of the room.

'Steve! Steve! There's fucking thousands of them! Steve! What do we do?'

'Shoot, Will, shoot!' Leaning over, pressing the button to open the roller doors, lifting them a couple of feet, just enough for Will to lay down and blast a magazine into the night, just enough for several smoke bombs and flash bombs to roll underneath and ruin the atmosphere. Smith listens, as his eyes smart and his ears ring. A grenade exploding. Something heavy on the roof. Another explosion. Rapid fire. Single shots. Wondering how Abe's getting on. He had a shotgun, like the East End villain he truly is, a big fuck off shotgun, two barrels, not much good in a fire fight, but what a look for a little man! And Peter, with his own and his wife's pearl handled pistols, going down like Captain Horatio

Hornbeam in a blaze of establishment bullets out in the yard. What a film they are making together. Will is hit.

'It hurts! Fuck! Shit! It hurts! I'm bleeding, I'm really bleeding!'

Smith has the police gear on now, the cap, the balaclava, the vest, the armband – all correct. He has a regulation SIG pistol, a happy coincidence that the Swiss army use the same weapons as our MD Police. Lost on Will as he puts the poor boy out of his misery with a shot to his head. No future for you. The shots continue. Screaming. Tedi? Definitely a woman. More shots. A call to cease fire, through a megaphone, but someone is ignoring the order, merrily blasting away around the back. He presses the button and the door rises, this time to its limit and the scene is revealed, lights blazing from the tops of vans, oh, look, two helicopters now, smoke everywhere, more shouts, another shot. Shadowy figures, balaclavas and caps, just like him, crouching, just like him, guns outstretched, scuttling, low. He moves, blends. Heading for the back. He finds Abe, his throat blown away, the shotgun unfired. A gentle man really, was Abe. He lights a fuse. He runs back to the main room, screaming:

'Get out! It's wired! It's gonna blow!' Waving his hands, back, back, back, running past the crouching figures, diving to the ground just past the gate, in the adrenalised confusion counting a little too fast and seeing a large man, who might be in charge begin to walk towards him when – the factory splits the dark like a firework, the roof blowing up and off and flames stabbing the sky. A big bang! A lot of smoke. Smith is on his feet and calmly helping another cop along, a woman, he can tell, by how light she is and her protesting voice:

'No, I'm alright, you don't have to.' So he leaves her by one of the vans and slips back, back. Unbelievably, he can now hear debris still falling, plop, splish, splash into the reservoir and he hopes the filters are efficient at the processing plant. Possibly bits of people, his people and perhaps a couple of cops or bad guys or bystanders, added to the drinking water – not healthy. A hand to his ear – it's his radio, stupid – talking, heading for an empty patrol car. In he gets and away he goes, while the dust is still settling and the bullets and bombs still echo round the houses and roads and factories and shops, distracting the residents and winding up their dogs.

16

Chapter 16: Inspiration

A pond, surrounded by tape and cones, rubble and several police cars and an outside broadcasting unit. Sherriff had managed to ease his way through by being very quiet. Expecting a huge crowd, but instead, a couple of men in high visibility jackets and safety helmets, a few journalists, lots of police. Where are the citizens, the outraged revolutionaries, sparked by this massacre? Bit too far to walk, hard to get there because of the roadblocks. Spotting a vantage point, Sherriff makes his way up the bank a few yards away from what's left of the factory. The blast had broken the banks of the reservoir and a steady trickle had filled the hole where the building had stood. The leak plugged by sandbags, the water, still, reflecting the sky, the flashing lights. Sherriff takes out his notebook and pencil and looks through tears. A duck lands on the pond, adventuring from the great reservoir to a new pasture. Sherriff scribbles, a little poem for his friends, a Robin Hood ditty for his hero.

At the bottom of the bank, police are searching the undergrowth. One of them is already climbing towards him, getting ready to move him on when, clearly, Sheriff hears someone say:

'Sarge! We've got another one here!'

Which is just too much and Sherriff turns and flees as ducks quack and radios crackle.

*   *   *

Toby, hurtling through nettles and whipping boughs along a stony path crossed with exposed roots and decorated with crumpled sheets from newspapers and magazines, spunk and shit drying on the headlines and pink fleshy print. Small insects pelt his face, hard peas that feel bigger than the twitching greenfly he washes off in the family bathroom. Showered and shaved – a new affectation as the blonde cobwebs on his chin only appear when they catch the sunlight – creamed and blessed with flags of lotion, running a hand over the half an inch of even growth, soft animal down nervously covering his scalp. Hears his mother calling him for lunch and he is suddenly ravenous.

Sedately taking the stairs, two at a time, feeling the inch difference in height from a year ago, giant stepping into the kitchen. Where ham and pickle and poppy seed buns coated with butter, fresh orange juice and midsummer breeze hangs on the curtains like chip fat on a shell suit. And a reasonable mother, standing back, but, in her mind, tucking in a bib, spooning sweet and savoury, wiping his mouth and loving him with all her heart – allows herself a dainty step forward and the lightest of touches on her son's nape. Rewarded with the brightest smile from her sunny, brave boy, who is going to be, an explorer, a fireman, a soldier, a rock star, an accountant like his dad – no – a policeman. He told her this morning he will be joining the last British police cadet training scheme in Inverness, Scotland, just as soon as he gets his place confirmed. Which, she knows, is just a formality. Her son would make a wonderful policeman! Anyone can see that.

* * *

*   *   *

In the Holiday Inn, next to Edinburgh Zoo, fresh from the number 26 bus, stripping ready to shower, Stephen Smith receives a phone call. On the counterpane, naked apart from his underwear, looking a little weary, a bit underfed.

'Yes?' he asks.

'Yes it did.' He agrees.

'Yes I will.' He promises.

'Sleep.' He states.

'I know you do. And I love you, too, boss.' He lies.

The phone replaced, he changes his mind about the shower and instead crawls beneath the sheets where he looks for but can't quite reach the sorrow in his heart that must be there.

End

Printed in Great Britain
by Amazon